ALSO BY MATT BENDORIS

Killing With Confidence

ALSO BY MATT BENDORIS

Killing With Confidence

DM FOR MURDER

MATT BENDORIS

CONTRABAND

Contraband is an imprint of Saraband

Published by Saraband,
Suite 202, 98 Woodlands Road,
Glasgow, G3 6HB, Scotland

www.saraband.net

ISBN: 9781910192009
ebook: 9781910192016

Printed in the EU on sustainably sourced paper.

1 2 3 4 5 6 7 8 9 10

To my wife, Amanda;
children, Andrew and Brooke;
and Aunt Sam for always being there for us.

My mum, Annie, for never giving up the fight,
and my brother, Sean, for his constant support.

Finally, this book is for
beleaguered journalists everywhere.

Prologue

Bryce Horrigan couldn't speak after the first bullet ripped open his throat. It was the first time the shock jock television presenter and chat show host had been lost for words in years. The only sound he made was the audible hiss of air escaping from his lungs through the horrendous wound. He clawed desperately at his neck, in the same manner as John F Kennedy when the first bullet had struck in Dallas. Ironically, if Bryce could have chosen a celebrity death, he would have wanted to be ranked alongside such luminaries as JFK.

But Christ how it hurt.

The shock in his eyes was exactly what his killer wanted to see. The giant ego of the man Americans loved to loathe had finally been burst.

Bryce slumped to his knees, clutching the mass of blood and sinew that was once his neck.

How had it come to this? Scottish-born Bryce had been one of the UK's brightest Fleet Street stars, before becoming one of the highest-paid television presenters in America. He continually made headlines in his adopted homeland with his outspoken views, especially standing up for the pro-abortion lobby. Privately, he cared little for the plight of expectant mothers or their unwanted babies. But he loved how it riled the right-wing Bible bashers and helped fuel his nightly talk show, which was broadcast coast to coast across the States and beamed around the world by satellite. He revelled in the number of threats upon his life he had received via his Twitter account – '90,000 and rising,' he'd proudly say – and would deliberately goad his haters: *Come on, you lot, let's see if we can make it six figures by the end of the week.* Naturally, they were only too happy to oblige. Bryce Horrigan was smugly satisfied about his ten-million-plus followers on the micro-blogging site – easily outstripping some of the biggest Hollywood stars.

The second bullet hit his shoulder, exiting through his spinal column, paralysing Horrigan completely. He knew his time was up.

His killer smiled, before slowly taking aim and emptying the rest of the 9mm's magazine into his head and face, destroying all that expensive plastic surgery Horrigan had always denied having.

The murderer had been very careful and would leave behind no trace of his own DNA. But it wasn't the forensics that would prove to be the most problematic issue for detectives – it was Horrigan's Twitter account.

Just where do you start investigating 100,000 serious death threats from all fifty states and beyond?

1

#Doughnuts

'Did I ever tell you about the time I worked in a doughnut factory?'

April Lavender was speaking to her younger colleague Connor 'Elvis' Presley as they made their way from the staff car park to their usual breakfast pit stop at the Peccadillo Café.

Connor thought he'd heard about all of April's previous jobs since they had been thrown together a year ago as the *Daily Chronicle*'s special investigations team and given their own office, which was little more than a converted broom cupboard. To date, they included barmaid, cleaner, secretary and Royal Navy Wren. Then there was her stint as something called a 'Go-Go Dancer', which Connor was pretty sure was some early form of lap dancing.

So his ears pricked up at this new occupation to add to the list. 'Nope, can't say you did.'

'Well,' she continued, 'on my first day on the production line one of the guys asked if I wanted a doughnut, but I said, "No thanks, they'll make me fat." But this guy, Rick Fullerton, thought I said, "No thanks – they make me FART," and told everyone. Well, I tell you, I have never been so embarrassed – make me fart, indeed! From that day on, until I left, I had to put up with gas jibes; about it being "windy in April" and how "Lavender smells".'

'They're some pretty sophisticated insults,' Connor said sarcastically.

Ignoring him, April said, 'What a terrible first impression, though.'

Connor was quickly losing interest. 'If I were you, I would have farted whenever I was around this Rick character, just to get him back – what did you have to lose?'

'Oh, I did,' April replied. 'I used to break wind in his vicinity all the time – so much so that everyone eventually thought he had a serious bowel problem.'

'Ah, revenge of the reekie woman – you never fail to amaze me, April. Sailor, secretary, lap dancer, doughnut factory worker and able to break wind on demand. I have to admit the latter is probably your most impressive attribute. Now, how do you fancy some beans on toast at the café? That should clear the pipes.'

He didn't need to ask twice; April loved her food. He would regularly tease her, saying that she continually grazed throughout the day, like a cow. The insults sailed over her head. She'd grown a very thick skin during her thirty years in the rough and tumble world of journalism.

2
#TweetToWho?

Captain Sorrell surveyed the crime scene, taking in everything. Technically, he didn't possess a photographic memory, but he had the next nearest thing. His attention to detail and powers of recall were almost freaky. All his detectives needed to do was mention a suspect's name and he would repeat it a few times, then the light bulb would burst on somewhere in his head and he'd declare something like, 'We picked him up four years ago on a grand theft auto,' before his subordinates had even logged on.

Sorrell had ordered that no one should roll the body, or touch anything until he got there. He looked at the wrecked corpse and stood up to his full 6'2". Although Sorrell was tall, it did little to conceal the fact that he was overweight, passing the 300-pound mark long ago. He put his overeating down to his poor upbringing, when food had been scarce.

Bernard Sorrell was born and bred in Baltimore, Maryland, to a large African-American family. His father had been a plumber while his mum had the toughest job of all – raising Bernard and his eight brothers and sisters, trying to keep them from the wrong side of the tracks, what with the area's gang problems.

The teenage Bernard had just one close brush with the law when a friend shot dead a convenience store owner during a bungled robbery. Sorrell was meant to be there, but fate had intervened and he had failed to meet up, which meant he narrowly escaped an accessory to homicide charge. From that moment on he'd decided enough was enough and buckled down to his studies to graduate from high school. He distanced himself once and for all from the pack when he enrolled at the state's police academy. In his twenty-five years on the force since then, he had personally investigated more than 300 murders.

It's said you never forget your first case, but after a while Sorrell discovered he became numb to witnessing the expressions of the victims' last moments on earth, forever frozen onto their faces. Eventually all those tortured souls just blended into one. Except those of the children. As a father of two daughters, those were always the hardest cases to deal with.

Smell is one of the strongest of the senses, which was a pity for detectives like Sorrell. He could never forget the stench of decomposing flesh on the hot summer day he discovered the body of a ten-year-old boy killed by his mother's boyfriend, who turned out to be a predatory paedophile. The odour was so overpowering that Sorrell swears he can still taste it. The detective had literally stepped on the boy's body – hideously bloated from the searing heat of a Maryland summer – disturbing a swarm of flies that had been feeding on the corpse's multiple stab wounds.

When Sorrell had brought in the killer, he confessed immediately, claiming to have been in love with the boy and flying into a jealous rage when he got himself a little schoolyard girlfriend. But the love affair had all been inside the killer's own head. That had been what's termed a 'dunker' – a slam dunk – as Sorrell had wrapped up the case by the end of the day.

His attention returned to the here and present in a hotel suite of the Baltimore City Hotel by the city's bustling waterfront.

Sorrell took one look at what was left of Horrigan's face and muttered, 'Robbery, my ass.' That was before he looked towards the bed, where he saw a wallet lying open with its contents apparently intact.

The tinkling of melting ice in the champagne bucket suddenly caught his attention. Sorrell noted there were four champagne glasses, an unusual number, and all of them filled and untouched. The bed was also still made up, the starched white sheets pulled tight flat in the way only chambermaids and nurses seem able to do.

Lieutenant Haye disturbed his boss's thought process when he approached brandishing his iPhone. 'You gotta take a look at this, cap'n.'

'Can't this wait, Haye? I'm kinda busy,' Sorrell snapped back.

'No, sir. Someone has already tweeted a photo of the crime scene,' Haye replied, with the look of a worried man.

Captain Sorrell took his reading glasses from his top pocket, perched them on the end of his nose and squinted as he tried to focus on the smartphone's tiny screen. He then said in his slow, steady, measured drawl, 'Can someone please explain to me, what the hell is a tweet?'

3

#Teabagging

'I'm reading that *Fifty Shades Of Grey*,' April announced, her mouth half-full with food, as was always the case when she was in the Peccadillo Café.

'That was all the rage ages ago,' Connor replied dismissively.

'I ended up having to Google "fisting". I had no idea what it was.'

Connor had not expected that. He laughed and said, 'Do you not remember the comic Julian Clary? He practically ended his TV career when he claimed he had been fisting the Chancellor of the Exchequer.'

'Yes, yes, I remember all that,' April said impatiently, 'but I didn't know what it meant back then, either. I mean, how does it even fit?'

Connor decided he'd have some fun. 'What about rimming? A donkey punch. DP? I'm sure as a former Wren you've tried all of them, even if you didn't know their names.'

'No, I certainly have not. You're a dirty boy. Honestly, the things people do to each other. Where's the romance?'

Connor ordered the bill from Martel, the waitress and his occasional lover, then said to her, 'April's going to try a spot of teabagging later.'

'Oh, good luck with that,' Martel said, stifling a laugh.

April ignored them both, saying, 'That reminds me, I need to buy a box of Earl Grey.'

They made their way to the newspaper's Glasgow city centre office where April switched to her favourite topic – her retirement plans.

Connor loved winding her up whenever she mentioned it: 'You'd miss the broom cupboard, my relentless wit, my occasional practical jokes that keep you on your toes.'

'Nope,' she'd reply confidently, 'I won't miss any of it. When I leave I'll finally have the time to lose weight and write the book, just like I've always wanted to do.'

The book. For as long as Connor had known April Lavender she'd always talked about writing *the book*. She had bought not one, but two laptops; eventually both ended up in the care of her eternally ungrateful daughter from one of her three failed marriages, with *the book* not even started, never mind completed. April had attempted to move with the times and bought an iPad, but she couldn't master the touchscreen keyboard and began moaning how this new technology was all that stood between her and writing a bestseller. So Connor convinced her to buy a wireless keyboard for the iPad, which effectively just turned it back into a laptop. Still, she did not commit one word to screen. Eventually, after relentless ribbing by her colleague, she confessed, 'The problem is, I don't have a single idea for a plot in my head. Not one. My brain is a blank canvas.'

'Well, it perfectly matches your face,' Connor retorted. 'Did you know E L James wrote *Fifty Shades* on her BlackBerry on her way to work? So there's no excuse for not writing your book.'

'It's not even very well written,' April said a little bitterly.

'Who cares? One hundred million people can't be wrong. It's mummy porn. To get your old boiler fired up. Talking of which, how is the Italian stallion?'

'Hmm, not too sure about old Luigi.' Widowed Luigi owned April's favourite restaurant in the city's Shawlands district. She had been a shoulder to cry on after his wife had died. Now the ageing lothario had April in his sights, repeatedly asking her to marry him.

'He's obsessed with my boobs.' For the second time that morning April had said something Connor wasn't expecting. 'He's always finding excuses to give them a feel. I wouldn't mind so much but it's usually in front of his customers. He even jokes about it. "April, I a-love your a-boobies,"' she said, giving a near perfect impression of Luigi's curious half-Glaswegian/half-Italian accent.

'At least he leaves your growler alone,' Connor said thoughtfully.

'Eh, yeuk. Where do you get such language from?' April responded.

'Don't you get sick of the old sex pest?' Connor asked.

'What, Luigi? He's harmless. You should have seen the Navy. They'd grab you everywhere. All ranks. All time of day. Pulling your skirt down and all the rest. You had to literally beat them off. Newspapers used to be even worse. There was a guy on the picture desk nicknamed Radio Luxembourg, because on nights out he'd turn women's nipples like tuning a radio. I was constantly called "that daft lassie" or "Barbie doll".'

'Better than "dumpy wee woman",' Connor smiled.

'That came later. I've heard it all. So please spare me all the sexism stuff. Girls today need to toughen up. A swift kick in the balls usually sorted it out. Now they call the police.'

'People have been banged up for less than your old perv Luigi,' Connor remarked.

'Look, at my age it's nice to still be an object of someone's desire. However ugly he is.'

'You know, I could do a book on you: *Diary of a Menopausal Woman*,' Connor teased.

'Oh, I'm way past that.'

'I'll make it a prequel, then,' he retorted. 'Come on, better get moving. We've got another digital presentation this morning.'

April shuddered at the thought.

4

#ThisIsNotAHoax

Bryce Horrigan @BryceTripleB
R.I.P. @BryceTripleB

The police tape had only just gone up over the hotel suite's door when Bryce Horrigan's death made headlines around the world after it was tweeted from his own Twitter account, along with the photo of the crime scene. Within an hour, the television presenter's name began trending. Not for the first time. Before his untimely death, Bryce had trended twenty-one times.

'That's more than any other television personality on the planet,' he would tell anyone who would listen.

Once, even a hoax death tweet had seen him trend. He had loved responding with his usual bullishness: *Sorry to disappoint, but rumours of my demise are greatly exaggerated. My haters will have to get the corks back in those champagne bottles.* His response got more retweets than the US president's re-election post.

Cautious after that false alarm, most of the reputable media websites resisted posting the crime scene picture at first. But when calls to Horrigan's agent and his private mobile went unanswered, they had no choice but to run with it for fear of being left behind by the social media sites. For in the world of Internet journalism, speed is everything.

At first, many of the headlines were non-committal: *TV star Bryce Horrigan at centre of death riddle*. But when Bryce's employers at ABT News released a short statement saying that they were concerned over the whereabouts of their star host, it was open season.

Baltimore Police didn't know what had hit them. The communications division was more used to handling daily calls from the local newspapers, like the *Baltimore Sun*, *Times* and *Examiner*. In the past, there had also been national and international press enquiries on the back of the popular television series *The Wire*. Hopeful journalists wanted to accompany police units working the city's housing projects. Or they'd ask whether the show's detective Jimmy McNulty, played by Dominic West, was based on a real cop and, if so, could they interview him?

But the communications division had never experienced a volume of calls and emails like this. When Horrigan's employers confirmed the presenter had gone missing in Baltimore, the police received over 800 requests for comments from media outlets around the world. Amongst them were frantic calls from Horrigan's television executives, along with various members of the presenter's family, all desperate to speak to someone. As the switchboard struggled to cope, they were either put through to voicemail or received a busy tone.

Captain Sorrell had just left the crime scene for the hotel lobby when he was met by a throng of cameras. He muttered, 'What the f…' before quickly censoring himself.

'Captain, over here for CNN – can you confirm you are investigating Bryce Horrigan's homicide?'

Another reporter, brandishing a microphone, shouted, 'Is it true he's been shot?'

'Have you any leads yet on the Twitter Killer?'

Sorrell issued a gruff 'No comment' before getting into the passenger seat of the sedan. He'd barely closed the door when Haye hit the gas.

'The Twitter Killer?' For the second time that morning the captain swore. 'This is gonna be one big shit storm, Haye.'

Sorrell had been inside the hotel for a little over two hours before stepping outside into the chaos. He needed to get back to HQ for time to think.

5

#BraveNewWorld

Like most newspapers in the English-speaking world, the *Daily Chronicle's* circulation had gone into terminal freefall. Scotland had once enjoyed a thriving print media business with more than a million people a day buying a newspaper in a country with just five million inhabitants. And not just one newspaper. It wasn't unheard of for the working man to buy two papers on the morning commute and an evening paper on the way home again.

But the working day had changed. When traditional tea breaks were phased out of many industries, including the shipyards, circulation began to slip in the mid-1990s. Then came the Internet age and the new media phenomenon, which the old media, printed on dead trees, had struggled to understand, never mind adapt to. At first, the race was on for readers, so they gave away all their content for free online, despite it costing millions of pounds to produce. Even April thought it had been commercial suicide to allow people using the Internet in the comfort of their own homes to read the exact same stories as the loyal customers who walked through rain or shine to buy an old-fashioned newspaper.

'And they wonder why circulation has plummeted,' April would remark.

When the proprietors gingerly thought of asking the online community for a contribution for reading all of their expensive content, the Internet readers disappeared in their droves rather than type in their credit card details. That's because there was always plenty of newsgathering sites still prepared to give it away for nothing. And even the major sites with over ten million hits a day were losing money hand over fist.

Now management were convinced the 'multi-platform' revolution would save their eternal decline, with journalists producing fast, accurate content several times a day to be consumed on customers' smartphones, tablets, laptops, Kindles and any other device that appeared on the market.

April turned her customary whiter shade of pale at the start of the latest digital presentation when the speaker explained how they would need to become 'platform agnostic' – a phrase she was convinced had been invented just to deliberately bamboozle her.

There was talk of writers taking photos and videos on smartphones to upload them directly onto the website. This, the speaker predicted, would eventually generate enough online advertising to allow the business to stand on its own two feet before the time came when rolling out trucks full of paper was no longer a viable option.

April sat in each of these company meetings with a fixed grin, fastidiously taking notes, desperately trying to appear like she knew what was going on. In truth, these presentations gave April a blinding headache.

Afterwards Connor muttered angrily, 'Management are trying to reinvent the wheel. You don't get firm directions now – you get feelings. It's all a wish list. "If we get enough readers…" "If we get enough advertising…" "Imagine how you could change your working day…" I like my tech, but this is all whimsical bullshit.

'And another thing, the people put in charge of "future proofing" the company are all broken arrows – useless and can't be fired. That guy giving the talk today felt up his secretary at the Christmas party. She complained. But he was too expensive to give the bump, so he's put in charge of digital operations instead. The whole digital department is full of people who have been shunted sideways. Then they just repeat parrot fashion what they've heard at other training sessions. There're certainly no Mark Zuckerbergs at the *Daily Chronicle*.'

By April's expression, Connor knew she didn't have a clue who the Facebook founder was.

'They don't even use good old-fashioned newspaper jargon any more,' Connor said, continuing his moan. 'It's "narrative" and "line manager". What was wrong with "copy" and "desk head"? They're so obsessed with the future they're forgetting what we do best. Produce stories. Get splashes. No matter what the platform is, good words and pictures will never go out of fashion.'

Conversations about the future actually made April feel physically sick. She desperately tried to end the conversation as she needed to get some 'fresh air' – code for a cigarette – but she knew there was no stopping her younger colleague when he was in full flow.

'Remember all the chat about podcasts a while back?' Connor recalled. 'How we'd be giving running commentaries from our desks, with millions of listeners hanging on to our every word? What a load of bollocks that turned out to be.'

April did actually remember podcasts. 'Why would anyone want to listen to my ramblings? I confuse myself at times.'

She tried to change the subject. 'Did I ever tell you about the time I was driving the chairman of my local newspaper group around Glasgow? He was an Englishman so I took it upon myself to give him a guided tour. We're driving past Ibrox Stadium when he asked me if that was where Rangers played. I said, "Oh yes. That's called Ibrox. But it's also known as Hampden Park. That's where Scotland play, too." He was very quiet in the car after that. It's incredible the crap I come up with.'

Her diversionary tactic didn't work. Connor ploughed on as if she hadn't spoken. 'Vidcasts were next. If anything, they were even worse, with dodgy sound and shaky camera work. We're not trained broadcasters. We're journalists.'

'When I sit down with my G&T to watch something, it certainly wouldn't be some journalist at work,' April admitted.

'Exactly. But we're told we have to raise our profiles. The

number of Twitter followers you have is the modern day equivalent of "how big is your cock?"'

'I remember seeing a big one once,' April announced in her usual random fashion. 'It was my nineteenth birthday. I'd been to a Navy dance and went back to this guy's place and he got it out. I couldn't believe my eyes.'

'Sweet memories?' Connor smiled.

'Hardly. I said to him, "You can piss off with that thing, pal," put my knickers back on and left.'

'Another snapshot of your life that was neither asked for nor wanted,' Connor retorted. But at least April's teenage encounter finally concluded Connor's rant. 'I think I should rename you Edward Scissorhands,' he mused. 'As you have an uncanny knack of cutting any thread.'

Connor checked his Twitter feed on his BlackBerry on their way back to their broom cupboard office, and whistled softly. 'I take it all back. Twitter has just got us a splash.'

6

#HeHadItComing

Bryce Horrigan @BryceTripleB
This is what happens to baby killers.

Connor had received his Twitter alert announcing the death of Bryce Horrigan at the exact same time as the murdered presenter's millions of followers. With the American east coast five hours behind the UK, it had just gone 1pm when he returned from digital training with April and opened the tweet. He would have been dismissive of it as he'd read news of Horrigan's demise before, but it was quickly followed by another tweet from Horrigan declaring, *This is what happens to baby killers.*

This time the attached photo link got his full attention.

There was something so eerily sinister about a crime scene photograph. It had been poorly lit by the camera phone's flash, but you could still make out a figure lying face down. The back of its head was a misshapen mass of dark sticky blood and brain matter disgorged from what was clearly a deep, cavernous hole. It looked too authentic to be just a screen grab from a TV show or film. There was also something about the angle the picture had been taken, triumphantly towering over the victim. Whoever took the snap had probably pulled the trigger too.

Connor decided the quickest way to determine the tweet's authenticity would be simply to call Bryce directly. The pair had worked together for three years at Scotland's biggest selling newspaper, the *Daily Chronicle*.

Bryce Horrigan was the product of a private school education at

Fettes College, nicknamed the 'Eton of the north'. His life was one of privilege and he was imbued with the born-to-rule demeanour that is ingrained in the elite classes. But instead of following family tradition and becoming a solicitor, Bryce almost had himself disinherited when he opted for a career in newspapers.

He had started at the *Daily Chronicle* in the same week as Connor, whose route into the national title couldn't have been any more different. Connor had been raised by his single mum and had struggled his way through school before turning up at his local newspaper, asking for a job. His timing couldn't have been better as desktop publishing was sweeping through the antiquated industry – the paper's straight-talking editor told him, 'If you can use a computer you're in.' But Connor soon discovered he had that unique journalistic skill that simply can't be taught in a classroom – an eye for a story. Within a year he was working at his first national newspaper. By the age of twenty he was taken on as staff at the *Daily Chronicle*, at exactly the same time as Bryce, the blue-eyed boy, arrived on the scene.

Despite their many differences the pair instantly hit it off. But Bryce, six years Connor's senior, was clearly earmarked for greater things. Within months Bryce had been promoted to deputy features editor. But like anyone on the make, he needed allies and Connor became one of Bryce's closest confidants. While Connor would quietly and doggedly go about his work, Bryce was the showman, a braggart, who liked the sound of his own voice, earning him the nickname of Triple B – Bryce Big Balls. He liked the moniker so much it would form part of his Twitter handle in years to come. But being loud and opinionated with an unflinching confidence in his own abilities, it was little wonder Bryce had his detractors.

However, nothing could derail Horrigan from his career path, and less than a year after starting at the *Daily Chronicle* he bagged another executive post, with the title of features editor at the age of twenty-seven. Five years later, Horrigan achieved what seemed impossible when he made editor of the *Sunday Courier* in London, part of the *Daily Chronicle*'s stable of newspapers.

He took Connor with him to the Big Smoke, but while Bryce embraced London life, Connor struggled to adapt. It was too much of a rat race. Even an early morning run in the park was a crowded affair.

Then there were the drugs. It seemed almost every journalist did cocaine back then. It was a culture shock to Connor, who thought all that had been a thing of the past with the yuppies in the Eighties. Connor was as sociable as the next man, but the more his colleagues kept disappearing to the toilet, the more he felt like an outsider. Like Connor, Bryce was staunchly against drug use… at first, before he too was soon seduced.

Then there were the women. Bryce Horrigan was tall and slim, but not a good-looking man. However, power is said to be the greatest aphrodisiac and being a Fleet Street editor meant he had his pick of the single – and, often, the married – female report-ers and attractive PRs. That's when Connor knew they had to go their separate ways. To some, it all seemed like the dream ticket, but to Connor, the world of drugs and women who wouldn't look at you unless you had a title was all too phoney. By the end of two years he had come to hate London with a passion and had drifted so far from Bryce they barely even spoke. On the day Connor gave into the inevitable and tendered his resignation, Bryce summoned him for a meeting in his office, which over-looked the Thames.

It surprised Connor when the editor then offered him a pay rise before asking, 'Why on earth would you want to go back to Scotland, Elvis?'

It was right there and then that Connor knew their relation-ship was over. He was homesick and missed being around his own people more than anything, but Bryce clearly no longer even thought of himself as a Scot. His accent had been diluted and he never made any reference to his country of birth, almost exactly like the chameleon Prime Minister, Tony Blair, who was born and educated in Edinburgh, although you'd never know it.

'Stay in touch,' Bryce said half-heartedly, knowing they wouldn't.

Now, Connor picked up his BlackBerry and did something he hadn't done in over a decade, and called Horrigan's number. The reporter heard that familiar sound of being connected overseas with the ring tone longer than in the UK. Ten rings later it was answered by a male voice.

7

#AnOrdinaryLife

While Bryce Horrigan burnt the candle at both ends, Geoffrey Schroeder lived a largely uneventful life until a week before his thirtieth birthday. In the months leading up till then, he had been working overtime in a local tyre factory, doing double shifts for time-and-a-half pay, which just about made the money bearable.

When Geoffrey arrived back at his mobile home late on the Thursday before his Big Three-Oh, exhausted after a long day, he wasn't surprised to find his fiancée, Carol-Ann, not there. She'd said she was spending the weekend with her folks, so he didn't expect to see her until the following Monday.

Geoffrey and Carol-Ann lived on Bunker Down trailer park, seven miles from the centre of Kansas City in the Midwestern state of Missouri. It was the type of place where dogs roamed wild and the owner had once been cautioned for shooting cats for fun. The couple dreamed of a time when they could move out to a proper home, made of bricks and mortar.

The first inkling Geoffrey had that there was something wrong was when the local sheriff pulled up outside his home just after 7am the next morning.

'Are you Geoffrey Schroeder?' the sheriff asked in a slow drawl.

'Yeah, what appears to be the problem, sir?' Geoffrey replied respectfully, as he had never been in trouble with the law before nor ever intended to be.

'You mind if I come inside, Geoffrey?' the cop said in his most soothing manner.

The sheriff had remained standing as he delivered the news: Carol-Ann was dead. But there was more, she had died in mysterious circumstances in a motel room.

'Was ma girl having an affair?' he asked the cop.

'No, Geoffrey, she was having an abortion,' the sheriff replied grimly.

Geoffrey felt like he'd been kicked in the stomach. He hadn't even known she was pregnant and that he was to be a first-time dad. He'd thought she was just putting on weight and used to gently tease her about it. He slumped down on the couch, his head spinning, before vomiting on the floor.

'There's more, Geoffrey. The procedure was carried out by a doctor. You may or may not know that late-term abortions are illegal in the state of Missouri – and she was very late.'

'How late?' Geoffrey asked in a daze.

'Almost eight months,' the cop said, lowering his eyes to the ground.

'What was the "procedure"?' Geoffrey asked, drawing out the word as if it was poison.

'I don't know if you should hear this part,' the sheriff replied, before Geoffrey urged him to continue. 'The doctor had stuck a needle into Carol-Ann's belly to inject a drug directly into the baby's heart to stop it beating. After that, she was supposed to give a stillbirth delivery over the weekend. But something went wrong, Geoffrey. Very wrong.'

The cop kept talking, but Geoffrey could barely concentrate, hearing only the odd key word like, 'morgue', 'autopsy' and 'identification'.

Eventually the sheriff drove off, leaving Geoffrey with only grief that soon turned to anger. That had been just over a decade ago. Over the years, Geoffrey had joined various pro-life protest groups. He had picketed the abortion clinic where the doctor worked and harassed the man he considered had murdered his wife-to-be and unborn son.

Under Missouri law, aborting a viable foetus – i.e. one that is capable of surviving outside the womb – is only permissible when two independent medical experts agree that the mother's health could be impaired. The doctor had escaped all charges relating to Carol-Ann's death and the illegal abortion after another complicit medic, who happened to be a fellow director at the same practice, had countersigned all the necessary forms.

While the doctor walked free, Geoffrey was left to brandish gruesome placards outside the clinic depicting dissected foetuses. He would sometimes vandalise staff cars or glue the locks on gates and doors. But it all seemed so futile. For every day the clinic would continue to operate its business of mass infanticide no matter how uncomfortable he made life for the medics. Geoffrey began to drift away from the pro-life groups. He became tired of their constant chanting and talking. He had never been much of a talker. He was more of a doer.

However, one man would become the new focus of Geoffrey's obsessions – Bryce Horrigan. Geoffrey would watch the TV host with the plummy British accent talking about his pro-choice views – how all women should have the right for late terminations. Well, Carol-Ann had made her choice. She chose to get rid of his unborn child without telling him. It turned out she planned to leave him for another man. Her 'choice' had cost Carol-Ann her life. People needed to know that with choice came great responsibilities. Or repercussions.

Geoffrey had already caught the attention of law enforcement agencies. Then there were the explosives that had once been found in his car. He had dodged that rap on a legal technicality. But intelligence reports branded him as a dangerous loner, and 'one to watch'.

The authorities had kept tabs on him. But three weeks before Bryce Horrigan was shot dead, Geoffrey Schroeder went completely off the radar.

8

#MysteryCaller

BBC News @BBCNews
US police confirm they are treating the sudden death of
television presenter @BryceTripleB as homicide.

'Who is this?' Captain Sorrell demanded as he answered Horrigan's
iPhone, which he held in his latex-gloved hand to make sure he
didn't contaminate a potentially important exhibit. Bryce had
long since ditched Connor's contact details so it was just a random
phone number that flashed up on the screen.

'It's Connor Presley. I'm a reporter from Scotland.'

'Well, this is Captain Sorrell of Baltimore Homicide. Call my
press department. I'm trying to run an investigation here,' the irritated detective responded.

'So it's true, then?' Connor asked.

'Yeah, it's true, and now your time is up,' Sorrell said abruptly,
wrapping up the call.

'Of course. But you have my number on Bryce's phone now if I
can be of help,' Connor said, trying to keep the cop on line as long
as possible.

'Yeah, you and every other person who's called.'

Connor detected a slight softening in the weary detective's
tone. 'If you don't mind me asking, why did you answer my call?'
he asked politely.

Sorrell sighed heavily. 'Because your name didn't flash up. Just
a number. Yours and two others.'

'Who were the others, captain?' Connor asked, sensing he was
onto something.

'Wouldn't I love to know. They hung up,' Sorrell snorted.

'Listen, I worked with Bryce back on his first paper in Scotland. So if there's anything you need to know...' Connor said helpfully.

'We'll see,' Sorrell drawled, before the line went dead.

9

#FacingTheMusic

ABT News @ABTNews
Baltimore Police Dept. will give press conference over
the homicide of TV star @BryceTripleB @ 11am EST.

Captain Sorrell was already dog tired when he was told he would be facing the world's media just six hours after he'd first been to the crime scene.

The corpse was at the city morgue, where, just as in life, Bryce received the VIP treatment, jumping to the head of the autopsy queue in front of the other suspicious deaths from the previous night.

Sorrell felt he hadn't even begun his investigation proper yet. Media outlets were already flagging up the numerous death threats Horrigan had received via his Twitter account. Many had been so serious in the past that Bryce's employers had called in the authorities. This concerned Sorrell's boss, Colonel Cowan, immensely.

'We need to get a team ploughing through these threats right now,' Cowan said. 'We also need to find out the ones who have been questioned before by police. This is going to be a logistical nightmare.'

Sorrell wasn't sure. Even stranger killers didn't normally notify their victims first. Mark Chapman gave little away when in 1980 he asked for John Lennon's autograph before he shot him dead a few hours later outside the Dakota building in New York. Sorrell decided to keep his own counsel on the matter.

He took his place at the press conference next to Colonel Cowan. His boss was a natural in front of the camera and clearly enjoyed it. Rumour was, Cowan had aspirations to run for office. Sorrell, on the other hand, would be a policeman until the day he died or retired, whichever came first. He didn't like dealing with the press. As far as he was concerned, journalists were a nuisance who got in the way of his job.

Most of the questions were about Twitter. It all sounded like French to Sorrell. Retweets. Favourites. Were there any DMs – direct messages?

Did they know how the crime scene photo had been posted from Bryce Horrigan's own account?

Had his account been hacked?

Had it been sent from his own iPhone?

Was it a real crime scene photo?

Were police investigating the thousands of Twitter-related death threats?

Why had Bryce been in town?

Sorrell sat bored, staring into the middle distance while his boss partially answered and deflected the questions as he saw fit before reluctantly calling a halt to the conference – no performer likes to step off the stage.

Afterwards Colonel Cowan warned Sorrell in private, 'We better get answers to those questions soon.' By 'we', Sorrell knew Cowan meant 'he' had to get the answers soon.

'Haye, get in here,' Sorrell said, summoning his lieutenant into his office. 'Right, explain to me how a dead man tweets his own murder scene.'

10

#BluePill

Bryce Horrigan's New York office was almost in complete silence – except for the muffled sounds from the city below – when his computer screen flickered into life. The gentle hum of the cooling fans began to whirr on the late presenter's PC as its processors kicked into life. Moments later, the monitor lit up with the log in screen. The username 'BHorrigan' was typed in followed by the password in the space below.

But there was no one tapping on his keyboard, or anyone even in Horrigan's office. The PC was being accessed remotely, via a securely connected tunnel that had been proxied through half a dozen 'zombie' machines from North Korea, Russia, Georgia and North Africa before accessing Bryce's office computer. It was a complicated procedure used by hackers and government agencies across the globe. But these days at least 200 'off the shelf' programs, with zany names such as 'I Spy' and 'Hide My Ass', are instantly available to download for free, meaning you no longer have to be a computer whizz-kid to become a hacker.

All that's required is a 'Trojan' application inadvertently opened by an unsuspecting user receiving a phishing email, usually enticing them with the offer of free porn. Once accessed, the program is hidden deep within their computer. Although the zombie machines need to be switched on and connected to the Internet to be used by the hacker's command and control program, there are so many hidden Trojans undetected by anti-virus software on computers that the program just bounces around until it finds a 'live' machine. Then it hops to the next country and the next before ending up at its intended target. The process leaves the hacker's IP address 100 per cent masked.

Bryce Horrigan's infected PC had been powered up remotely using a 'Wake-on-LAN' application. Normally, the rogue software would almost instantly be detected by the daily anti-virus sweep carried out automatically by the IT department at ABT News. However, a nearly undetectable root kit called the 'blue pill' – a hacker's geeky reference to *The Matrix* film – had been installed on Bryce's computer, rendering it completely and inconspicuously at the hacker's disposal. It meant that the hacker could not only power it up, usually in the early hours of the morning when they knew the office was likely to be empty, but could use the system as fully as if they were sitting at Horrigan's keyboard.

After successfully logging on to Horrigan's computer, the mysterious user accessed his Twitter account then tapped out another tweet:

Bryce Horrigan @BryceTripleB
Hello everyone. This is what the baby killer looks like begging for his life. #TerrorFace

The cursor then moved to the camera icon and uploaded one of the crime scene photos that had been stored earlier on the desktop of Bryce's PC. Moments later, the picture was attached to the tweet and sent. His ten million followers instantly received a new post – with the picture showing Bryce Horrigan's expression of abject horror right before he was shot at almost point-blank range.

11

#RoundTwo

Daily Chronicle @DailyChronicle
BREAKING NEWS Gruesome pic of murdered TV host's
last moments posted from HIS Twitter account.

By staff reporter

A PHOTO thought to be taken moments before Bryce
Horrigan was shot dead has been posted from the murdered
TV star's Twitter account.

The gruesome image shows the Scots-born presenter
clearly in distress.

It appears to be from his Baltimore hotel room, where he
was found dead from multiple gunshot wounds.

But in a chilling new twist, the photo was posted from
Horrigan's own Twitter account – possibly by his murderer.

It read: 'Hello everyone. This is what the baby killer looks
like begging for his life. #TerrorFace'

Authorities in America are trying to establish whether the
45-year-old broadcaster's Twitter account was hacked – or if
his password was known to his killer.

An insider said: 'This tweet has been a bombshell to the
homicide investigation.

'It's as if the hacker is goading the police and they appear
to be powerless to stop it.'

30

'Sorrell,' Colonel Cowan shouted almost at the top of his voice, sending the heads of staff ducking down beneath their computer screens for cover.

The captain appeared, falling in behind Cowan as he marched to his private office, before the door was slammed behind them. It was the quickest anyone had seen Sorrell move in years.

The colonel threw his weight into his chair and tapped on his keyboard, bringing up the tweet sent from Bryce Horrigan's account.

'This is the second picture from MY crime scene. Are we no closer to finding out how it's being sent?'

'We're trying to work out how, colonel. The killer could have hacked his Twitter account.'

'I am fed up hearing "could have" done this, "might have" done that. Answers, Captain Sorrell. That's what I'm after. Get every IT expert we have to find out how he's doing it.'

The colonel returned to his screen without saying another word. Sorrell headed for the door thinking to himself, *I guess the meeting's over*.

12

#DeadManTalking

Bryce Horrigan @BryceTripleB
Thanks for all your tweets folks, but don't act so
surprised. #IDeservedIt

It was followed a minute later by:

Bryce Horrigan @BryceTripleB
Someone needs to protect the innocents. #BabyKiller

Connor showed the tweets to April, who adopted the fixed
smile that he knew only too well, which meant she didn't have the
slightest idea what was going on.

'It's so weird to read tweets from a dead man,' Connor said,
returning to his keyboard to rattle out the Bryce Horrigan 'copy'
for what would appear online for the *Daily Chronicle* in a matter
of minutes and form the basis for the next day's newsprint splash.

'It's not really Bryce. He's dead, of course,' Connor added, seeing
that April's fixed smile expression was starting to morph into one
of total confusion. 'Someone has hacked his account and is sending tweets and photos. It's cocky as hell. A bit like the real Bryce.'

'How on earth can they do that?' April asked in genuine
amazement.

'I honestly don't know. But it's a safe bet the US authorities
will be trying to work that out right now. However the hacker's
doing it, they're confident enough they won't get caught,' Connor
explained.

'And what's all this "baby killer" stuff? What am I missing?' April asked.

'About six months ago Bryce started banging the drum for the pro-choice groups in America. It's totally alien to us, but in the States abortion is still a big issue. He clearly liked the publicity, so he really ramped it up, getting anti-abortion lobbyists on his show and basically shouting at them.

'The liberal showbiz lot loved him for it. All the actors he got on his talk show at night would praise him for his stance – without going as far as endorsing his view, of course, in case it wrecked their careers. It gave Bryce huge kudos. And as you'll remember, Bryce liked kudos. But it also earned him some serious death threats. He was taking one hell of a risk. Which is weird because, for all his faults, he was one smart bastard. But he was almost goading the nutters to take a pot shot at him.'

'Which they duly obliged,' April replied glibly.

'Yeah, so it would seem. Anyway, the newsdesk already has someone hitting his folks' house; why don't you try Pasty? Remember her?'

'No,' April said truthfully.

'Pasty Tolan. Bryce's girlfriend. She'd always turn up at our nights out,' Connor said, dropping in the clues until he saw that familiar flicker of recognition.

'Ah, Pasty – the very pale girl. Posh voice. Torn-faced,' April said, pleased with her powers of recall.

'Yeah, she was in public relations. Went out with Bryce for years. Moved to London with him until… well, his head was turned. She's back in Scotland now with her own firm,' Connor explained.

'Pasty Public Relations has a certain ring to it,' April said, giggling at her own joke.

'She's probably used her actual name, Patricia Tolan, I think you'll find. Right, go and clear it with Big Fergie.'

Big Fergie was the acting news editor after the sudden departure of their last boss, the Weasel. He was named Big Fergie as he looked uncannily like a fat version of Manchester United's legendary manager, Alex Ferguson.

'Pasty will be a great hit. Might be a good one to get in the bag for a day two follow-up. All that "I've lost the love of my life" crap you're good at,' Connor added, thinking in headlines. Like many journalists he had been taught to work a story backwards with the belief that a decent headline was the foundation to every good article.

Connor was buzzing with the adrenalin that came with working on a big, breaking news story. And they didn't get much bigger than this.

13

#Taunting

Bryce Horrigan @BryceTripleB
Have the Keystone Cops caught my killer yet?
#CluelessCops

'So we still don't know even which country these tweets are being sent from?' Sorrell was exasperated, trying to grasp this new tech.

'No, cap'n. It appears they are using a borrowed proxy router,' Haye replied.

'Does nobody speak goddamn English around here anymore? Just pretend, for one minute, that I know nothing of proxy thinga-majiggies and explain it to me as though I were a child,' Sorrell said through gritted teeth.

'Okay, so this person is tweeting crime scene pictures. The first one was tweeted soon after the murder. Any good detective would reason that this person would have been at the crime scene in order to take and post that first photo, right?'

'Right,' Sorrel replied cautiously.

'Not necessarily, cap'n. Someone needed to be there to take the photo all right, but that doesn't mean the picture was posted online from there. We've now pulled all the records from the cell phone towers and no one tweeted from a mobile device in the area at the time the photo hit the net.'

'This is like being back to school.' Sorrell sighed heavily.

'Right, so someone took that pic in that hotel room then, I'm figuring, emailed it to someone else. But they didn't do it on their cell phone. Or rather, they probably did use their cell phone but didn't use the cell network to send it.'

'Haye, you are stretching my patience to limits. Cell phone, no cell phones. Just get to the goddamn point,' Sorrell demanded.

'He'd have switched his cell phone's carrier service off and sent the photo over the net. Virtually untraceable, cap'n. There's a McDonald's with free Wi-Fi a few blocks away. But their CCTV has come up with nothing.'

'Pull all the street CCTV, then?' Sorrell replied.

'We are doing so, cap'n. But all the person needed to do was walk past the shop window to get the connection and email the picture. And if they didn't use McDonald's, they could have done it from a Starbucks or any number of places with free Wi-Fi. I think we're gonna have to let them have that one on us. But once we figure out how they're sending the tweets anonymously from Horrigan's account then we'll close right in on them,' Haye said with a confidence not fully reflected in his tone.

'What about finding all the trolls that threatened Horrigan? Can you trace someone on Twitter if they don't use their real name?' Sorrell asked.

'Simple answer is, you can't. We can track the IP addresses to find out where the tweets were sent from or where the profile was set up. But if the tweets are sent from a pay-as-you-go phone, that's a tough nut to crack. Although we can get an approximate location from the nearest cell tower. Most trolls aren't too smart though; they normally use their own contract cell phone, then boom, we've got their address. No contract without an address. If the troll used a McDonald's Wi-Fi or whatever, we can track the source. Then you time match. Pain in the ass job, but very doable. You take the time the tweet was sent then scour the McDonald's or coffee shop CCTV and try to ID your troll from there. Even better if they've used a card to pay for their goods or Internet usage.'

'This is gonna be some operation,' Sorrell sighed.

'It will be, cap'n, but you'll be surprised how quickly we can mop up. Many will 'fess up when they receive a tweet from the police asking them to identify themselves. Others will come forward once we start getting some publicity out that we're round-ing up Horrigan's haters. Sending abuse is one thing, but they won't wanna be linked with any homicide. We can also try to get it trending. Once the message gets out we're chasing down the trolls, it will spread like wildfire.'

'Sounds like we're giving ourselves more work. Throwing the net even wider,' Sorrell said dubiously.

'Easy enough to sort the wheat from the chaff. If all they've done is sent "Bryce is a cocksucker", we can put them in the wast-ers' pile. With just about every state's law enforcement involved we'll soon work out the real persons of interest from the keyboard warriors. We'll find his killer,' Haye said cockily.

The captain looked anything but confident as his lieutenant drafted up a tweet:

Baltimore Police @BaltimorePolice
We are investigating the homicide of @BryceTripleB, whose life you once threatened. Contact us ASAP to help with our inquiries.

'That should put the fear of God into them. These trolls are like schoolyard bullies. Hit them back and they crap themselves. Let's get working through the list. With five or six of us, it shouldn't take us more than a day to fire this out to all of Horrigan's trolls. This is going to be fun.' Haye beamed.

'Homicides have just gotten a lot more complicated. But as far as I'm concerned, new tech or not, murders are all the same. Someone had a motive to kill this guy. Find that out and we've got our killer,' Sorrell replied wryly.

14

#WhoseBillIsItAnyway?

Patricia Tolan @PastyGirl70
My deepest sympathies and condolences to the friends
and family of @BryceTripleB. I feel your pain.

There was no doubt Patricia 'Pasty' Tolan had been expecting a
call.

'I suppose you'll want to know how I feel about Bryce,' she said,
coolly adding, 'Well, that depends if you plan to snatch me or
allow me to supply my own photos.'

It was a strange opening gambit from someone whose ex-fiancé
had just been shot, execution-style. But, being in PR, she figured
image always came first.

'Your own pictures will be fine and I wouldn't pull a fast one
like that on you, anyway,' April said, having fully intended to have
a photographer 'snatch' Patricia leaving work or while they met
for coffee. 'Do you have any of you both together?' she asked
hopefully.

'You mean the ones I didn't destroy? Sure, I'll email them over
before we meet,' Patricia replied in her Edinburgh accent, which
sounded more English than Scottish.

Patricia 'Pasty' Tolan looked little like the picture she'd emailed
of herself, glass of champagne in hand, laughing at an unheard
joke at some function or another, beside a suited and booted
Bryce Horrigan. There was a hint of faded glory emanating
from the still slim figure of Tolan as she smoked a cigarette from
behind oversized sunglasses, sitting cross-legged outside a coffee

shop on Glasgow's Royal Exchange Square and enjoying the late September sunshine. She had spotted the reporter long before she had seen her as April waddled past, with her hips swinging from side to side, towards the front door.

'I'm glad you didn't bring a sneaky photographer as we agreed,' Patricia announced, peering over the top of her shades.

'Oh, there you are. What am I like? Trained observer, eh? And here I am walking straight past you,' April replied in her usual cheery manner before they embraced briefly.

April took her seat, using the empty chair for her overflowing handbag and assortment of jackets and layers. 'Connor says I'm like a bag lady wherever I go,' April chuckled.

'I forgot Elvis had pitched up here again. Bryce had been so disappointed when he quit London. He said together they could really go places. That it was a retrograde step. Career suicide,' Patricia said, blowing a plume of cigarette smoke out the corner of her thin lips.

'I'd call it a wise decision. Connor's still here and Bryce is dead.' The words were out before April could stop herself.

The first mention of the murder seemed to visibly jolt Patricia Tolan before she regained her cool, taking a long draw of her cigarette. She eventually replied, 'Well, ain't that the truth.'

April announced they should 'get down to business', as she fished around in her bulging bag for her digital recorder – that she could barely work – and her notepad and pen.

'I'd like to start with some basics if you don't mind.' April whizzed through the usual: name, age and where Patricia was from, before she got down to her relationship with Bryce.

They had met at Fettes College in Edinburgh, where they were both destined for a life as lawyers until Bryce broke ranks and headed to the world of newspapers. Patricia followed him and soon moved into PR, which she found time-consuming but incredibly easy. When Bryce relocated to London, she followed again, opening up her own PR agency with some very big corporate clients who were prepared to pay top dollar for someone with the ear of a national newspaper editor. But she admitted London had put their relationship under immense strain.

April paused a moment before asking, 'Because of other women?'

It was a loaded question. Connor had told April about the time when he and Bryce had arrived at the *Sunday Courier* offices and an attractive, leggy, blonde reporter from New Zealand completely ignored Connor's offer of a handshake, walking straight past him to Bryce, basically to swoon all over him. That night, the Kiwi, who had been in a long-term relationship with a photographer from the paper, stayed behind late then pounced as Bryce was leaving at 10pm, asking if he wanted a drink. She had joined Bryce, Connor and the other execs in a bar after work, where she never left his side. Connor became convinced Bryce wouldn't be able to go to the toilet without her.

From that moment on, Connor knew Bryce's head had been well and truly turned. Horrigan had never been a ladies' man and had been an item with Patricia for as long as Connor had known him. But suddenly he found himself completely irresistible to the opposite sex – and he was loving every minute of it.

Surprisingly, Patricia was now defending her ex to April. 'It was understandable, I guess. In his first week in the job, the fucking Prime Minister had us over for tea at Number 10. And if it wasn't the politicians throwing themselves at his feet, it was women. I could keep my eye on him if we attended functions together; other nights he would be working late, but not late enough to explain the hours he came rolling in at. At first I went crazy, shouting and screaming and throwing things around. But I soon realised that'd get me nowhere – he'd just stay out even later the next night or wouldn't come home at all. So I learned to bite my tongue and turn a blind eye.'

Patricia paused to take another long draw of her cigarette, before adding, 'Of course, none of that's for publication. As far as quotes are concerned then I am of course shocked, shattered and appalled that his life should end so tragically. I'm also there for his family if they should need me. Although we split up, you can't spend as long as I did with Bryce without still having feelings for him.'

'When did you split up, incidentally?' April asked.

Patricia took another long draw on her ciggie, which was nearly done now. April was beginning to spot the routine, for whenever she needed to think before replying she would take a puff to gather her thoughts. This was one cool customer.

'That,' Patricia said, taking her time, 'is complicated. I moved to New York with him when he became this big TV star. But within a month he decided I should stay in my own apartment, for obvious reasons.'

'Obvious reasons?' April asked. 'As in, he was seeing someone new?'

'Again, this part is not for publication, but yes, he was seeing someone else,' Patricia admitted.

April sensed a lead and probed deeper. 'But this wasn't just another starlet, was it? This was someone he cared about. Someone who was going to move in with him. Take your place?'

Patricia did the whole cigarette routine again, before tilting her head to the side and letting out a long stream of smoke. 'You're very astute, aren't you?'

April chuckled. 'I guess looks can be deceiving,' she said whilst eyeing Patricia's packet of cigarettes enviously, trying to resist asking for one after all her promises to her daughter Jayne.

Patricia spotted the direction of her interrogator's gaze and laughed loudly. 'Trying to quit – or not start again? Here have one. I'm having another.'

As April leaned forwards for a light, she couldn't help noticing some scarring on Patricia's alabaster white chest. It had only become visible when her blouse fell open as she lit April's cigarette. It looked like an old injury, but was still red and angry. April chose not to mention it.

'Yes, he had a new woman and he wanted me out of the way. I got set up in a tiny flat a few blocks from his penthouse. He even paid for it… at first.'

'Were you working in New York?' April continued, enjoying her cigarette almost too much.

'That was the problem. I'd come on a tourist visa so couldn't really work. I would have to go back home to apply. I asked Bryce if he'd help, but in truth he saw it as a perfect way to get shot of me. On the day my visa expired, I came home on a one-way ticket with no job to go to and no fiancé. Not a good day,' Patricia said grimly.

'Men, huh?' April said sympathetically.

'No. Bryce was unique. I knew he'd become huge in America. His pro-abortion stance was a perfect cause célèbre. It took the debate to the next level. It got him noticed.'

'It certainly did. Do you think it cost him his life?' April asked while stubbing her cigarette out in the ashtray.

'It's America, isn't it?' she shrugged. 'They shoot their own presidents, don't they? So a television host would be no problem.'

'Did it ever bother you, being called Pasty?' April said out of personal curiosity more than anything else.

Tolan threw her head back and laughed. 'With this milk bottle skin? There wasn't a lot I could about it do even if I did. Bryce always called me Pasty no matter how much I protested.'

Patricia's phone rang. She was immediately all business, promising the caller she'd phone back as soon as she finished a meeting. 'Got to go,' she said to April. 'I need to speak to a potentially big customer. Let me pay though. I insist.'

Before April could protest, Patricia had disappeared inside to settle the bill. She returned and gave April another of her cigarettes. 'For later. You look like you need them as much as I do. Just do me one favour. Don't make me sound like a needy psycho. And please don't mention my nickname's Pasty. I really do hate it. It's not my fault I don't take a tan.'

April examined Patricia Tolan from top to bottom as the PR gathered her belongings and left. The reporter then asked for a light from a neighbouring table to smoke her gifted cigarette. She was just finishing it off when the waiter came out with the bill. 'For your coffees, madam.'

'But my friend paid?' April protested.

'No, madam,' the waiter said, most insistently. 'She came in to use the bathroom. She didn't pay.'

April settled up. She needed to get back to work and didn't have time to argue.

'Did she sing like a canary?' Connor asked when April arrived back in their broom cupboard office.

'Yes, sort of. I've got what we wanted but it was all very strange,' she replied.

'Strange how?'

'She didn't ask much about the investigation. You know, "Have they found anyone yet?" All the usual stuff you'd expect to ask if your ex had just been shot. She's been through the mill with Bryce, all right. Treated her like crap. But I didn't feel much sympathy for her. She's the one who clung on to his shirt tails, ignoring his affairs and all the rest of it. And she had some weird scarring on her chest.'

'How weird?' Connor asked.

'Like a burn. Or a scratch, or bite, or something. Whatever it was, it was deep and bloody sore looking.'

'Recent?'

'No. Healed. But not ancient.'

'Unlike yourself,' Connor said, now shifting his interest to his screen as he continued writing an updated report into Bryce's death.

'She also forgot to pay for the bill. Or maybe we paid twice. It was just very strange,' April said, trailing off as she too got busy typing.

15

#Room1410

Captain Sorrell looked harassed. Colonel Cowan was demanding results immediately and the whole police department felt like it was under siege.

'So, we have a murder in a hotel room that was vacant,' Sorrell said to Haye. 'No one had booked it out. Horrigan's killer got in with an all-access swipe card – which means a maid took a kick-back, right?'

'Don't forget hookers too, cap'n,' Haye replied. 'Some of the high class ones strike a deal with hotel security. They get an empty room for a few hours or the whole night. Depends how much back work they've got going. Of course, there has to be more than just the security man in on the scam. You're right, though, they also need a maid to clean up all the mess afterwards.'

'That's a lot of witnesses,' Sorrell replied, doubting Haye's hooker theory.

'Not so, boss. The killer gets a call girl to book it out. Gets to the room. Pays her off. Maybe fucks her first to get his money's worth. I know I would,' Haye smiled.

'Yeah, I know you would. But this killer isn't a dumb-ass like you.'

The captain looked at his computer screen, sighed with relief. 'Finally,' he said, 'the CCTV footage.'

A large media file had been emailed to him after the IT department had spliced together the timeline he'd requested. Sorrell intensely studied the black and white footage, which had been taken from the security cameras from the Baltimore City Hotel. It showed a man in a long coat, with a trilby hat that perfectly obscured his face from the ceiling-mounted cameras. He entered the lobby, striding purposefully past the front desk, like he knew exactly where he was going, and took the elevator to the fourteenth floor. The suspect kept his face pointing almost directly at the ground, meaning you couldn't even tell his skin colour from the angle of the elevator's cameras. The next shot showed the suspect leaving the elevator and walking towards room 1410, keeping as close to the left wall as possible, which wasn't as well lit as the middle of the corridor. Sorrell thought it was no coincidence that the room was situated at the furthest point between the corridor's cameras. Minutes later, a well-dressed black female left the room. In the elevator she indiscreetly thumbed through a wad of notes before putting them in her purse.

'I need her. Fast,' Sorrell commanded. Haye resisted making any smart-ass quip.

The CCTV clock imprint jumped to twenty-eight minutes later, when Bryce Horrigan pulled up in a cab, having come straight from the airport. He headed across the lobby to the elevator, for even though he had never been to this hotel before, he'd stayed in more than enough to know how to find a room without troubling the front desk staff. Bryce walked confidently, with his chin jutting out, which meant he looked down his nose at people, both physically and metaphorically, before admiring himself in the elevator's mirrors.

'He was one cocky son of a bitch,' Haye scoffed. Sorrell thought the remark was pretty observant. Bryce knocked on the door of room 1410 and entered moments later. It would be the last time he was seen alive.

Exactly eleven minutes and twenty-three seconds later, 'hat

man' left the room, sticking to his same routine of hogging the corridor walls and keeping his head tilted down. But this time the elevator was packed and he shuffled to the side, staring at his shoes and trying to sink into the background.

'I want to speak to every one of them, too,' Sorrell instructed, pointing to his screen.

'Looks like a bachelorette party, cap'n. Shouldn't be too hard to trace, but they look pretty wasted.'

'Hat man' walked through the lobby, almost more slowly than when he arrived, to make sure he attracted as little attention to himself as possible.

The Baltimore Police Department computer whizz-kids, as Sorrell called them, had made sure all the images were in 'real time', with footage of the suspect walking along Fleet Street, taking a left onto South Central Avenue, before all trace of him was lost on Doyle Alley.

'Hit the hotel management hard,' Sorrell demanded. 'If they don't play ball, threaten to bring every maid, security man and receptionist downtown. I want whoever rented out that room, whoever planned to clean it and the hooker who planned to use it, in an interview room by the end of play.'

'What about the Twitter trolls and the pro-lifers, boss?' Haye protested. 'Shouldn't we be working on them, too?'

'I guess. The press seem to like all that bull. Cowan, too. But last time I checked we were detectives. It's not our job to sell papers or chase ratings. We just follow the facts. Hitting the hotel is definitely our main priority. We can keep working the Twitter angle as well, but it's absolutely not going to be the focus of this investigation.'

Haye had worked with Sorrell long enough to know that was the end of the conversation. Sorrell was a hard ass all right, but Haye had to admit he was right more often than not. Like the time Haye was working on the case of a married woman who had gone off with some guy, after a night dancing, before she turned up dead in a disused car park. Sorrell had insisted Haye hit her best friend hard – really apply the pressure – under the assumption that women always share things with their girlfriends. Haye had been convinced his boss was wrong on that occasion. But, sure enough, the best friend eventually admitted her cousin had gone off with the victim. The cousin got life in jail.

But Haye really feared his boss might have got it wrong this time – and that he should be placing more importance on the social media side of things. His iPhone was constantly vibrating with Twitter alerts about the case.

16

#WarpedSenseOfHumour

Edwina Tolan @QueenBee
Just done 2 hours at the gym, now ready for lunch with
the girls at Jenners.

Patricia Tolan's mother, Edwina, was an Edinburgh ladies-who-
lunch walking stereotype. When she wasn't in the gym, or pound-
ing the capital's cobbled streets training for a 10k, she filled her time
with charity fundraising drives. Known as Eddi, she knew everyone
who was anyone in Edinburgh. Her sharp features mirrored her
sharp manner, although she could ooze with charm when required.

But Edwina was definitely a doer. If something had to get
done, then she did it. Her no-nonsense approach, and intimidat-
ing demeanour, meant she wasn't someone you said no to easily.
It was this drive and determination that made her a prized and
sought-after asset for the charity boards. Lately though, much of
her attention had been focused on her daughter, Patricia.

'Pasty' Tolan had been carefully moulded in her mother's
image. Edwina had watched with glee as Patricia's status soared,
albeit on the coat-tails of Bryce Horrigan – like her mother, it was
the way she had been tutored to be.

Of course, Edwina had been a shoulder to cry on, too. Advising
Patricia to keep a stiff upper lip when she suspected Bryce of
having several affairs.

'Turn a blind eye, dear. Act as if nothing has happened. God
knows I had to do it often enough with your father,' would be her
general advice.

But Mr Tolan had never flaunted his affairs. Far from it. In fact, there had been only one, with his secretary-cum-mistress, which had lasted nearly as long as his marriage. And contrary to what she told her daughter, Edwina had failed to handle it with dignity and respect. She had instead burst into her husband's office, grabbed a dagger-shaped letter opener from his secretary's desk and tried to gouge her love rival's eyes out, until her husband had dragged her away. The affair had petered out shortly afterwards when the secretary was moved to another branch as far away as possible from Mr Tolan, and more importantly for her safety, from Mrs Tolan.

But Bryce had been unusually cruel with his affairs. He had boasted about them to Patricia, tormenting the poor girl until she could take no more. She had come back from New York an emotional and physical wreck and desperately needed her mother's comfort and protection. And there was no one more protective than the human lioness Edwina Tolan.

Patricia called her shortly after being interviewed by April.

'How did it go, dear?' Edwina asked.

'Exactly as planned, Mama. I even gave her some old photos to show what a sweet boy Bryce had once been. That chubby little reporter lapped it all up for the rag,' Patricia replied with a smile. 'I didn't even pay for the coffees.'

Both women laughed at an in-joke that no one in their right minds would find funny.

17

#MakingAHashOfIt

Connor Presley @ElvisTheWriter
Off Stateside to cover the @BryceTripleB case.
#FeelsSurreal

'I'm off to Maryland,' Connor announced within the confines of the broom cupboard. The news editor, Big Fergie, had just got the go-ahead from the managing editor to send Connor to the US. With falling revenues and tightening budgets, all travel now had to be approved at the most senior levels.

'Oh, what'll you be doing there?' April asked.

'Bryce Horrigan. Dead. Remember?' Connor said impatiently.

'Eh, in Maryhill?' April asked quizzically.

'MaryLAND. I swear your hearing is getting worse.'

'Pardon?' April asked with her trademark throaty laugh.

'You were random enough even before you became deaf as a post,' Connor replied.

'I've been to America, you know,' April said. 'I went to New York on a press trip.'

'I can see you being like dipsy Carrie in *Sex And The City*,' Connor said, half bored. 'Apart from all the sex. Right, I'm off home to throw some clothes in a bag; my plane leaves tonight. You've to keep working the Bryce case, this end. So stay in touch, I'll be picking up all my emails. In fact, I really should give you a crash course in Twitter,' Connor added, checking his watch.

The colour drained from April's face. She wasn't just scared of new technology, but wide-eyed terrified. Connor only needed to mention the latest piece of social media and her heart would skip a beat.

'How has a technophobe like you managed to survive so long in newspapers?' Connor said, teasing her.

'It wasn't like this when I started, that's for sure. I had a phone, a typewriter and an ashtray – and the ashtray was used more than anything else.'

The truth was that by sheer determination and bloody-minded stubbornness, April had eventually overcome the technological obstacles put in her way, like when emails and the Internet had come along in the late-Nineties. She had slowly but surely learned to use them, even though she never truly understood how they worked. But it was the constant advancements of new technology that kept giving her cause for alarm. She would moan, 'Have they not invented enough already without giving me something else to worry about?'

'Okay, are you paying attention?' Connor began. 'A tweet is like a text message. But instead of being on your mobile phone it's on the Internet. With me so far?' he asked hopefully.

'But you read your tweets on your mobile,' April interjected.

Connor sighed heavily. 'Yeah, but I'm reading them on my Twitter app… Anyway, that's not important. Try to focus. So a tweet is 140 characters long and they can be seen by anyone who looks up your username. But your followers will be able to see what you write in their timelines.'

'Followers?' April asked quizzically.

'Yeah, people who "follow" your tweets,' Connor replied slowly as if speaking to a child. 'Also, if I follow you, and you follow me, we can then DM – direct message – each other in private. Okay?'

'Not really, but that's nothing new,' April replied truthfully.

'Then there're hashtags,' Connor added.

April stifled a giggle.

'Would Miss Lavender like to share what's funny with the whole class?' Connor said in a headmaster's tone.

'I remember doing hash once. I had a laughing fit. I couldn't stop for hours. Then I got the munchies and couldn't stop eating.'

'So I see,' Connor muttered under his breath. 'Hashtags can be used to group tweets together by topic. And an RT is a retweet. So if I like something you have posted, I'll retweet it to all my followers to show what a clever thing you've said, or what a complete idiot you are. Or perhaps I'll just favourite it. That's like a "well done" nod of approval. Either way it gets you noticed. Then there's trending.' Connor paused momentarily as he looked at April's blank expression. 'I do hope you are just taking the time to soak all this information in rather than stroking out on me?'

'Yes, please continue,' April said, snapping out of her trance-like state.

'Trending is when a word, phrase, topic or name is tagged faster than anything else – so it starts trending. For example, the name Bryce Horrigan has been trending for most of the day. But he's been replaced with Justin Bieber now.'

'So his death was just a flash in the pan to Twitter users?' April asked.

'Bingo. Welcome to the Twitter generation, who are always hungry for the next trending topic.'

Connor took the time to set up an account and password for April then announced he had to go. April stood up, clutching her right hip, which had been giving her bother of late, before lightly touching Connor's arm. 'Be careful over there. I don't want you ending up like you friend.'

'Thanks, Mum,' Connor said mockingly, 'but Bryce and I were friends a lifetime ago. Somewhere down the line he lost his way. I'd love to find out when.'

18

#Fidel

'People just post bullshit all the time?' Sorrell said, irritated after reading pages of tweets from people Haye followed.

'Granted, the majority is babble, cap'n,' Haye replied almost apologetically.

'Jeez, so my homicide investigation is competing with people talking about the latest boyband song?'

'Yeah, you've summed it up pretty well there, cap'n,' Haye replied.

Haye had never truly respected his superiors until working for the captain. He saw them as either career suits or seeing out their days till their pensions. But Sorrell was different. He still had the instinct of a street detective, in spite of his senior position.

He had also stopped Haye going off the rails. In the early days, it wasn't unusual for the young detective to turn up at work reeking of stale alcohol and cheap perfume. That all changed when Sorrell was promoted to head up the homicide squad. The captain hadn't brought Haye back on track; he'd fallen into line on his own free will with renewed purpose and enthusiasm. Haye was soon hitting the gym at night instead of the bars. A year later, the captain had promoted him to be his deputy. He had genuinely not expected nor coveted it. He hadn't even applied for the post until he was told to. Instead, he was given it during a typically brief conversation with Sorrell.

His captain had just finished talking about a case, when he casually concluded, 'Oh, and Haye, you're my new deputy. You start Monday.'

Haye had been totally shell-shocked. 'But cap'n, I didn't ask. Everyone else has been desperate for it.'

'Exactly, they've been kissing my ass for months. Makes me sick. That's why you've got the job.'

'Aw jeez, cap'n, and I thought it was because of my detective skills and management potential.'

'You'll get there in time, Haye.'

And that had been the end of the job 'interview'. But that was just the way Haye liked it. All work conversations with the cap'n were short and concise. That's because Sorrell actually took time to think things through instead of just 'bumping his gums' – a phrase the cap'n was fond of using.

When Haye turned forty, Sorrell had taken the department to a bar to celebrate. As a surprise, the cap'n had even invited Haye's twenty-two-year-old daughter, Sam. It was, without question, one of the happiest moments of his life when he hugged his daughter surrounded by his close work colleagues and a boss he had nothing but the utmost respect for.

But Haye was more than just a hard-working and loyal cop; he also had ambitions. The last thing on his mind would be to groom himself for the captain's job, even though that would be the natural conclusion. Instead, with the permission and blessing of Sorrell, he was seconded to the Baltimore Police Department's new cybercrime division. There, he attended seminar after seminar, given by everyone from Internet security experts to various visiting IT professors. However, it was a talk given by an ex-felon, Peter Genasi, that resonated.

Genasi had been a low-level street thug before turning his attentions to cybercrime. Haye had asked him why.

'It's easy, that's why. Cops forget all these yos have been raised on Xbox, man. They know all about systems, broadbands, hacks and cheats. Hell, I was playing the Box before I could speak. Working your way around a company's security systems is just a matter of perseverance. So while you guys are busy lifting yos,

I was breaking into company systems and encrypting their data with ransom-ware. I could earn $5,000 a day. Easy.'

'And these company's would actually pay you?' Haye asked incredulously.

'Not the corporations. They call the FBI on your ass. But medium-sized companies? Twenty, thirty, forty workers? It's cheaper for them to pay 5k to get their company back than pay an IT crisis company 20k to take a month to fix it.'

Haye shook his head in disbelief. 'So if you're so smart, Genasi, how come you got caught?'

'The usual: greed. Greed and laziness. After I made my first $100,000 I couldn't be bothered doing the hours of research into new targets. So I went back to hitting old ones. But this time they were prepared, weren't they? Once bitten, as the saying goes. I got lifted still sitting in my boxer shorts, man. Red-fucking-handed. So now I do this shit. Tell you good folks about how bad men like me operate.'

Haye liked Genasi. He was a crook, but he was honest about being a crook. 'Bet you'd go back to your old ways if you could?'

'Yeah, but this time I won't get caught.'

'That, my friend, is what they all say. Next time the judge won't be so forgiving,' Haye retorted.

'Next time I'll be sending you a photo from a beach in Cuba. Some lovely cutie serving me cocktails.'

'Shit, you've really thought this out. The communists could run riot with someone with your skills,' Haye replied.

'Damn straight. Just call me Fidel Genasi from now on.' And so he did. From then on the cyber-crook-turned-security-expert Peter Genasi was always called 'Fidel' by Haye. They formed a close personal and working relationship when the company who hired Genasi won a year-long contract with the new Baltimore cybercrimes unit.

Haye would need all of Fidel's expertise and guile now more than ever.

19

#AvengingAngel

Baby Angel @BabyAngel
(to **Geoffrey Schroeder** @GeoffreySchroeder)
Do you want to know where BH is going to be?

Geoffrey Schroeder could remember with great clarity the moment it had happened. He'd been in two minds over his next move and was browsing through his timeline as usual, when he received the tweet just moments after he'd been notified he had a new follower. The Twitter user's profile didn't give much away. There was a picture – or avatar – of a newborn baby, along with a short profile which made for ominous reading: *God's assassin. My mission is to destroy all baby killers.*

It came as something of a surprise to Schroeder as he only had around a dozen followers, and most of those were spam accounts promising thousands of followers if you signed up to their service. The others were from the dwindling handful of friends he still had left. But Geoffrey followed thousands of other tweeters, all related to pro-life and pro-choice groups, or those connected with the medical profession who carried out abortions. He'd spend hours each day sifting through the various posts.

He was also one of Bryce Horrigan's ten million followers. Geoffrey had read all of Horrigan's messages, of which there were many as Bryce was a serial tweeter. The chat show host was constantly bragging about what famous person he'd met and what they had said to him, and how they'd become such 'great mates'. Even someone of limited intelligence like Geoffrey Schroeder knew a phoney when he saw one. But from the fluff of the show-biz world, Horrigan would work himself up into a rage online over the latest attack on some abortion clinic, or he'd speak in the defence of whatever doctor had had his life threatened for carrying out terminations.

Geoffrey scrolled back through Horrigan's many thousands of messages to the first time the presenter had voiced his pro-choice opinion. It was as if the seasoned broadcaster was dipping his toe in the water to gauge the temperature, to see what sort of response he'd get. His retweets and replies seemed to spread like wildfire across Twitter. The torrents of abuse he received from pro-lifers were unanimous in their condemnation. It didn't seem to deter him at all. On the contrary, Horrigan decided to ramp up the rhetoric.

But Bryce hadn't known what it was like to have his heart ripped out of his life; not like Geoffrey had. Horrigan had never suffered real pain and loss… until he went to Baltimore, that is.

Bryce was dead, just as Schroeder had fantasised. But now he had to carefully plan his next move if he was to escape capture.

20

#VirginTweeter

Bernard Sorrell @BernardSorrell
This is my first tweet – I hope I don't screw it up.

Captain Sorrell had only provided the bare minimum personal information for his profile, which simply stated, *Born and bred in Baltimore*. His avatar was a picture of the city's landmark, the Key Monument. There was no mention of the police department, or any hint he worked in law enforcement. He was determined to keep his two teenage daughters out of his online existence. He already worried about them enough after his wife had pointed out their casual use of social media, and he regularly berated his kids over what they were posting.

'What have I told you about posting all these pictures of your-selves and your friends, then telling the world where you are going to be on a Saturday night? This is a bad guy's dream. He has your names, what you look like and even your location. It's like you're begging for trouble,' was how one of his rants would go. His daughters would give a half-baked apology, go quiet online for a while before they were back to the idle chitter-chatter their dad hated so much. The truth was, like many cops' kids, they were tired of the lectures they'd had all their lives about the bad men lurking in the shadows. Why should they worry when their lives were full of friends, parties and boys?

It was their father who had the dubious pleasure of having to witness the other side of humanity. The things he'd seen would regularly keep him awake at night. It was the burden those on the frontline had to bear. He was now beginning to believe that ignorance really was bliss.

Sorrell remembered how, as a rookie cop, he had wrestled a knife off a man who was threatening to slit the throats of his partner and three-year-old child. It had been a block from where Sorrell's oldest school friend lived. He had later warned his high school pal to be careful as there were dangerous men in his neighbourhood. His friend had calmly put a hand on Sorrell's shoulder and in a reassuring manner said, 'Bernard, I have lived here all my life and I've never so much as seen a knife, never mind a gun, on these streets. Some fruitcake trying to slice up his family can happen anywhere.'

It had made Sorrell realise a plain truth – that it was the cops who saw society's underbelly. They were the ones who had to tackle the mad, bad and mentally deranged. Meanwhile, the innocents would just go about their daily routines, laughing, joking, making love, drinking beer, moaning about their bosses, having affairs, going to the ball game and basically living their humdrum lives.

Twenty-five years on, Sorrell had stopped trying to metaphorically clean up the city. He realised a long time ago that it was a losing battle. But although he was now cynical with age and battle weary with the bureaucracy of the police department, he had never lost his core belief that if you murdered someone, you should be caught and sent to jail.

Early on in his career, Sorrell had discovered he had a knack for homicides. On entering a crime scene he could usually suss out within minutes what had gone on. His talents were soon recognised by his superiors and he began to climb the career ladder and humble pay scales. But Sorrell also realised the higher up the chain of command he got, the further removed he was from catching the bad guys.

He had become something of a control freak over homicides. He'd despair at some of the botched investigations carried out by his underlings or how they'd try to over-complicate their murder theories. Sorrell would berate them: 'Stop watching *CSI: Zip Code* and get back to basics. The victim almost always knows their killer. And someone ALWAYS knows who the killer is. You've just got to find the right people to lean on.'

Sorrell prided himself on getting the right man, for the killers were rarely women. He'd never had an unsafe conviction or attempted to frame someone just because he was a strong suspect. Instead, Sorrell let the detective work take him to where the killer was. Then he'd nail them good. Although it didn't allow him to sleep any easier, it did allow him to be able to face himself in the mirror each morning knowing he had done right.

An email arrived on his iPad informing him he had a new follower.

'Hey, what do you know, honey, I've got myself a disciple,' he chuckled.

'It's probably just spam, babe,' his wife, Denise, hollered back from the kitchen.

Sorrell decided to follow back his mysterious new follower, called Baby Angel.

Moments later he received his first direct message. It simply stated, *Do you want to know who killed Bryce Horrigan?*

21

#BryceSuspects

Before the FBI had released pictures of 'people of interest' for the Boston marathon bombing, the Internet sleuths had already swung into top gear. Less than twenty-four hours after the attack that killed three spectators at the finishing line and left 280 people injured, the faces of two suspects, carrying heavy objects in their backpacks, had been posted online. They turned out to be genuine 'people of interest' to the authorities.

The same was happening with Bryce Horrigan's homicide. Not out of any great love for the presenter – quite the opposite – but as a way of proving the Twittersphere could police itself. The hashtag #BryceSuspects was set up with the purpose of identifying all the people who had posted death threats to Horrigan.

Twitter users went into overdrive. They tracked down personal information about the abusive users, including their real names and where they lived and worked. Each new bit of information was tweeted with the same hashtag so it could all be shared. The 'targets' were hit with a barrage of personal details about themselves and threats to reveal them as Bryce Horrigan homicide suspects to their bosses, families and friends. Most of them relented straight away, apologised profusely for their offensive tweets, claiming they were drunk. Others immediately deleted their accounts and went into hiding, but would still later receive letters from across the States from the self-appointed Twitter guardians, proving there was no hiding place. Some were just insane, getting into incredibly heated and abusive slanging matches with their accusers.

But Geoffrey Schroeder had gone unnoticed by the Internet sleuths, having never once sent a death threat to Bryce Horrigan. Why on earth would he want to alert someone he was going to kill?

'Haye, look at this. There's a "Top 10 Bryce Suspects" trending,' Sorrell said, much to the surprise of his detective team, who greeted his announcement with mock cheers and tongue-in-cheek congratulations.

'Welcome to the twenty-first century, cap'n,' one wag shouted. 'You related to Bill Gates, boss?' said another.

'Yeah, yeah, very funny. Don't you all have work to do?' Sorrell replied, his deep dark cheeks slightly more flushed than usual.

Haye peered over at his boss's screen and let out a low whistle. 'Jeez, is nothing sacred?' Sorrell clicked on the trend. Sure enough, people had been contributing their suspect suggestions – from the humorous to the ludicrous to the downright libellous.

'I used to think the press were out of order,' Sorrell said, 'but even they wouldn't try a stunt like this. Printing suspects' names – even as a joke – is unheard of.'

'That's the information super highway, boss. Wanna make a bomb to blow up the Boston marathon? It's just a few clicks away. Child porn? Fundamentalism? Hell, I even came across a how-to-kill-a-cop guide. It's all there,' Haye said with a shrug.

'Well, if this is the future, I don't care much for it. I mean what's with these trolls in the first place? Grown men abusing folks. I just don't get it,' Sorrell replied.

'Not just adults, cap'n. It's the kids, too. Have you heard of One Direction?'

'Who, or what, are One Direction?' Sorrell asked.

'Come on, cap'n. One Direction. 1D. Harry Styles. They're the latest boyband. Your daughters will know them.'

Sorrell stared at Haye with unblinking eyes. He was probably right, his daughters kept up to date with all the latest music trends. 'So what?' he shrugged.

'Well, whoever the band members start dating get the most vile abuse and death threat tweets from their fans. They have more than twenty million Twitter followers. At least double that of Horrigan.'

'I am more than capable of doing the math,' Sorrell drawled.

'The point is, these are just kids, cap'n,' Haye said, while tapping at his keyboard. 'But listen to this: "Harry is too good for a slut like you. If you don't leave him alone I am going to stab your slut pussy then my brother will rape you." Here's another: "Get your ugly, filthy, whore hands off Niall or you will die. I'm gonna shoot you in the pussy." That one included the address of the bastard's poor girlfriend. And that's just some of over 300,000 threatening tweets. And these were the ones serious enough to be investigated. The first girl was thirteen years old. The other, fourteen. Good families. Good schools.'

Sorrell sat in stunned silence before he offered, 'Teenage hormones?'

'More than that, cap'n. I'm sure your daughters had a crush on someone at that age…'

Haye was cut off with a warning look from his boss. 'Careful where you're going with this, Haye.'

'Sorry, cap'n. What I mean is, teenage girls may have confused thoughts at that age, but instead of sharing it with their diary they now share it on Twitter. It's given them a voice. And direct access to the stars.'

'But this is more than just trash talk, Haye. That girl actively went out to obtain an address. That's a serious threat. Real cause and motive. They have mental health issues,' Sorrell reckoned.

'I don't know, cap'n. I think people can adopt different personas online. An alter ego. That's why many hide behind avatars. They can be someone else online. Live out their fantasies, however warped.'

'Talking of which, what do you make of this?' Sorrell said in hushed tones as he clicked on the direct message from Baby Angel asking if he'd like to know who murdered Bryce Horrigan.

'Could be a time-waster, boss?' Haye reasoned.

'I don't think so. I got this about ten minutes after I set up my account,' Sorrell replied.

'Ten minutes? Someone either knew you were going to open a Twitter account or was waiting for you to do it, cap'n,' Haye figured.

'Waiting? How?' Sorrell wanted to know more.

'Well, anyone with Google could find out with one search you were heading up the case. So they check Twitter for someone matching your profile and find nothing, right? But this is a Twitter killer – the whole case is being built round that. They just know you have gotta go online at some point. So they keep searching and searching until, hey bingo, Sorrell pops up. Resident of Maryland. Now even if you're not the Captain Sorrell they're looking for, and they tweet the wrong person, what does it matter? They know they're safe. They're hidden where we can't find them. It's a fishing exercise, then they reel you in.'

Sorrell appreciated Haye's layman terms explanation – it made it perfectly clear to him that, for Baby Angel, this was all just a game. He decided to play along... for now. He sent a direct message reply in his typically forthright manner:

Who are you?

22

#WhatsAMatterYou?

April felt drained from the day's events, once the adrenalin had worn off. She found it harder and harder to motivate herself every morning. She just didn't have the energy anymore for the demands of working on a national newspaper.

April decided she couldn't be bothered cooking so decided to eat at her favourite restaurant on the way home. Its owner, Luigi, may have wandering arms like an octopus, but he made the finest Italian food on Glasgow's Southside.

The portly proprietor was busy serving a table of six when she arrived, which suited her fine as April wanted to take her table with the bare minimum of fuss. She ordered her usual dish of meatballs and a large glass of house red wine, then decided she'd try to tweet from her phone, as Connor had showed her.

Minutes later, Luigi was by her side, bending down to give elaborate kisses to both of April's cheeks, smudging her half-moon spectacles in the process.

'Ma a-favourite customer. Always good tae see ye, hen.' Luigi had been born in Naples but spent almost all his life in Scotland, leaving him with a ridiculous Neapolitan twang that would break into strong Glaswegian mid-sentence. 'But today, you ignore Luigi, for your phone. Why you ignore Luigi, eh?' he said in mock hurt.

'I am tweeting, Luigi. Or trying to,' April explained. 'It's all about raising my profile, you see. It is going to save the newspaper industry, apparently.'

'What pish are you a-telling Luigi?' The restaurateur nearly always referred to himself in the third person. 'The only people who make a-money from the Internet are fraudsters and porn-sters. You wanna make a-porno with Luigi?' he said, smiling, with his eyebrows arched sky high. April knew he was only half-joking.

'I don't think there would be much demand to see me in the buff, Luigi. Not when you can have the pick of all these skinny little minxes online.'

'What, with their fake a-titties? They make Luigi sad. Why ruin their bodies with these horrible things. I like a-real titties, like a-yours,' Luigi said, giving April a bear hug and making sure he discreetly managed to get a feel of her ample breasts in the process.

'Technically, Luigi, that is sexual assault,' April cautioned her eager suitor.

'I a-know. Luigi is an old sex pest. But I'm a nice old a-sex pest, don't you think?'

April would have to concede that point. 'With the juiciest meatballs in Glasgow,' she added with a wink.

Luigi blushed. 'April. You know I a-love you. And I wanna marry you. But you are a big cock tease.'

23

#PersonOfInterest

Baby Angel @BabyAngel
You shouldn't be worried about who I am. But
@GeoffreySchroeder might be a POI.

Captain Sorrell received the direct message less than three minutes after sending his own DM to Baby Angel.

'Do we have a Geoffrey Schroeder as a Person Of Interest?' Sorrell asked Haye.

'I'll check him out, cap'n. We're still waiting for a complete list of all those who were investigated for threatening Horrigan,' Haye replied.

'Be helpful to know if he's on the radar as soon as,' Sorrell said, returning to his screen.

The captain typed back:

Bernard Sorrell @BernardSorrell
I like to know who I'm talking to. Why would Geoffrey
Schroeder be of interest?'

It took less than thirty seconds for a reply to come through.

Baby Angel @BabyAngel
Ask yourself why he's not in Kansas City anymore.

Bernard Sorrell @BernardSorrell
Why don't you tell me?

Baby Angel @BabyAngel
Because he was in Baltimore, stupid.

Sorrell sat back in his chair and clasped his hands behind his head, staring at the last DM. His thought process was interrupted by Haye, who came into Sorrell's office reading out sheets he'd just printed off.

'Geoffrey Schroeder you said, cap'n? His background is usual minimum wage stuff, trailer trash from Shitsville, Missouri. With a good motive: he lost his beloved wife and unborn son to an illegal abortion. Poor bastard didn't even know his wife was pregnant, never mind the fact she'd gone for a termination.'

Sorrell let out a slow-whistle response.

'As you can imagine, cap'n, he bore a grudge against the doctor who fucked up his family. Loads of harassment charges and all the usual stuff you'd expect. He ramps things up a notch when he's later discovered with explosives in his car. We never discovered what he planned to do with them as his lawyer got him off on the wrap before it even went to court. But Bryce Horrigan became his new focus of attention this year with all the pro-choice stuff, and Schroeder sent him loads of pictures of late abortions. State police gave him a formal warning and kept regular tabs on him – dropping by his trailer, just letting him know they were still interested in him. But get this. Less than a month ago, he's a no-show. He hasn't been seen since.'

'I take it we have his mugshot?' Sorrell enquired.

'Of course, cap'n,' Haye said, brandishing a police photo of Schroeder. 'Want me to send it as an all-rounder before he makes a run for the border?'

'No. Not yet,' Sorrell said. 'Let's keep Geoffrey Schroeder to ourselves for the time being,' he added thoughtfully.

24

#Help

Geoffrey Schroeder took refuge in a cheap motel about seventy miles north along the I-81 highway towards Scranton – the middle-of-nowhere city that was now indelibly associated with the comedy series *The Office*. He planned eventually to hang left along the I-90 highway to Buffalo and cross the border into Canada at Niagara Falls.

He parked his pick-up truck two blocks from the motel, but it was still within sight, should the authorities take any interest in it. He gave a false name at reception, demanded a front-facing room, paid in cash, and put the TV on for background noise. He desperately needed to work out his next move and fast. His only saving grace was the motel receptionist had barely given him a second glance. Still, he knew it wouldn't be long until law enforcement came calling – after all, he certainly wasn't the first wanted man to try to flee to Canada.

Schroeder decided to send a direct message to the person who had guided him.

There was nothing left to do but wait for the reply.

25

#ProfessorPainInAss

Bryce Horrigan @BryceTripleB
Hello everyone. This is what the baby killer looks like
begging for his life. #TerrorFace

As Captain Sorrell looked at the image of Bryce Horrigan's face
moments before he was murdered – a picture that had now been
retweeted around two million times since it had been posted –
he couldn't help but think that the accompanying hashtag was a
pretty accurate description.

'Someone really took a lot of time to plan this,' he said to himself. 'They didn't just want you dead. They wanted you to know
you were going to die. To feel the fear.'

His solitary musing was broken by Haye rapping on his door
and letting himself in before Sorrell had time to answer. 'The prof
is on the premises,' Haye announced without preamble. Under his
breath, Sorrell swore.

Professor Benedict Watson was head of criminology at
Maryland University. He had been fully dedicated to his life of
academia until he felt the seductive touch of celebrity when he was
hired as a 'talking head' for a low budget documentary on serial
killers, which ended up getting high ratings when it was picked
up by a number of TV networks across America. Suddenly, the
fifty-year-old professor was a serial killer 'expert' and 'top criminal profiler'. Whenever he appeared on television, Sorrell used to
scoff, 'That dude ain't ever met a killer, never mind caught one.'

Sorrell was correct on both accounts. The professor had led a very privileged and sheltered life, never leaving an educational institution since kindergarten. All his criminal profiling came from theory, books and discussions in the lecture hall. He'd never had to look into a murder suspect's eyes and tell them the game was up, as Sorrell had countless times.

Unfortunately for Sorrell, his boss Colonel Cowan had met the professor when the academic was a guest speaker at a criminology conference. The pair hit it off and the colonel invited Watson to become Baltimore Police Department's official profiler on a crime-by-crime basis. It was the final stamp of approval the professor craved. But Sorrell was not so enthusiastic about the appointment; he didn't care much to be lectured on the theory of the criminal mind. His job was to bring people who do bad things to justice. What else was there to know? Colonel Cowan didn't see it that way, telling Sorrell, 'Think of the professor as offering a different perspective. That'll be the extent of his involvement in cases. To be used by you like a tool.'

'He's a tool, all right,' Sorrell had remarked to himself.

By and large, Sorrell had been able to avoid the professor when he was on the premises due to a network of lookouts and tip-offs from his staff. And anyway, the prof would rather be giving lucrative soundbites for TV news and documentaries than getting his hands dirty with painstaking police work.

But the Bryce Horrigan case was very different. This wasn't just network news, it was a worldwide event and the professor's massive ego could sense the related glory from helping to track down the perpetrator. This time, Sorrell wouldn't be able to avoid him, especially when he was summoned to a meeting with Professor Watson in the colonel's office.

'I believe you two gentlemen know each other,' the colonel said by way of an introduction, adding, 'Professor Watson might have some useful advice for you, captain.'

A little show had clearly been pre-arranged between the two men for Sorrell's benefit as the professor brought the captain's attention to his laptop, which was already booted up on the edge of the colonel's desk.

'I've been studying the hacker's tweets sent from Bryce Horrigan's Twitter account after his death. Take this one, for example. It begins with "Hello everyone". That is someone who feels comfortable in the knowledge that they haven't been caught. They are confident enough to post yet another photograph of the crime scene from Bryce's account because law enforcement hasn't been able to work out how they've done it.'

'We're working on it,' Sorrell said bluntly.

The colonel intervened. 'Now now, Bernard. I'm sure the professor didn't mean that as a personal slight. It's no wonder we haven't traced them yet. People can hide behind an electronic trail going all around the world. And no police force in America's history has faced a case like this, with over 100,000 potential suspects. You're doing a great job. But the professor will be able to build a profile of the killer, which will help you sift out the possibles from the time-wasters.'

Sorrell kept his thoughts on the professor's profile to himself.

The academic continued as if the interruption had never happened. 'Now, look at this taunt: "This is what a baby killer looks like begging for his life." Again, notice the confidence from the statement. This is someone who is careful and meticulously plans his moves. And when the coast is clear – i.e. their technique for delivering an untraceable tweet proves to be effective – they do it again. These will increase in frequency as the killer's arrogance and confidence swells to even greater proportions.'

By this point, Sorrell wasn't sure if Watson was talking about himself or the killer.

The professor prattled on. 'They also know that they have an audience. I notice it's ironic that Bryce Horrigan has nearly a million more followers since his death because of these gruesome posts by the impostor. This will present a window of opportunity to trace the killer,' he concluded, a tad smugly.

'And what about the killer's profile. What sort of person are we looking for?' the colonel prompted.

Sorrell used some profiling skills of his own, noticing how the professor would almost puff out his chest to engage with the colonel, but would barely give the lower ranks like himself the time of day. The academic was a snob, Sorrell concluded.

'A pro-life fundamentalist, of course, but working in unison with A N Other. The tweeter needs a fairly high level of understanding of computer networks. They are also intelligent enough not to be putting themselves directly in the firing line. Being behind a laptop or smartphone keeps them metaphorically and physically away from the crime scene and the shooter – the person who actually pulled the trigger. The shooter will be someone of much lower intelligence. Another pro-lifer, but someone already known to the authorities. They may have convictions for intimidation of abortion clinic staff; sending death threats, that sort of thing. Bryce Horrigan would have become a focal point for his anger. However, the mystery tweeter is the person pulling the strings. They would have orchestrated the assassination.'

'And the puppetmaster's profile?' the colonel asked in hope.

'White male. University educated. Deeply religious. Early thirties. Unfortunately, it's unlikely they'll have previous convictions.'

A needle in a haystack, Sorrell managed to prevent himself from saying.

'But as I have said, their growing confidence will be their undoing. The more he tweets, the more chance we will have of catching him,' the professor said dramatically, giving the sort of soundbite that the TV cameras love so much.

'Any suspects fit the professor's profiles, captain?' the colonel asked.

'Not per se, but the professor's profile might throw up some names that have slipped through the net,' Sorrell said, playing the game. He added, 'Thank you, professor, I'll let you know how it pans out.'

The colonel beamed at Sorrell's compliance, dismissing him with a friendly, 'Thanks for your time, captain.'

Captain Sorrell had absolutely no intention of keeping the publicity-seeking professor in the loop. He thought the profile of the Twitter impostor using Bryce Horrigan's name was pathetic. However, he did agree that the description of the potential shooter was a match.

Back in his office, Sorrell pulled up Geoffrey Schroeder's image on his computer. It was taken from a street CCTV camera near the Baltimore City Hotel on the day of Bryce Horrigan's death. He'd already had the picture before the meeting with the professor, but he certainly wasn't going to share any of his information with someone all too willing to go blabbing in front of the cameras.

26

#DeadCheerleader

ABT News @ABTnews
All the staff and colleagues send their condolences
to the friends and family of @BryceTripleB. He will be
sorely missed.

In the weeks prior to his death, Bryce Horrigan had been even
more infuriating to work with than usual.

There was no doubt Horrigan was supremely talented as a journalist, but the transformation to chat show host had not been an
easy one. His TV show was a curious affair, originally setting out
in the vein of David Letterman, Conan O'Brien, Jay Leno and
fellow Scot Craig Ferguson. But there was one major flaw with
Bryce sticking to the tried and tested late night format – he just
wasn't funny, with no comedic timing whatsoever. So he shifted
direction to add a more current affairs feel, with congressmen sitting on the same couches as TV celebrities and film stars. The
politicians would get a rough ride, while he would fawn over the
film stars and TV personalities. It was a ratings disaster. Bryce had
been heading for a very public and humiliating sacking and began
to present his show like a condemned man, trying too hard to get
arguments going with political guests, making his interviews look
stilted and contrived.

That all changed with the case of Tiffany Wilson-Jones, a mid-
dle-class sophomore college girl from the University of Virginia,
who had undergone an illegal abortion and died from the botched
procedure. The tragedy had occurred after the Virginia House of

Delegates had effectively outlawed all abortions in 2012 – declaring the rights of a person apply from the moment the sperm and egg unite. Being the natural newshound that he was, Bryce sunk his teeth straight into the story and made it his own.

'It's very simple,' he declared the day after Tiffany's death had become a national talking point. 'Had abortions been legal in her state, Tiffany would be alive today. This is a girl who had it all: top of her class with a bright future ahead of her. Yet she died in agony, her insides shredded by a BUTCHER,' he said with great emphasis, loving his use of emotive, headline-grabbing phrases. 'But this isn't the eighteenth century, people. This is America. The best country in the world, I'm repeatedly being told. Yet it is a country where you force your youngest and most talented citizens to pay with their lives just because they've made a simple mistake.'

The fact that Tiffany Wilson-Jones was a blonde, all-American girl, who looked damn sexy in her cheerleading pictures, only helped his cause. For it is an indisputable fact that had a poor, less attractive girl died in such circumstances, then her passing would have hardly troubled the headline writers at her local newspaper – which is just the way the media cookie crumbles.

Bryce seized the fortuitous timing. Now he had a campaign he could throw himself into. He steered any conversation on his show onto his own pro-abortion agenda, which had suddenly become a hot potato in America once again thanks to a dead cheerleader.

27

#Blagger

Connor sat in Edinburgh airport's departure lounge waiting to catch the Continental flight to Newark before flying to Baltimore. He was hoping he'd get lucky. Like most journalists, Connor was a blagger. Whether it was a holiday or dining out at a restaurant, journalists would try to get money off, or the whole thing for free.

Connor wasn't the worst offender. He'd once had an editor who was able to blag gratis holidays for himself, his wife, their six kids and his mother-in-law, who was dragged along as an unpaid babysitter. When the editor and his brood had been late for one flight, missing it entirely, he had casually phoned the harassed travel firm PR and demanded she got him on the next departure – in business class, of course.

That was taking the piss as far as Connor was concerned. But that didn't stop him firing off an email to an attractive airline PR he had once met at a function. At least Connor was up front about his intentions, openly asking if there was any chance of an upgrade before handily supplying the flight number. He got the desired response: 'I'll see what I can do – chancer.' He promised the PR lunch on him the next time she was in Glasgow. It was a welcome relief because business class flights for reporters had long since been scrapped.

Continental airlines made an announcement for a Mr Presley to make himself known to the check-in desk. He'd be flying business class, after all, meaning Connor could rest fully then hit the ground running.

He was soon settled into his spacious seat, with a complimentary glass of champagne. The economy passengers were still boarding, which gave Connor time to scroll through his tweets when he spotted one from ABT News and suddenly had a thought. He knew someor e who worked for Bryce. He tapped in the name Tom O'Neill and saw his name and picture pop up. He 'followed' Tom before typing, *Hi Tommy. Long time no speak. Please follow me as I need to DM you.*

Seconds later, Connor received the notification email: *@DerryDude1887 is now following you.*

Connor whispered to himself, 'Yes – contact.'

The next message he received was a DM from O'Neill: *What's your phone no. Elvis?* Moments after sending it, Connor received a call: 'You were supposed to have my job in New York, you know,' Tom said in his thick Northern Irish accent.

'Get lost, really?' Connor said in genuine amazement after taking the transatlantic call. Connor had known Tom O'Neill only briefly after handing in his notice to Bryce, when the Irishman was recruited as his replacement.

'Whenever Bryce got pissed off with me, he'd say things like, "I should have brought Elvis with me instead," or, "I wouldn't have had the same problems with Elvis." I don't mind admitting I hated hearing your name. Even now, when *Blue Suede Shoes* comes on the radio I still turn it over,' Tom laughed.

'I guess I'd hate me too after that,' Connor replied.

'I thought he was deadly serious at one point. I'm surprised he never contacted you?' Tom asked, with something sounding like a touch of paranoia.

'Well, I can tell you I didn't hear a peep,' Connor assured him. 'Of course, I couldn't help thinking "what if" when he became a big name in America. But then again, at least I'm not in your situation now.'

Connor was greeted with total silence down the line.

Eventually Tom replied, 'Couldn't have put it more bluntly myself, to be honest, Elvis. I'm fucked. No Bryce. No show. No job.

I'll be back before my visa runs out. This is the inherent danger of being so reliant on someone else's career, I guess.'

Connor changed tack. 'Listen, Tommy, they're just closing the plane doors so I'm going to have to go. But I'll be in Baltimore soon. Do you think you could keep me in the loop?'

'Sure. I can be your insider – no direct quotes, though. And I'll need paying. I'm going to need all the money I can get.'

'Great, I'll DM you,' Connor said with a smile.

28

#OldDogsNewTricks

The email alert on April's Samsung Galaxy let her know she had been sent a new tweet. She could of course use the app Connor had installed on her phone, but she found it hard to type anything on the screen, cursing her 'little sausage fingers'. She decided to use what Connor called her 'glorified laptop' – the iPad with the wireless keyboard. April searched for Twitter on Google, then was met with the object of her many fears – the log on screen. She could remember her username easy enough, but then became stumped at her password. Which was strange as she only ever used a variation of the name of her cat, Cheeka, with a selection of numbers ranging from her own date of birth to the moggy's.

April placed her nightly generous helping of gin and tonic on the side table and plonked herself in her favourite chair. She was determined she could conquer this. Her daughter Jayne was always moaning at her that technophobia was all in the mind. But as far as April was concerned, technology wasn't there to help and enhance her life. It was to be tolerated. Given the choice, April still hankered for the days of old, with her typewriter and overflowing ashtray. How she missed smoking all day at her desk. 'Puff, puff, puff, tap, tap, tap,' April said.

April loved her sound effects. They occasionally even made it into her copy; like the time she wrote a feature about a couple who had turned their home into an owlery. Her intro had begun, *HOOT believe it!* That didn't make it into the paper but onto the wall of shame instead, which was an old cork message board where the sub-editors – the journalists who edit, re-write and make articles fit the spaces on the pages – printed out and pinned the funniest copy filed by the reporters and agencies.

Officially, April was meant to have given up smoking. A strong lecture from her doctor at her annual company health check-up warned of high blood pressure and of being at risk from a stroke. An even sterner lecture from her daughter concluded with the emotional blackmail that April was being cruel to her one and only granddaughter Alana. Connor had also got on her case when she nipped off for one of her increasingly frequent cigarette breaks. He even helpfully compiled a time and motion sheet for her.

'I've timed that your average fag break lasts around eight minutes, including the time it takes your wee stubby legs to walk out of the building. So, at six ciggies a day, that is forty-eight minutes lost every day. Which is 240 minutes per week,' he said, sounding like a maths teacher as he tapped numbers into his BlackBerry calculator. 'That's four hours a week. So over your forty-four working weeks, that comes to 176 hours a year. Divide that by an eight-hour shift and it comes to… twenty-two days.

With a smile spreading across his face, Connor concluded, 'You are stealing twenty-two days a year from the company with your nicotine habit.'

'Everyone needs a screen break. It's the law,' April replied feebly. She hated when Connor went on one of his little rants. She also hated having her smoking habit laid bare in such brutal fashion. But a newsroom wasn't for the thin-skinned or fainthearted.

But still she couldn't stop herself. April had actually given up smoking years ago – more or less – but she only replaced one vice with another: eating. Her weight had ballooned and Connor would tease that her hips were now as 'wide as the Clyde'. So after almost a decade-long hiatus, she began secretly smoking again, in so much as she tried to hide her habit from her daughter. Whether it was being older she wasn't sure, but she still had an insatiable appetite. But now she also had the hunger pangs mixed with nicotine cravings. She'd curse herself for being so stupid, yet at the same time come to the conclusion that she simply loved eating, drinking and smoking.

'Well, when the sex goes, we need something else to keep us entertained,' she announced to no one in particular.

Although she felt like she was losing the battle against her weight and habits, she was determined to try to conquer her fears of technology. 'Right, you little bastard,' she said to the iPad, 'let's do this thing.'

29

#HardAss

Lieutenant Haye was already in Colin Cooper's office when the head of security for the Baltimore City Hotel arrived at 7am for the start of his shift. If he was surprised to see a cop sitting in his chair, he didn't show it.

'It's the captain's little bitch – getting plenty of cock these days?' Cooper said while taking off his suit jacket and placing it on the hook at the back of his door.

'You always were a silver-tongued bastard, Coops,' Haye smirked back, refusing to take the bait.

'Rather be a bastard than a brown nose.'

Colin Cooper was a squat man with wide shoulders, which could just about accommodate the massive chip he'd carried around for most of his life. Cooper had been a homicide detective for twenty-two years before being forced to take early retirement, after his bosses discovered a prostitution racket he had going as a lucrative sideline. It had been the straw that broke the camel's back, with rumours of police brutality following him throughout his career. So much so, Cooper was nicknamed 'Blackbeard' by defence lawyers as their clients would inevitably turn up wearing eyepatches after being in his custody. Following on from his enforced dismissal and the threat of feeling the full weight of the law if he tried to set up his prostitution business again, Cooper had been left deeply resentful of the police – and in particular of his former colleagues, who had gleefully shown him the door.

'So how can I assist Baltimore's finest today?' Cooper said with his usual sneer.

'In case you haven't noticed, there was a homicide on your watch. Room 1410? High-profile dude. Goes by the name of Bryce Horrigan. Ring any bells?' It was Haye's turn to be sarcastic.

'Oh yeah, think I heard something on the news. How are the brains of homicide getting on catching his killer?' Cooper replied nonchalantly. He took a seat at his desk, which was crowded by three large Mac screens that systematically flicked through the hotel's several surveillance cameras, displaying the images in black and white. 'First thing I did was download all the footage we had and hand it over to you guys,' Cooper said, indicating towards the screens.

'That was very public-spirited of you, Coops. But I guess we'd get on a lot quicker if you told us the name of the hooker you rented the room out to?' Haye wasn't smiling any more.

'What?' Coops replied as if he hadn't heard, before continuing, 'What the fuck does that mean?'

'It means you had a deal going with room 1410,' Haye said stony-faced.

'Good to see the homicide department has developed a sense of humour since I left. About time, as it's full of clowns.'

'C'mon, Coops, you're the one who's clowning around. We're not after you. We need to speak to the whore. She saw the killer. She's our only eyewitness.'

'How do you know she saw him?' Coops said, changing tack.

'Your cameras. She counted her dough in the lift. Classy girl. She was in there long enough to blow him, so we're hoping she looked up and saw his face. Now stop fucking around or you're coming with me. I'm sure your old buddies will give you a warm welcome,' Haye warned.

'Fuck them and fuck you too, Haye. If that's the way you want to play it, then let's play,' Cooper snarled back.

'Right, screw this. You have the right to remain stupid, fucknuts,' Haye said, grabbing Cooper by the shoulders and snapping on the cuffs behind his back. 'You always were a stubborn bastard, Coops.'

'And you always were an asshole,' he replied in kind.

30

#CouncilHolmes

At the same time that Colin Cooper was being taken downtown, another policeman was slamming the phone down on his superior nearly three-and-a-half thousand miles away in Glasgow's Pitt Street – the former HQ for Strathclyde Police, before all eight of the country's regional forces were merged together in 2013. Detective Chief Inspector David 'Bing' Crosbie had just taken a new set of orders from Superintendent Cruickshank. He was to be the chief liaison officer for 'our American cousins' after an official request had come in via the Foreign Office and London's Scotland Yard from Baltimore Police Department.

'Fuckity bumhole,' Crosbie fumed. 'Now I'm a lackey for a bunch of Yankee doodle wankies.'

DCI Crosbie had once been the archetypical policeman – straight-laced, methodical in his work, never cutting corners, and with a ruthless determination that saw him always get his man. He also abhorred swearing. But that had been the old Crosbie. A year ago he had undergone a complete personality change, becoming outspoken, opinionated and cocky. He also swore. A lot. Crosbie believed his inner monologue suffered from a kind of Tourette's syndrome, a neuro-disorder that made him think the most offensive and inappropriate thoughts. Now those thoughts were well and truly out in the open, and aired on a frequent basis. It had endeared him to the rank and file, who had always thought of 'Bing' as a cold fish, but now he was the life and soul of the party – though it was not the best persona for a crime scene.

At a recent 'domestic' in a basement council flat in Glasgow's perpetually deprived Easterhouse scheme – Scotland's equivalent to the projects in the US – Crosbie had adopted an aloof Sherlock Holmes-style manner for the benefit of his subordinates. The couple had got into a drunken fight, with the wife fatally stabbing her husband. Her husband had retaliated by stabbing her back. The result was utter carnage, with two dead bodies and hardly a surface in the two-bedroom flat untouched by their crimson stains. The only witnesses had been their two young children, now orphaned and with memories to shatter any childhood.

'I see what has happened here,' Crosbie announced while studying the crime scene. 'The male, let's call him "Jimmy" for talking's sake, has come in late on the Friday night, rather the worse for drink. The female, "Senga" seems an appropriate moniker I'd say, has not approved of his lifestyle choices. She has probably used an opening gambit along the lines of, "Where the fuck have you been, shitface? Chatting up that slutty old barmaid again, huv ye?" Jimmy, full of bravado and cheap booze, might have retorted, "Away ye go and fuck yersel'," or words to that effect, and perhaps encouraged her to "go greetin' tae yer ma as ye always fucking dae." Jimmy has then slumped into this armchair to watch the oversized, flat-screen television, which they can ill afford and rather dominates this meagre living space,' Crosbie said, pointing like a game show hostess at the giant TV screen that almost filled one entire wall of the room.

'Now, Senga has been none too happy with Jimmy's tone, and demonstrates this by grabbing the largest knife she can get hold of from this cutlery drawer here,' Crosbie said while marching to the kitchen and pointing to the half-opened utensil drawer. 'She has then walked in a determined fashion back to the living room and plunged said knife into Jimmy's neck, with words to the effect of "Take this, ya bastit,"' Crosbie continued, indicating the suspicious dark staining around the headrest of the armchair.

'But instead of "taking it", Jimmy has surprised Senga by leaping to his feet, removing the blade from his neck, then stabbing her in the heart. The next few minutes involve them staggering around with their arterial spurts of blood giving the flat a rather fetching red makeover. Chuck in a couple of kids traumatised for life and it's typical Friday night fare in the schemes, ladies and gentlemen. A tragic Shakespearean ending for the Romeo and Juliet of Easterhouse. Elementary, my dear wanker,' Crosbie said, patting the shoulder of a young police recruit who was desperately trying to stifle his laughter. 'El-e-fucking-mentary.'

Crosbie's career trajectory had in fact been on a rapid rise ever since he had solved the murder of a high-profile Scottish businesswoman by the name of Selina Seth. But his split personality was getting worse – with the sweary Crosbie he had tried so hard to suppress now appearing in full control. While the detective's new outgoing personality may have provided the laughs for his colleagues, it deeply worried his superiors, who were now determined to sideline Crosbie. And he knew it.

'Baltimore Homicide department,' Crosbie said, reading an email from Superintendent Cruickshank. 'I better buy the boxset of *The Wire* so I know what the fuck I'm talking about,' the detective mused.

31

#TheRingRound

Tom O'Neill @DerryDude1887
Can't believe he's gone. RIP @BryceTripleB

The staff at ABT News were still in a state of shock, wandering around in a trance. There was no procedure for an event like this, when your star presenter is suddenly no more. Apart from having to deal with the media maelstrom, senior executives now had a forty-five-minute hole to fill in their schedules every night.

There was also the question of what sort of tribute piece should be done for the first show in Bryce's absence. Should it be a montage of clips from his best, most combative interviews, or should they hurriedly try to arrange on-camera pieces from his celebrity friends giving glowing tributes to the deceased presenter?

Tom O'Neill knew all too well that celebrity ring rounds were the bane of every reporter's life. Whenever an editor or one of his minions wanted an opinion on some topic or another, they ordered their staff to phone celebrities. The problem was, editors came up with the idea so often it was always the same faces, which was mostly ageing soap actors or fading pop stars – basically anyone a journalist could get instantly on the end of a phone.

Whenever the topic was really important, editors would add the proviso, 'And no crap celebs this time – I want A-listers.' That meant going through agents and managers and, given the deadlines and time constraints, this was a completely futile exercise. So, forced with nothing better to run, they would end up using the same old faces yet again. Tom had always made a point of calling the Krankies for a quote whenever he was ordered to do a celeb ring round.

The Krankies were a veteran husband-and-wife showbiz act, who had been on the go for nearly half a century. Tom called so often, the pair just told him to 'make up whatever you want us to say', the sort of open invitation a journalist has wet dreams about. There wasn't a topic too trivial or too big for the family entertainers to tackle: from nuclear disarmament to the death of Nelson Mandela, the Krankies always had something poignant and meaningful to say.

Tom thought he had left all that behind when he had quit London for New York. He'd been installed as Bryce Horrigan's Head of Content. It had been a grand title, but he found himself doing almost the same job as he had in London – being at Bryce's beck and call to try to make his boss's cocaine-induced ideas work.

Now, in the wake of Bryce's death, the network chief arrived on the editorial floor, instantly commanding respect. 'I know you're all suffering, folks. But you are professionals and we have a show to put together. I want to get a bunch of celebrities to give tributes to Bryce for tonight's show. No Z-listers. I want A-listers.'

New country. Different medium. But same old shit as far as Tom was concerned. He sat in his late boss's chair for the first time and swivelled around to take in the city. There was nothing like the Manhattan skyline. It was such a pity Tom never had the time to appreciate it. He was perpetually busy, doing at least four-teen-hour days. And Bryce was even more demanding as a TV host than he was as a national newspaper editor.

After replacing Connor Presley, Tom had eventually risen to become Bryce's deputy editor. But in New York he had hit the glass ceiling. As Horrigan's deputy, he could rise no further. There was virtually no prospect of taking the editor's chair from him in London or unseating him in New York. In one late-night boozy session after work, Tom had been crying into his drink, bemoaning the lack of advancement opportunities, when Bryce had announced he was taking a rare week's holiday to return to the UK. Tom assumed he would finally get to anchor the TV show in his absence. But the network chief had decided to run a bunch of Bryce re-runs instead. In a bustling bar off Second Avenue, where the real New Yorkers like to drink away from the tourists, Bryce gave it to Tom straight.

'They just don't want you in front of camera, I'm afraid,' he said casually.

Tom was appalled; he had been hoping this would be his big break. 'I've been waiting for this, Bryce. It's what I came for,' he said in his Derry accent. Tom felt he was far more suited to television than Bryce. He was better looking for a start.

'The problem is your voice, old bean. The Americans haven't a clue what you're saying. To be truthful, I didn't have a fucking clue what you were banging on about for the first year you worked for me, but your copy was always spot-on. So I'm afraid a Northern Irish brogue just ain't going to cut it with our American friends.'

Bryce's words had been like a dagger to Tom's heart. It felt like his whole career was a sham. That he was destined to forever live in Bryce's shadow.

32

#BridgeToNowhere

Geoffrey Schroeder looked at the Buffalo and Fort Erie Bridge that linked the US with Canada. A highway display showed that the waiting time for border crossings was currently less than twenty minutes. Now would be as good a time as any. He was about to pull out of a lay-by when his notifications revealed he had received a DM. He stopped the car to read the message.

'About time,' Schroeder mumbled to himself.

The DM read:

Baby Angel @BabyAngel
Hold tight, you are on the righteous path. Help is on the way.

Now Schroeder had the unenviable task of finding somewhere safe to hide out, which was easier said than done when you are in a strange state with dwindling resources.

He wrote back:

Geoffrey Schroeder @GeoffreySchroeder
Who are you sending?

Baby Angel @BabyAngel
One of my disciples will give you a passage to safety.
Keep the faith.

Schroeder did not reply and he was not placated. He felt like a hunted animal and now knew he could trust no one.

33

#JetLagged

In his twenties Connor travelled a lot, but he had given up on long-haul flights by his mid-thirties as it took him longer and longer to recover. He remembered reading somewhere that President Ronald Reagan was almost incapacitated by jet lag. As a young man, Connor had failed to understand the concept. Now he knew exactly where Reagan was coming from. Even sleeping much of the journey in business class, the five-hour time difference left Connor feeling physically sick.

Instead of being fresh to hit the ground running as he hoped, Connor felt groggy, lead-footed and disorientated. 'This is why I holiday in Europe,' he said to himself as he waited for his luggage. He knew he'd better shake his malaise fast. His first stop would be the hotel where his old friend and boss had been murdered. He suspected the place would be swarming with reporters, but it would at least allow him to touch base with some of the local journalists. It would also give him some colour for his copy describing what the hotel looked like.

But something was nagging Connor even through the fug of his jet lag-muddled mind. Just what the heck was Bryce Horrigan doing in Baltimore, anyway? His bosses at ABT News hadn't released any information in their statements to explain why their anchorman had come to Maryland. There weren't even any off-the-record briefings about Bryce being on an assignment, or being due to interview someone here. A quick check through an online what's-on guide confirmed there was no one of note in the state the weekend Bryce died – neither a well-known actor nor a world-famous band that Bryce had arranged to interview mid-tour. In fact, nothing appeared to be happening in Baltimore that weekend at all. Bryce would normally hang out in the top celebrity joints of Los Angeles and New York, to make sure he was seen and to also try to personally pick up some big names for his TV show, knowing the ratings boost that they'd bring.

Yet something had brought him to Baltimore. Connor corrected himself: 'Not something. Some*one*.'

He picked up his battered old man bag, containing his recorder and notepad, and headed out into the Maryland capital to do his job. He would contact his boss, Big Fergie, in the taxi to say he was in situ then start asking around to see if anyone knew why Bryce had been in town.

34

#HeavenSent?

Bryce Horrigan's own Twitter account had taken to mocking the Baltimore Police Department on a regular basis. The retweets alone would run into thousands, with the hashtag #CluelessCops remaining in the top ten trending topics. If that wasn't enough of a headache for Sorrell, he also began to receive more DMs from Baby Angel:

Baby Angel @BabyAngel
Found Schroeder yet, captain?

Bernard Sorrell @BernardSorrell
Nope, but working on it. Amongst others.

Baby Angel @BabyAngel
Why waste your time? He's your murderer, although a hero in my eyes. He made the world a better place.

Bernard Sorrell @BernardSorrell
Why you so certain Schroeder's involved?

Baby Angel @BabyAngel
Oh come on, captain. A pro-life whackjob who happens to be 100s of miles from home in a strange city when Bryce's brains are blown out?

Bernard Sorrell @BernardSorrell
But how do YOU know about him? You have never said who you are.

Baby Angel @BabyAngel
I am the Baby Angel. A voice of good for those who have no voice.

Bernard Sorrell @BernardSorrell
So you say. But really you could be any keyboard warrior, pretending to be someone you're not.

Baby Angel @BabyAngel
Why are you wasting your time with me in the middle of a homicide investigation?

Bernard Sorrell @BernardSorrell
Because I'm trying to figure out what makes crazies like you tick. My theory is Social Media has put knives in the hands of lunatics.

Baby Angel @BabyAngel
Or powerful handguns, like Schroeder.

Bernard Sorrell @BernardSorrell
Again, so you say.

Baby Angel @BabyAngel
Ah, still an unbeliever, captain? Check out the Sunrise Motel. I think you'll find someone matching Schroeder's description was there.

The captain looked at the last message and sat back in his seat. He knew the motel well. It's where he had picked up several bail jumpers enjoying a last night on US soil before heading to the Canadian border.

Whoever Baby Angel was, they certainly knew their stuff. But the captain couldn't help wondering if this angel was heaven sent or doing the devil's work.

35

#LetTrainTakeStrain

'You know someone else you should try to track down?' Connor said as he checked in with April after phoning his newsdesk. 'Lacey Lanning.'

'Who?' April said through her customary mouthful of food.

'The DJ, Lacey Lanning. Bryce ended up giving her a weekly column in the paper – and probably another column in bed.'

'Don't be disgusting,' April protested.

'Who's being disgusting? Me with my double entendres or you spraying food all over the café while talking?' Connor said. April conceded he had a point.

'Lacey was unbelievably ambitious. She was like a Bryce groupie. I remember he hired a karaoke machine for his birthday party, to be ironic or something. Lacey made sure she clapped the loudest and danced the wildest when Bryce sang. She ended up on stage as his backing singer. Pasty could barely conceal her fury, but that's what the worshippers in the court of King Horrigan had to do – fight for his attention.'

'No wonder you left,' April said before taking a noisy slurp of tea.

'Yeah, there was only so long I could keep up the charade. But Lacey was a master at it. Then it all went tits-up. I'd left London by that point so I don't know exactly what happened. As far as I know she's back home in Inverness. I bet she has a tale to tell. You should speak to her.'

'Brilliant plan,' April replied, although the enthusiasm in her voice didn't match her thoughts. April hated long drives. Or short drives, for that matter. They always seemed to end in an incident, for she was a truly terrible driver. She didn't set out to annoy her fellow road users, but somehow she nearly always managed to, whether sitting at 45mph in the fast lane, or driving with her full beam on for nearly a whole winter until Connor spotted it.

She still remembered how he leaned in through her driver's window in the staff car park and flicked the switch on her steering column with the words, 'You may be blind as an old bat – but it doesn't mean everyone else has to be.'

Her Daewoo, which was a hideous purple colour, was covered in scrapes, dents and bumps, most of them inflicted by the car's hapless driver. There was even a considerable crater on the roof. April had no idea how it had come about and thought that one possible explanation was that perhaps the car had been struck by a meteor. She wished she'd kept her cosmos collision theory to herself, as she could still recall Connor's sarcastic reply.

'So you're telling me, an ancient lump of carbon travels millions of light years across the galaxy, survives the Earth's atmosphere, only to end its epic voyage by colliding with your old banger? That'll be the Daewoo,' Connor had snorted. 'Is it perhaps more feasible that you dented it with the garage door?'

'Come to think of it, I did hear a scraping noise on the roof one morning. What am I like?' April had recalled.

Another time, she'd said to Connor, 'I hadn't realised when you overtake another car you have to wait until you can see them in your rear view mirror before pulling in – I was always nipping in straight away, cutting them up.'

That was greeted with another of Connor's stinging rebukes. 'Let me get this right. For years, possibly decades, you have been causing road rage incidents wherever you go? Did you never think you might be doing something wrong with all the beeping of horns and flashing lights?'

'I thought they were just saying "thank you". I used to give them a friendly little "toot, toot" back.'

'Dear Lord. You shouldn't be allowed out by yourself.'

April Lavender really was a liability let loose on the roads. Connor seemed to read her thoughts from several thousand miles away. 'Don't worry, you don't have to drive the A9. Let the train take the strain. Beautiful countryside, although you'll probably end up snoring your head off as usual. Why not buy yourself a nice Marks & Spencer's lunch for the journey? That's what I do.'

April smiled. She couldn't even remember the last time she'd taken a train. She looked forward to it. Especially the lunch.

36

#NonCompliant

Colin Cooper sat slumped in the interview room's chair, looking for all intents and purposes like he couldn't care less. He'd been left to stew for almost an hour but knew the drill better than most. When Haye and Sorrell entered the room, Cooper barely looked up. 'The monkey and the organ grinder. I'm honoured.'

Sorrell ignored the jibe, as he was determined to keep his cool. 'Good to see you again, Colin. Sorry to keep you waiting, things have been a little hectic today, what with the incident at your hotel.'

'Yeah, then Lieutenant Asshole here brings me out front in cuffs and I end up on the news, with half the world and my bosses thinking I killed the English prick,' Cooper said bitterly.

'Scottish, dumb-ass. Bryce Horrigan was Scottish,' Haye responded, taking the bait.

Cooper completely ignored Haye, refusing to even look in his direction.

'We cleared that up, Colin. Released a statement saying an employee had been arrested for an unrelated matter,' Sorrell said in his most reassuring manner.

'Yeah, but who's gonna believe that, captain?' Cooper said, eye-balling his former colleague.

'You brought it on yourself, Coops,' Haye spat back. 'I was being all civil. You were being an asshole.'

'Captain, can't you tell shit-for-brains to shut the fuck up? He's like a yappy dog: yelp, yelp, yelp. I don't know how you put up with that every day. I'd have stuck a slug in his head long ago. Put him out of his misery and do us all a favour.'

Haye leapt across the table, grabbing Cooper by the collar. 'Come on then, let's see how tough you really are.'

Sorrell pulled the men apart, and decided to play devil's advocate. 'Colin is just yanking your chain, lieutenant.'

Cooper laughed as he fixed his collar. 'Jeez, these youngsters are so easily wound up. You need to relax a little, Haye. Get some relief.'

'Yeah, maybe your hooker at the hotel could blow me,' Haye smirked.

This time it was Cooper's turn to leap across the table and grab Haye. 'I don't work no fucking hookers, okay?'

'Gentlemen, gentlemen, please,' Sorrell pleaded. 'Haye, time out. Give Colin and me a moment, would you?'

Haye stared manically at Cooper, just itching to be allowed at him. Cooper responded by blowing him a kiss then silently mouthing, 'Bye, bye.'

'Okay, Colin, the fun and games are over,' Sorrell announced after Haye had left the room.

'Shame, I was just starting to enjoy myself,' Cooper grinned.

'I need to speak to the girl who was in room 1410 the night Bryce Horrigan was killed. I don't care what she was doing there and I don't care what arrangement you both have, if any. None of this will go any further. No press. Nothing said to your bosses. In fact, I can happily call your boss at the hotel and say it was all one big misunderstanding, or that you'd been lifted for unpaid parking tickets. But I need to speak to that girl now,' Sorrell said, leaving no room for negotiation.

'I'll tell you what I told your bitch. I don't know any girl and I don't know anything about room 1410. So let me go, or give me my fucking phone call.' Cooper sat back with his arms tightly folded, indicating it was the end of the conversation.

Sorrell sighed, stood up and left the interview room. Haye was waiting outside, having watched and listened to events unfold on the room's CCTV.

'What a fucking scumbag. Want me to go fuck him up? Give him a taste of his own medicine?' Haye asked enthusiastically.

'No, but I do need you to goad him. See if he'll confess to beating on anyone. Get him to boast about it. We need any sort of leverage to make him hand over that girl. In the meantime, I'll get onto vice and see if any of them recognise her,' Sorrell said.

Haye went back into the interview room and was greeted by Cooper smirking at him again.

'Just asked the cap'n if I could beat the hooker's name out of you, but he says I'm not to stoop to your level. So who did you beat up when you were a detective, Coops? A couple of ten-year-old kids or something?' Haye said, following the captain's instructions to the letter.

Cooper's smirk just got wider. 'Is that all you've got? Trying to get me to confess to slapping around some yos? Fuck you, Haye.'

'Oh yeah, as if a grand jury would be interested in that shit. A washed-up, old brothel creeper ex-cop says he used to beat on suspects? No, I'm just curious, Coops. I want to know if you're as tough as they say you are. So give me a name. Any name. The toughest yo you ever fucked up. Go on, try me. I bet I've heard of him.'

Cooper laughed loudly. 'Okay, let's play your little game, if only to pass the time. I've got a name for you, ever heard of Tre Paul Beckett?'

'TP?' Haye asked. 'No fucking way. Didn't he once box at welterweight?'

'Yup, could have been a contender too until I lifted him for dealing. I fucked him up good in this very room,' Cooper said proudly.

'Was he high? Handcuffed? Both?' Haye asked.

'Nope. Took the cuffs off. Just knew he was gonna swing for me. Nearly caught me too with that lethal right of his. That was his last fight and he lost fair and square. I never let no fucker take a free swipe at me. Welterweights or no welterweights.'

Haye decided to go for the sucker punch himself. 'Try me with another?'

But Cooper shot him a suspicious look and crossed his arms again. 'Time's up. Charge me or let me go.'

Haye knew he'd come to the end of the line. Tre Paul Beckett was not the type who would be ready to help the police, but he was all Haye had.

37

#PressPack

Connor stood outside the Baltimore City Hotel and realised the futility of it all. He had travelled 3,000 miles to join the chattering, gossipy throng of yet another press pack. They sounded different from back home, with the big-haired female television reporters who have marginally more make-up and Botox than their male counterparts. But no matter the gender they were all experts in talking complete and utter bullshit.

Every broadcast was essentially the same. The news anchor would announce they were going over live to their reporter at the scene for an 'update', where it would be quickly established within thirty seconds that they didn't have one. Each journalist would try to match the other in banality, generalisations and complete and utter waffle. Fortunately, as is true of all TV folk, they loved the sound of their own voices and could continue in this vein for hours, long after their viewers had given up.

Connor never understood why TV news journalists had such a high opinion of themselves. But they seemed to revel in their minor celebrity status and the odd occasion they were spotted in supermarkets or complimented on their new hairdo – and that was just the blokes.

Back home in Scotland, Connor hated it if a local news crew got to a job before he did, as they would attempt to commandeer the whole event, trampling over print journalists' interview time slots. As if it was their God-given right because they were TV news, despite the fact they had fewer viewers than his paper's circulation. He recalled Bryce's words when he once berated his news and sports colleagues by claiming that they were 'all sheep – they follow the herd and are too scared to break free. If you are ever going to get something different, you have to break away from the pack.'

That's exactly what Connor needed to do now. He had one major advantage over the herd here in Baltimore: he had already established a direct line with the captain in charge of the case, and he knew the dead man's deputy. He would need to start cashing in on his contacts.

38

#HeadingNorth

For the first time in her life, Lacey Lanning didn't crave the oxygen of publicity. Since she had quietly slipped back to her Highland home after the bright lights of London, she had deliberately stayed out of the limelight. She was given the 8pm till midnight slot on the local radio station she'd first started with, which suited her fine. The money was truly appalling, just £30 a show, but it was the only income she had and she wasn't in a position to negotiate.

In the early days, she'd had an affair with the station manager, a vain, married middle-aged man, who insisted on being called 'The Gaffer'. She had cynically used him to get on air then engineer her move to London by threatening to withhold her sexual services if he didn't help her out. Now, the Gaffer was the one holding all the cards as Lacey returned home to Inverness, very much the broken woman. He had taken a great deal of pleasure in beating her wage demand down to a pittance, then sadistically enjoyed telling her that sex wouldn't advance her career this time around.

'I'll be keeping it in my pants. There are a lot younger girls wanting a piece of the Gaffer.' He eyed her cleavage, which he'd once so desired, and added needlessly, 'Younger and more pert girls.'

The Gaffer had a point: the intervening decade had not been kind to Lacey. So much so, the once youngest female broadcaster in the land was now forced to lie about her age, lopping five years from her actual thirty. Sadly for her, she looked at least ten years older.

The Gaffer looked at her almost distastefully. 'What the hell happened to you in London, anyway? You're a mess.'

She didn't answer, choosing to stare at her feet instead.

'Well, that's not my concern now. I don't even know why I'm giving you a show after you turned your back on me. I made you, Lacey. You were once a great broadcaster. Anyway, thirty quid a show, take it or leave it. Maybe it will help you get back on your feet.' The £150 a week was hardly going to get her back on her feet, especially with the debts that had followed her home from London. But she was desperate. Desperate enough to even move back in with her parents.

And she knew she needed to recuperate. To recover from the trauma. She just couldn't get over the guilt she felt that would wake her up every night in a cold sweat. She repeatedly asked herself, *What have I got myself into? What have I done?* There was no one she could turn to for help. She needed to lie low or they would come looking for her.

Lacey's return to Inverness had gone as well as expected. The Gaffer had predictably been horrible to her, but the listeners seemed to welcome the return of a familiar voice. Being on air in the evening meant she also bypassed having to meet most of the station staff, which made it easier for Lacey to keep herself to herself.

Then April Lavender came calling. Lacey had told her she didn't want to talk, especially about Bryce, but the journalist had been most insistent. There was also money involved – £1,000. Hardly a king's ransom, but still more than a month's wages. It would certainly help keep the wolves from the door a while longer.

Reluctantly, she agreed to the interview. As usual, Lacey had her own agenda and she planned to paint a very one-sided picture to the reporter currently making her way north.

April was as excited as a schoolgirl as she boarded the train at Glasgow Queen Street for the three-and-a-quarter hours direct service to Inverness. As Connor had suggested, she had stocked up on supplies from Marks & Spencer on Argyle Street first. Although, admittedly, it was a lot more than Connor would have bought. Along with a prawn mayonnaise sandwich, orange juice and packet of crisps from the 'meal deal', she'd also bought a bucket of Chinese chicken wings, commenting to a complete stranger in the aisle, 'Oh, I just can't resist these – mmmm. Delicious.' At the check-out, she picked up a packet of bon-bons, only to be told that the sweets were actually part of a three-for-two offer.

'Oh, you are awful,' she said to the check-out man, pushing him playfully on the shoulder. 'I think you're just trying to make me fat,' she added while throwing a couple more bags of sweets into her basket.

April was to meet a freelance photographer, Kenny Black, in Inverness, which meant she had the journey to herself, to feast in peace. Shortly after trundling through the long tunnel out of Queen Street, the train made its way north of Glasgow and into the countryside, passing parallel to the Campsie and Kilsyth hills before turning north through Stirling towards Perth and the Highland main line. April was glued to the window as she munched her variety of supplies and took in the scenery; the train stopping at stations with an old-world charm, including Dunkeld & Birnam and Pitlochry, through Blair Atholl, which has the only private army in Britain, and over the 1,500ft Drumochter summit, where the lush Perthshire forests and rivers are replaced by bleak moorland.

It trundled on through Dalwhinnie, home of the famous whisky distillery, into Newtonmore and Kingussie before pulling into the toy-town station of Aviemore, where the Strathspey steam engines run side by side with the modern Scotrail locomotives. From there it was thirty miles or so to Carrbridge and on to the final destination of Inverness. By that point, April was fast asleep, her snores being heard the length and breadth of the entire carriage.

She was woken with a start by the train conductor after pulling in at Inverness. She hated the moment's panic that came when she woke only to realise she didn't know where she was. Her mouth felt dry, which could only mean it had been hanging open – 'catching flies', as Connor once observed, having stumbled upon her having a sneaky wee nap in their broom cupboard office. April apologised to the conductor, took an age to gather her belongings and headed outside to meet the photographer.

Lacey Lanning had agreed to meet at a four-star hotel on the outskirts of the city. April couldn't help but be impressed by the hustle and bustle of Inverness, which only officially became a city in 2001. It was a hive of activity, from the shops in the city centre, to the flow of heavy goods vehicles to the business parks on the outskirts. Inverness had clearly become so much more than just a mecca for all the monster hunters using the city as a base to visit Loch Ness.

That myth fascinated April. Even in this day and age, when almost everyone has powerful cameras on their mobile phones, there was no solid proof whatsoever that the beast existed. Yet still they came in their droves. Some so-called Nessie watchers dedicated their lives to staring out at the loch surface, longing to catch a glimpse of the creature from the murky depths. Tourists travelled from across the globe, pumping millions of pounds into the local economy, captivated by the thought that a dinosaur had been trapped in modern times.

'I know how you feel, Nessie,' April chuckled to herself.

Kenny, the photographer, met April outside the station and drove her to the hotel. He was a nice chap and, like April, had been working in newspapers for decades.

'So I take it you must have photographed Lacey Lanning before? What's she like?' asked April.

'A real looker in her day,' Kenny said in his lilting Highland accent, 'and probably the most ambitious girl to come out of Inverness. She was going to the top and nothing was going to stop her. Rumours are she slept her way there, mind you.'

April was saddened that any career woman was always tarred with the same brush. Ambition equalled ruthlessness. Success meant she'd turned favours on her way to the top. April recalled being accused of such in her early days. If only she'd had the opportunity to have some fun, because by the time she got a foothold in the industry she was already a divorced single mother.

No, she would take Lacey Lanning as she found her, like she did with everyone she met. And anyway, she really wanted to know the truth: why such a high flier had returned home. Growing in stature as Inverness surely was, it wasn't London, where she imagined a girl like Lacey would have thrived. April often wondered how she herself would have taken to London, given the chance. But the opportunity never arose. She imagined she would have liked it, unlike Connor who couldn't wait to return home to Scotland after his time working with Bryce Horrigan.

The thought of the deceased sharpened her focus. Despite her own curiosity about Lacey's life, April had travelled a long way and she needed her interview subject to spill the beans.

39

#CheshireCat

Tom O'Neill had been dispatched to Baltimore by his bosses at ABT News. He was needed as a man on the ground to liaise between the police department and the television executives. O'Neill knew it gave his bosses an excuse to get him out from under their feet as they ran down his contract. The police were also asking a lot of questions, the main one being why Bryce Horrigan was in Baltimore in the first place.

O'Neill had been briefed intensely by his bosses, who were desperate to be kept as far away from any potential scandal as possible. He could still hear the words from his CEO ringing in his ears: 'I don't care if Horrigan was snorting coke off the ass of a Puerto Rican hooker – as long as the network is kept clean.'

Kept clean. There was a laugh. The bosses had deliberately been turning a blind eye to Horrigan's increasingly erratic behaviour in recent months. For starters, there had been his barely concealed cocaine addiction, where it had become routine for the television host to do a line shortly before going on air.

Then there was his casting couch approach to hiring interns and the nicknames he gave them, including 'Guns' for a young graduate with big breasts, 'Brazil' for another who waxed off all her pubic hair, and 'Screamer' for a girl who made a lot of noise when she got real excited. They all came and went, either because Bryce grew tired of them, or because they could no longer take his public humiliation.

But Bryce had barely even had his knuckles rapped by the senior execs, despite their assurances to the Human Resources director that they would. From then on, Bryce knew he was untouchable and revelled in it. Unchecked bad behaviour has a habit of breeding. And though Horrigan thought his boorish and bullying ways helped drive his team to greater heights, all it really did was make him increasingly unbearable. O'Neill found it hard to believe he had once hero-worshipped Horrigan – the charismatic newspaper editor who had brought O'Neill to New York had turned into a grotesque character. O'Neill always figured Horrigan would one day end up with a bullet in his head. Although he hadn't figured on it happening so soon.

Now the police in Baltimore were asking awkward questions. They wanted to know if Horrigan had ever verbally, physically or sexually harassed any members of his ABT News team. How O'Neill would love to tell them he ticked all those boxes and more.

The police had also requested access to Horrigan's computer in his New York office. The network's bosses turned them down flat, citing the need to protect Bryce's sources. In truth, they were worried what investigators would find. The cops knew they were playing for time as it allowed ABT News's IT department to sift through their dead presenter's hard drive, making sure they left his PC in-situ, lest they be accused of tampering with evidence. The network's refusal to play ball forced the police's hand – they now needed to apply for a court order to seize the computer, which would only serve to slow down the investigation.

In the meantime, O'Neill had been sent to Baltimore with Horrigan's personnel file, albeit a heavily edited version. He doubted it would stand up to any serious scrutiny. The HR director was concerned she would be subpoenaed if the cops smelled a rat. O'Neill just hoped the police wouldn't shoot the messenger.

Lieutenant Haye was friendly enough when he welcomed Tom O'Neill at the station, but his lack of sleep with the Horrigan case meant Haye had little time for small talk.

'Did you bring the personnel file we asked for?' Haye asked.

'Right here,' O'Neill said, smiling a little too broadly while waving a thick brown envelope. He berated himself for his nervousness – after all, he hadn't personally deleted all the sexual harassment claims from Bryce's records.

Haye ripped open the envelope and thumbed quickly through the pages, indicating towards a chair outside an office for O'Neill to take a seat. The lieutenant disappeared through the door marked 'Captain Sorrell'. Over half an hour later, the door swung open again. Haye was even more brusque than before. 'Come in,' he ordered.

Sorrell was sitting behind his cluttered desk, with Horrigan's personnel file sitting open in front of him. Without introduction, he said, 'So Bryce Horrigan was a real Mother Teresa, huh?'

'Well, he had his moments,' O'Neill said as jovially as possible.

'Not according to this,' Sorrell snorted, throwing the personnel file across the table.

'Ha, well, you can't expect Human Resources to know everything that goes on,' O'Neill heard himself say, but couldn't fathom why.

Sorrell leaned on his desk, resting his chin on his meaty hands. He remained silent as his big, brown eyes bored into O'Neill. 'Why don't you cut the bull and tell me what working for Bryce Horrigan was really like?'

O'Neill had always thought of himself as a professional, hard-nosed journalist. But he was hugely disappointed by the effect the world-weary Baltimore police captain had on him. O'Neill had adopted the nervous Cheshire Cat grin favoured by former British Prime Minister Tony Blair. But it was beginning to ache after a few minutes. He had no idea how Blair managed to keep his going for nearly three terms in office.

Then Bryce's deputy started to unload. It felt good to finally get things off his chest. 'Well, first and foremost, Bryce was a brilliant journalist,' O'Neill said, having learned that in any interview you must always start with a positive. 'As a newspaper editor he had this incredible instinct to always find himself on the right side of the argument. That wasn't being populist for the sake of it. Often his newspaper's stance was highly controversial at first, but soon it would start finding support and when debates became a national talking point, they tended to side with Horrigan. I can say this with all honesty, that Bryce Horrigan was a genius.'

'But a flawed genius,' Sorrell said, by way of a statement rather than a question.

O'Neill's shoulders sagged slightly. 'Yeah, he was. I think the problem was, it all came too easy to him. He was so good that nothing was really a challenge. He was a national newspaper editor. His paper was putting on circulation while others were failing. He could hold court with the Prime Minister. He wined and dined with the music and film stars. He was charismatic and people listened to him. Heck, even the Queen thought he was highly entertaining and she spent her reign despising tabloid newspaper editors.'

'So he was a smart ass?' Sorrell asked.

'Yes, I guess that would be an American take on it. But it wasn't enough. That's when he turned to television and annoyingly discovered he was just as good at that. It was weird because I always thought television turned him into a bit of a monster – a stereotypical, loudmouthed, opinionated, arrogant editor. But he loved it. He played up to the role. He appeared on current affairs shows back home, arguing the toss with politicians. Very few ever scored points against him. He enjoyed having a new platform from which to show off. But the strangest thing of all was how much he enjoyed the fame.'

'How did it change him?' Haye asked, leaning back against the office wall next to his boss.

'Truthfully?' O'Neill asked. 'He became a bit of an asshole, as you'd say over here.'

'Sounds like he was already an asshole,' Haye snorted.

O'Neill leapt to his late boss's defence. 'No. He hadn't been before. Seriously. I've thought about this a lot. I watched his life change almost overnight. He was seduced by television. Slowly but surely his newspaper began to suffer as he focused his attentions on his television career. After lots of guest slots he landed his own series, *Bryce's Britain*, which involved him travelling around the UK speaking to ordinary people. It was a brilliant programme, full of the British eccentrics with a passionate love for everything that makes the country great. It showed Bryce in a new light. But then America came calling. It was the perfect parting point for Bryce and the newspaper. He was handed a contract even bigger than his newspaper one. But, surprisingly, money didn't seem to be his main motivation.'

'So you telling me he did it all for the fame?' Sorrell asked.

'Yes. Because fame equalled women.' O'Neill let his statement hang in the air.

'Go on,' Sorrell demanded.

'At first it was just the "groupies", if you like. Ironically, the type of girls who slept with famous folk and would then do a kiss-and-tell story with Bryce's old newspaper. But he quickly got bored with those. So his next targets were forbidden fruit – women he had no right to be with. He loved the thrill of the chase. The deceit turned him on more than the conquest.'

'And you know this how?' Haye enquired.

'I was not only his deputy but his confidant also. And besides, Bryce liked to boast. I'm sure I wasn't the only one he'd brag to.'

'Didn't he have a fiancée?' Sorrell asked, searching around his overflowing desk before he found his notepad. He flicked a few pages then added, 'A Patricia Tolan?'

'Yeah, poor Pasty. That was Patricia's nickname because she was so white it looked like she'd seen a ghost. I guess she had a hard time with Bryce. She'd known him since university. He ordered her to leave his New York penthouse, I gather. She returned home to Scotland and who could blame her? I think that was the worst thing about Bryce: his admirers held him up on a pedestal, meaning it was so disappointing when he let you down.'

'And did he let you down, Mr O'Neill?' Sorrell said, his eyes unblinking, searching for any flicker of emotion.

'Yes, he did as a matter of fact. He promised me I'd be his on-screen cover when he was on vacation. But then he said the bosses wanted a clip show instead. He kinda enjoyed telling me I was no longer going to get my chance in front of camera. He could be cruel that way. He could make career-changing decisions for you on a whim. Or life-changing in poor Pasty's case.'

'Did you feel betrayed?' Haye asked.

'Yes, but then no. Our relationship had started to become strained. Technically I was his deputy, but became no more than his PA. I was also getting fed up with the way he'd wear you down psychologically. He would always wind me up about how he wished his old pal Elvis had come to New York with him instead. His real name is Connor Presley, but he's called Elvis for obvious reasons.'

'Enough for you to wanna do something about it?' Haye asked pointedly.

'Yes, as a matter of fact. It made me want to quit. But Bryce would have liked that. He was an alpha male. Only losers quit and I knew Bryce now looked at me as a loser. I became something of a whipping boy to him and I didn't like it. But I only wanted another job in broadcasting, which I hoped filling in for him on air would have given me. He probably suspected as much and that's why he stopped me. Classic Bryce. As I said, he enjoyed toying with people and their lives. But some things are just not meant to be played with.'

O'Neill was excused only after he had agreed to supply Haye with a list of disgruntled employees, interns and ex-lovers who might bear a grudge towards the deceased Horrigan.

It was a very long list.

40

#Scarred

Lacey Lanning looked down at heel as she arrived at the plush hotel. After their introductions, April indicated a table she'd reserved in a quiet corner.

'I'd rather sit outside, if you don't mind, as I'll need a ciggie,' Lacey said. That suited April just fine as she was gasping for a puff herself. After her hiatus, she was more desperate to smoke than ever before.

The two women ordered coffees and lit up as the snapper made himself scarce, scouting the well-manicured grounds for a suitable spot to shoot a portrait picture of Lacey. April liked to be left alone anyway, as conducting a three-way interview is nowhere near as intimate as a one-on-one.

Lacey used the old DJ trick of smiling as she spoke – the theory being that it made you sound bright and breezy and helped lighten the listeners' mood. But she was betrayed by her eyes, which April thought were the saddest she'd ever seen. Something had happened to this girl, April just hoped she was willing to reveal exactly what. Part of her skill as an interviewer was to gently coax more out of a reluctant interviewee than they'd planned to give up. April discovered long ago that most celebrities' favourite topic was themselves, and Lacey was soon talking enthusiastically about her early career. But it was when April finally asked about Bryce Horrigan that the conversation momentarily dried up. Lacey leaned forward to scoop up her packet of menthol cigarettes from the table, tapping one free from the top of the packet. She lit it, inhaled deeply and sat back in her chair, crossing her legs.

'Bryce, Bryce, Bryce. Where do I begin?' Lacey said coolly, adding, 'Let's just say meeting Bryce Horrigan nearly destroyed me.'

April could see that quote being made into a 'talkie' headline already. It hadn't been a wasted journey, after all. Lacey went on to detail how she had met Bryce at some function in London and they had immediately hit it off. She was at pains to stress that it wasn't sexual… at first.

'Despite what you may have heard about my reputation, I don't jump straight into bed with anyone,' she insisted.

Whether that was true or not, April had no way of knowing, not that it mattered to her. But their relationship had 'moved on to the next phase' when Lacey was commissioned to write a weekly column, *Racy Lacey – The Girl in a Hurry*, for Bryce's newspaper. She explained how the strapline was a play on her hectic broadcasting style – speaking at ten to the dozen – and her chaotic Bridget Jones-style love life.

'Ironic, really, considering at that point I had a boyfriend and was banging Bryce,' Lacey offered.

April thought 'banging' was a strange term for a woman to use. Lacey almost looked disgusted with herself for saying it, her self-esteem at rock bottom.

'How long did the relationship last?' April asked.

Lacey blew smoke into the air, giving herself time to decide whether to be truthful or not. It was a routine April had seen before with Patricia Tolan. She wondered if they knew each other.

'Until nine months ago,' Lacey eventually replied.

April flicked through her notepad. She knew she'd jotted down somewhere a timeline of Bryce's career from cuts. She finally found it. Bryce had been working in New York for the last two years.

'So it continued after he'd gone to America?' she asked, already knowing the answer.

'Yeah. I'd fly to New York for the weekend. He'd pay for me, most of the time. After Bryce left the paper, my column was eventually dropped by the next editor. I don't mind telling you that everything started turning to shit,' Lacey said, lighting yet another ciggie.

'My boyfriend was also the producer of my radio show. When we fell out, management took the opportunity to move me to an evening show. They said it was because of personal conflict but that was crap. They wanted rid of me and I knew it.'

April knew there would be two sides to her story. She chanced her arm by asking, 'Were you doing drugs?'

That was one area of her life Lacey had not planned on going into. She still clung to the hope of one day rebuilding her once bright broadcasting career. But she sighed and gave in, 'Yeah, I was doing coke. All the time by the end. I was just so knackered living in London and trying to keep up this "Racy Lacey" persona. Then someone gave me a line of coke and suddenly I was my old self again. Eventually I was doing a line every morning before going on air – then midway through my show, too. Management spotted me once. I was behind the mic with white nostrils, but they turned a blind eye: my ratings were going through the roof, I had a national newspaper column. I was getting the station noticed. I was the girl of the moment,' Lacey said, smiling at the memory of when her star shone brightly.

'But you were doing more and more drugs?' April predicted correctly.

'Yeah. I was also in a circle where everyone was doing it too. It seemed the done thing,' Lacey said, as if it was just a matter of fact.

'Bryce too?' April asked.

'Oh God, yeah,' Lacey laughed, before trying to light another cigarette. But her lighter was empty and she leaned down to get a replacement from the handbag at her feet. Lacey's V-neck jumper gaped open to reveal most of her breasts, barely contained in a black bra. It wasn't that which caught April's eye, though. It was the angry-looking injuries on her chest, which looked suspiciously like bite and scratch marks, similar to 'Pasty' Tolan's.

'And what about Bryce's fiancée, Patricia Tolan?' April saw a marked change in Lacey's demeanour as soon as Patricia's name was mentioned. She suddenly looked wary.

'Pasty? I don't think she knew of our affair,' Lacey said unconvincingly.

'Did you know her? Ever meet her? Can't imagine your paths never crossed,' April enquired.

'Yeah, we knew each other. But only as nodding acquaintances,' Lacey said. April knew a lie when she heard one.

After an hour and a half, April had more than enough for her article. The interview was good without being great, although it helped paint the picture of Bryce as a predatory, sex-mad egotist and showed how far he was prepared to go in order to seduce his targets. It also told the sad story of a girl from the sticks who had it all and blew it. But April knew she didn't have the whole truth. Not even half of it. A cocaine addiction only partially explained her rapid fall. By the look of her, Lacey had clearly been through so much more. She was frightened – as if waiting for something from her past or present to catch up with her. April thought perhaps Lacey hadn't returned to Scotland to rebuild her life, but to hide from the old one.

Not getting the full story gnawed away at April for the whole of the return journey home. She knew she wouldn't be able to rest easy until she had filled in all the blanks. April's journalist instinct told her she was onto something important. She needed to speak to Connor.

'Whaddups, A-Lav?' Connor said on answering April's call.

'Are you drunk?' she replied.

'Nah, just gone Stateside.' But Connor could tell by his colleague's tone that she was all business.

'I spoke to Lacey Lanning. Same old story of Bryce being a bit of a bastard, ruined her life, etc,' April said unsympathetically.

'Pin all your problems on the dead guy?' Connor retorted.

'Exactly,' she said.

'But you don't believe her?' Connor continued.

'Not entirely. I think I got the heavily abbreviated version,' April explained.

'The radio edit?'

'Excuse me?'

'The radio edit – when all the bad bits and swearing are cut out of songs so they can be played on air.'

April got it now. 'Yes. I definitely got the broadcast version. She did cough to being a coke addict, but she can hardly blame Bryce for that. But the biggest revelation wasn't in what she said, but from her breasts.'

'I'm all ears,' Connor assured her.

'They were bitten or scratched to ribbons, a bit like Pasty's injuries. Then, when I mentioned Tolan's name, Lacey clammed up. Pretended she hardly knew her, which was a lie. They even smoked the same way.'

'And they both scurried home to Scotland at the same time, shortly before Bryce ended up dead. Interesting. Very interesting,' Connor said, pondering the possibilities.

'What the hell is going on, Connor?' April asked.

'Damned if I know, but I have a funny feeling you will find out.'

41

#TheWire

'Lieutenant Haye? This is Detective Chief Inspector Crosbie from Police Scotland. How are things in Bawlmore? Send any vics down the chop shop this morning?' Crosbie said, using a mixture of local dialect for Baltimore and police jargon he'd picked up from watching all five series of *The Wire* back to back.

Haye frowned, wondering what sort of fruit-loop had been assigned as his liaison officer. He decided to play him at his own game. 'No vics this morning for me. What about you, detective? Any running battles with English garrisons today?'

Crosbie laughed. 'A *Braveheart* fan, huh? That has to be the best Scottish film ever made by an Aussie, written by an American and shot in Ireland,' he said, before descending into raucous laughter at his own lame joke.

Haye was tired and now finding the conversation irksome. 'Hilarious, detective. Okay, let's move on from kilt-wearing freedom fighters and TV cop shows, if we may. The day Bryce Horrigan died his iPhone received hundreds of calls, as you can imagine. All of them were accounted for as they were in his phone's contacts. But two numbers weren't. One was a Scottish reporter, Connor Presley...'

Crosbie cut off his US counterpart. 'Ah, Elvis. He's in your neck of the woods right now, I believe.'

'Correct,' Haye said, not welcoming the interruption, 'but the other was a UK number from persons unknown. It's a cell. We've tried calling it, but it's dead now.'

'Ah, a ten-seven, as you Yanks would say,' Crosbie said, clearly enjoying himself.

'Indeed, detective. A ten-seven does mean "out of service".' Crosbie was now starting to really piss off Haye. 'My captain would like you to try to trace the caller, if that's okay?'

'Easy peasy. Your wish is my command. When I find them, do you want me to snap on the "silver bracelets"? What if they've been "aced" already? Will I wait for the medical examiner to "roll them"?' asked Crosbie, now in full swing.

'Goodbye, detective,' Haye replied, slamming the phone down. The lieutenant shook his head and stared at the receiver. 'That sonofabitch is crazy.'

42

#TheHerogram

April Lavender @AprilReporter1955
Lacey interview is spread. Tomorrow. How you?

Connor Presley @ElvisTheWriter
No need to communicate like a World War I telegram.
Stop. Can use conjunction in tweets. So please. Stop.

April Lavender @AprilReporter1955
You. Cheeky. Wee. Fecker.

April loved tweeting. She liked how instantaneous it was and the fact she could have a live conversation with someone like Connor so far away. She had fewer than a hundred followers, but wondered what it would be like to instantly speak to ten million with a single tweet, as Bryce had been able to do. April could see why Horrigan had become so addicted to the micro-blogging site.

She had filed her copy on the interview with Lacey Lanning from the train back to Glasgow and, on her way back to the broom cupboard, she received a herogram email from Big Fergie, informing her it was to make a two-page spread for tomorrow's paper.

April tweeted the news to Connor, but then she was interrupted by her office phone, which rarely rang these days. In an old-fashioned newsroom, phones were ringing all the time. Now, even the public tended to contact reporters by emails, or text lines, which were printed at the bottom of every article.

'Hello, is that April Lavender?' asked a well-spoken voice. 'This is Edwina Tolan. You know my daughter, Patricia?'

There was silence as April desperately wracked her brains. She was given a little prompt by the caller. 'You might know her as Pasty Tolan? Bryce Horrigan's fiancée?'

'Ah yes, Pasty. Sorry, Patricia. How can I help you?'

'I understand you've been to see Lacey Lanning in Inverness,' said Edwina, more as a statement of fact than a question.

April wondered how she knew.

'I don't know what she told you and frankly it's none of my business.'

You're right there, April thought to herself.

'It's just, Lacey isn't in a good place,' Edwina continued. 'I don't mean to speak ill of someone, but Patricia – Pasty – and Lacey were very close at one point.'

April knew Lacey hadn't been truthful when she claimed they were just 'passing acquaintances'.

'It's true Lacey cheated with Bryce behind Pasty's back. But my daughter was used to that. She knew he'd soon dump Lacey when he became bored, as he inevitably always did. But Lacey took it very badly. I'm afraid she has gone a bit off the rails. She really hasn't been the same. I'd just be careful with what she told you.'

April remained quiet. She didn't like being told how to take people – she was more than capable of making up her own mind. And anyway, apart from a few little white lies, Lacey Lanning had seemed perfectly sane to her.

'There's more to it, you see. A lot more. But I'd rather tell you face to face sometime,' Edwina said suggestively.

'How did you know I had been to see Lacey, anyway?'

'I have eyes everywhere. Actually, she told me and I was worried. I'm trying to protect Lacey from herself more than anything,' Edwina explained. But April wasn't buying it.

Edwina Tolan helpfully left her number, urging April to get in touch if she had any other questions. April rechecked the Lacey copy she had filed. She was satisfied with it. If anything, Edwina's phone call had only helped confirm Lacey's version of events about having an affair with Bryce Horrigan.

April concluded Edwina Tolan was a control freak, guessing correctly she had been head girl at her private school – the sporty type who would have clobbered any opponent with a hockey stick had they dared to get the better of her during a match, then offer them a firm handshake afterwards. She would have made life a misery for someone like April at school. Today, Edwina would never encounter April's type unless she'd been hired to do the housework. But that meant Edwina underestimated April Lavender, thinking of her as an inferior. It was a dangerous assumption to make.

43

#CyberAttack

Bryce Horrigan @BryceTripleB
Cops still haven't caught my killer. Tell captain
@BernardSorrell if you think he's doing a good job or not.

'Haye, Fidel,' Sorrell hollered from his office, 'I'm under attack here.'

Both Haye and the IT consultant burst into the captain's office. Haye had his gun cocked and ready.

'Not physically attacked, dumb-ass. Cyber attacked. Look,' Sorrell said, holding up his cell. He had over 10,000 notifications.

'Sorry, cap'n,' Haye said, putting his gun away. 'I've been on the phone to cops from just about every goddamn state in America. They've been lifting Horrigan trolls all day. I didn't see the tweet.'

'I can't work for all the alerts. My cell's pinging so much it's almost one continual sound,' Sorrell complained.

Fidel chuckled. 'You're trending, cap'n. Not so long ago, you were a Twitter virgin. Now you've gone viral.'

'I'm glad you find it funny.'

The IT man changed the captain's notifications settings and the cell fell silent.

'Here you go, that should give you some peace for a while,' Fidel said, still smiling. Haye gave him a discreet shake of the head behind Sorrell's back. He knew his boss well enough to know he wasn't in the mood for games.

'Funny how they're always at the same time of day,' Fidel said aloud as he flicked through Horrigan's Twitter feed.

'What?' Sorrell snapped.

'Look, cap'n, ever since Horrigan was killed, whoever has been tweeting from his account mainly does so at 3am or 3pm, like just now. They're rarely late. Maybe a few minutes either side, but that's it.'

'What do you think that means?' Sorrell asked.

'At first I thought the 3am tweets were designed for maximum effect, something for Twitter to wake up to and the news outlets to follow up. The same would almost work in reverse with the media picking up a 3pm tweet, while many Twitter users are at work. Now I'm starting to think it's either the only time the hacker can physically tweet, or it's a time when they're most confident they won't be caught using whatever method they've got to access his account.'

'Good. Over-confidence always leads to a mistake,' Sorrell said knowingly.

44

#Lonely

With Connor in America, April was alone in the cramped broom cupboard office. She was rarely lonely though, as she always had herself to talk to, but even that was starting to bore her, so she took herself one of her regular tea breaks to the breakout area.

'Why do they have to rename everything? It's not a breakout area, it's a cafeteria,' she moaned to anyone within earshot, while stirring three heaped teaspoons of sugar into her mug.

These days, apart from a few familiar old faces, she barely recognised any of the new staff. Since the beginning of the newspaper's eternal spiral of decline, management had been cost-cutting, with redundancies and early retirements eroding the workforce. It felt strange to be part of a dying industry that was still a big business, with the *Daily Chronicle* bought and read by over a million people per week. But success wasn't judged by growth anymore, just the hope you weren't dropping sales faster than your competitors.

The figures were there in front of their faces every day, with a round robin email sent from the circulation manager with the previous day's sale. Every email revealed that year on year sales were down by around fifteen per cent – and that figure was rising rapidly. It didn't take a mathematician to work out that losing around 40,000 of your customers every year was a pretty unsustainable business model.

Another bunch of seasoned journalists had recently gone to make way for the new online department, full of fuzzy-haired and weirdly-dressed kids on a fraction of the journalists' salaries.

April would eye them with suspicion whenever she saw them in the breakout area. It was as if they were a totally different breed of human being. When she strained her ears to overhear their conversations, it was like a foreign language: 'domains' this and 'streaming' that. Just what the hell did it all mean? All April knew was, despite the rhetoric and assurances from the experts that newspapers would never die, the sands of time were surely running out on the business. She treated each monthly salary as a bonus and told herself to make hay while the sun was shining.

April decided the 'hay' would extend to a packet of crisps from the vending machine, assuring herself she would finally slim down when she was inevitably made jobless.

'Why so glum, old yin?' asked Davie Paterson, one of the few real journalists left. Davie was a sub-editor but also a rough, old-fashioned union man. He was the paper's staff representative, helping April out the previous year with a series of trumped-up accusations from a boss determined to sack her. He may have only been around 5'4" and getting on a bit like April, but management were still scared of Davie Paterson.

'Aw, Davie, is it that obvious? I was just dreaming of the day they put me out of my misery,' April replied, unable to lift her gloom.

'Then whit?' he asked with his usual gruffness. 'Are you going to take up cookery classes? Get fit? Be a lady who lunches? My wife took early retirement and she's tried all that crap. Now she just drinks most of the day. She's desperate for me to retire too to be her booze buddy. I'm telling you, retirement is just a myth. A fantasy we build up in our heads to get us through the years. This is living. Right here, right now. Not out there, wandering around art galleries, trying to fill your day.'

April didn't like where this conversation was going at all. Retirement dreams were all she had.

'Listen, you and I may be old,' Davie continued, 'but we're only old in here. What are you fifty-eight, fifty-nine?'

'I'm fifty-seven,' April quickly corrected him.

'Well, you know what they say, the older the violin, the sweeter the music. These young'uns may have all the energy but we have all the wisdom. They still need us behind the scenes to pull the strings.' Davie gave her a nudge, collected his awful coffee from the vending machine and left April to pick up her shattered dreams.

But her mind soon wandered to Patricia Tolan's mother, Edwina. It was Edwina who had all the wisdom. She couldn't help thinking she was also trying to pull April's strings.

45

#Charade

Patricia Tolan @PastyGirl70
Busy day meeting clients. So wish I could be chilling
with a glass of Chardonnay.

Patricia 'Pasty' Tolan sent the tweet to her 5,000 followers. She had once boasted four times that amount, but that had been in the days when she was Bryce Horrigan's other half, working the London scene for new, exciting clients. Her tweets were always in the 'busy girl' style of a professional woman, bemoaning the fact she had business to attend to when all she wanted to do was kick back and enjoy herself.

Patricia took a swig straight from the neck of some brutal, cheap red plonk, purporting to be from the Bortelli vineyards around Italy's lush Lake Garda region, but tasting like Bulgarian anti-freeze. She wouldn't be meeting any clients today. She wouldn't be 'chilling' either.

She gazed out of the back window of her Edinburgh town flat at the mass of overgrown grass and weeds that were once an immaculate lawn. Just like Patricia, the garden had seen better days.

Just fifty miles away in Glasgow, April sat in front of her work's computer screen with her half-moon reading glasses perched on the end of her nose. She always concentrated fully while typing, as though the computer would suddenly bite her if she dropped her guard.

Before he'd left, Connor had told her to check out Pasty's PR company to try to get a feel for how well it was doing. He hadn't elaborated, insisting he was merely curious. He told her not to bother with an in-depth check at Companies House, where records and accounts of every public listed business are held, but to merely find out who her clients were.

April had googled the name of Patricia's firm and was soon on her slick-looking website. She scanned through the 'About us' tab, which was Pasty's opportunity to brag about her career, experience and contacts, and to explain why your company simply could not do without her PR expertise. April then clicked on 'Our clients' to see the logos of around twenty companies, some of them major businesses such as Scottish Power and British Telecom. She took a note of half a dozen of the biggest names, then set about calling the in-house press and marketing department of the first.

'Hello, this is April Lavender from the *Daily Chronicle*. Is it possible to speak to Patricia Tolan?'

'I'm sorry we have no one here by that name,' replied a young and eager woman. April suspected her enthusiasm meant she was new to the job.

'Oh, I'm sorry. I think she has her own agency, PTPR. Can you please check if you work with them at all?' April asked politely but firmly.

The girl put her on hold to speak to someone who had been at the company longer than five minutes. Eventually she came back on to inform April that PTPR had done a one-off event for them a few years ago. April got virtually the same response from the next five companies – that yes, PTPR had done some work for them, but in the dim and distant past.

She returned to the 'Our clients' page and decided to try some of the smaller companies, as it could be possible Patricia was still on their books. One was for a custom-made cake business, which was no longer operating, the other was for a bespoke Edinburgh ladies' boutique. The owner was as snooty as April had expected, but when she raised the name PTPR, she replied, 'Oh, Patricia's company. I only allowed my logo to be used on her website as a favour to her mother. But Patricia has never worked for me. I do my own press,' she declared proudly. Which is why, April thought, no one had ever heard of her company.

46

#ReluctantWitness

Lieutenant Haye had been a visitor to the maximum security North Branch Correctional Institution so often that almost every guard knew him.

'Who you here for today, detective?' one of them asked after Haye had routinely handed in his weapon.

'TP,' he responded.

The guard shook his head. 'Okay. Don't think he'll wanna talk to you though, but I'll ask.'

Fifteen minutes later, a black male in his late-twenties, wearing a regulation orange prison jumpsuit, sat eyeballing Haye from across a table in the interview room. TP may have been a welterweight on the outside, but inside he had turned into more of a heavyweight.

'Jeez, you've stuck on the beef, TP. Don't get me wrong, you look ripped, but twice the size,' Haye said as way of a compliment.

'So?' was all Tre Paul Beckett said in response.

'I watched you sparring once at Southside gym – boy, you could move. Like lightning. Lethal. I said to myself, "Now there's someone who could give Mayweather or Pacquiao a run for their money." Not saying you could have beat them. But you'd hold your own.'

TP showed the faintest of grins, before regaining his stony demeanour. 'You here to blow smoke up my ass, or is there a reason?'

'Sorry, TP. I just love my boxing. Crazy for it,' Haye continued. 'I'd love to see you box again. What are you, twenty-eight?

Twenty-nine? You're still young enough. Problem is, you've still got five years to do. What if I made that two? You'd be outta here when you're still 30.'

'I ain't no rat,' TP replied bluntly.

'I'm not asking you to rat on no brother. Jeez, give me some credit, TP. I'm asking you to rat on an ex-cop – Coops,' Haye said, playing all his hand.

A smile slowly spread across TP's face. 'The pigs are turning on themselves. What do I have to do?'

Haye smiled back. 'Sign a sworn affidavit saying he beat you in custody. He'll claim it was in self-defence, of course, after you swung for him...'

TP cut him off. 'How could I swing for him cuffed? I asked him for a fair fight, but he's chickenshit. The motherfucker beat me with my hands behind my back.'

'The lying bastard,' Haye replied. 'I knew there was no way he could have taken TP.'

'So, yeah. I'll sign your papers, mister policeman. Maybe I'll even get my rematch with Coops. No cuffs this time.'

Half an hour later, Haye left with what he needed. He knew whose version of events he believed and it wasn't the ex-detective's.

'You really are a lousy fucking scumbag, Coops,' Haye muttered to himself as his sedan roared into life.

47

#HeadingEast

Connor Presley @ElvisTheWriter
Just wanted to see if @AprilReporter1955 is tweeting or eating.

April Lavender @AprilReporter1955
Both. Just wondering if I should have healthy porridge or a bacon roll this morning. #dilemma

Connor Presley @ElvisTheWriter
Has someone hacked @AprilReporter1955's account? Correct Twitter jargon and a bacon dilemma. Why not have both? #Littlepiggy

April Lavender @AprilReporter1955
@ElvisTheWriter is a cheeky wee bastard.

Connor Presley @ElvisTheWriter
Ah it is really you, @AprilReporter1955. Remember breakfast is the most important meal of the day... before lunch/dinner.

April likened Twitter to having a private conversation that's shouted between two people across a busy street. She also found it a more stress-free way to keep in touch with her daughter. Sure, Jayne was still sarcastic as hell in her replies, but there was more humour in her online communication than speaking to her on the phone, where Jayne seemed to regress into the role of a surly teenager. Now, everything from Sunday dinner to looking after her granddaughter could be arranged in 140 characters or less. As far as April was concerned, tweeting was definitely the way to go.

'Pretty soon everyone will be communicating this way,' she laughed out loud.

'To whom are you talking?' Big Fergie asked sardonically. 'How about communicating something for my schedule? I'll take it in 140 characters or less.'

The schedule was the be-all and end-all of a newspaper desk head's day. It was when each head of department took whatever stories they were working on into the midday conference with the editor. Conference was one of the oldest newspaper traditions. The editor would sit at the top of the table, a bit like a messiah – something many editors actually believe they are – while their disciples brought their offerings. A good conference would see a mediocre idea or story bandied about between the executives and worked up into something brilliant. With headline, photograph and graphic suggestions flying in from all angles. But, more often than not, conferences were no more than talking shops, where executives would read from their schedule lists, the editor would make some barely humorous remark or observation, and generally the executives seemed to excel in posturing and jockeying for the editor's approval.

Connor had once flirted with an executive career before quickly deciding it was no way for grown adults to behave. He'd told April, 'It's supposed to be an ideas factory – it's more like a sausage factory churning out a barely digestible product.'

The old newspaper characters, people with a distinctive feel for a story, were being phased out and replaced with a new breed of executives. Before, the best reporters and production journalists rose to the top. Like a football field, newspapers are an easy place to spot the most talented players. Now, mediocrity seemed to be the key to success, along with having a malicious streak. That's why Big Fergie would never get the gig on a permanent basis. He was too good and far too nice. But staff responded to Big Fergie's style of management; everyone respected him so much they didn't want to disappoint by failing to get the story. As Connor once explained, 'The last thing you want is to see those big sad puppy eyes of his if you come back empty-handed.' But good guy or bad guy, a news editor still needed stories every day to fill the insatiable list.

April had a suggestion ready for today's schedule. 'Well, with Connor in Baltimore, I thought I would chase up Bryce Horrigan's family. What about his folks in Edinburgh? I could hit the door this morning.'

Big Fergie's eyes lit up, sensing a splash. 'Brilliant idea. They turned away everyone yesterday. But if they'll talk to anyone, they'll talk to April Lavender.'

April's strength was on the doorstep. There wasn't a grieving relative who could say no to her cherub moon face when it appeared at their home, offering to help. For 'helping' was the service April believed she offered. Like the successions of police, undertakers or the local GP who would give the shattered parents 'something' to make it through, it was April's job to tell the country about their wonderful son or daughter who had been so brutally murdered or killed in tragic circumstances.

Other reporters were unable to do the same. They were too heavy-handed, going immediately for the throat: 'How did you feel when the police told you your loved one was dead?' That kind of dumb questioning would make parents clam up or turn inconsolable – sometimes both. But April would never be so crass. She would come into their homes and she'd make them cups of tea, fussing around them like a mother hen. With the lightest of nudges it would then all come pouring out of them. Not once, in her thirty-plus years of reporting, did she receive a single complaint from the families. Only letters with words of thanks for 'writing what I was thinking'.

Newspaper code under the now defunct Press Complaints Commission dictated that journalists could only approach subjects once for comments before it was considered harassment. The loophole meant families of murder victims, like the Horrigans, could also be approached once by every news agency and newspaper in the land. This could be done right up until the moment the bereaved issued a statement through police or a lawyer asking to be left in peace. Under the new Independent Press Standards Organisation, the loophole was tightened up. But the Horrigans still hadn't issued any such statement. Therefore, Big Fergie believed they were fully justified knocking the door again as no reporter had even spoken to Bryce's parents yet, never mind got a knockback from them. April hoped they wouldn't issue a formal 'back off' statement while she was en route.

The first thing April needed to do was get some background info on the Horrigans, as she didn't even know Bryce's parents' names. That meant doing a cuttings search on the Factiva system, which logs newspaper archives on a daily basis from thousands of media outlets across the globe. Like every other piece of new technology, April hated Factiva. She had never managed to get the hang of refining her searches, with her requests throwing up hundreds of articles as wide-ranging as death notices in Florida to stories from the *India Times*, meaning time wasted trawling through them for the information required.

But her luck changed this morning. When she searched for 'Bryce Horrigan' and 'mother', the very first article revealed that her name was Flora, and that his dad was a solicitor called Donald.

'Good Scottish names,' April said to herself.

She then tapped in her password to Tracesmart, which held the electoral roll for the whole of the UK. It was the same system used by banks, debt companies and just about any other agency that needed to trace members of the public. Only one result came back: for Barnton in Edinburgh, one of the capital's most exclusive areas. The search also contained a phone number, but April preferred the face-to-face approach.

She sent the address to the picture desk and asked them to have a snapper meet her outside the property in an hour and a half. April then scooped up her bulging bag and coat and headed east. She hoped the Horrigans would let her in, not only for the story, but because she was a natural-born nosey parker and was desperate to see inside their home.

48

#TheNewVic

'I have a Mr Cooper on the line for you, captain,' the department secretary said, calling through to Sorrell's office.

Finally, Sorrell thought to himself. The captain decided to ditch the charm offensive this time as he was fed up dancing to Cooper's tune.

'You got a name for me Colin?' Sorrell said without any preamble.

'I've got a name for you. Cliff Walker,' Cooper replied, knowing he had wrong-footed the captain.

'And just who the hell is Cliff Walker?' the captain said, losing his cool.

'He's one of our longest serving porters. Nice old guy. Never forgets a face. It's his thing. He's also dead. I'm standing in his apartment right now. Don't worry, I've touched fuck all. But he's been wasted. His brains are everywhere,' Cooper said in the matter-of-fact fashion of a man who has seen many dead bodies.

Sorrell's head went into overdrive. The porter's death had to be connected to the Horrigan case. All the staff members who had been on duty that night had all been interviewed. But Cliff Walker must have witnessed something that hadn't aroused suspicion at the time. Either that or Cooper was clearing up some loose ends.

'Stay exactly where you are, Colin. We'll need to bring you in and this time you're gonna need that lawyer,' Sorrell warned.

'Yeah, yeah, whatever. But I didn't take out Cliff. You have my word on that. And fifty dollars says ballistics match the bullets to the Bryce shooting,' Cooper said with his usual over-confidence.

Sorrell had no reason to doubt him. He slammed the phone down and hollered at the top of his voice, 'HAYE, GET IN HERE.'

49

#DeadPorter

The blue lights surrounded Cliff Walker's downtown apartment within minutes of Colin Cooper's phone call to Captain Sorrell. Haye arrived shortly after, noting the porter lived within walking distance of the Baltimore City Hotel. It would have been easy enough to follow the old man home after he'd finished his shift.

The lieutenant took one look at the crime scene with the porter's destroyed head, then turned to Colin Cooper, who had stayed rooted to the spot on Sorrell's instructions. He was grinning as usual. 'Not got the stomach for brains and blood, Haye?'

'Shut the fuck up, Coops,' Haye said, shoving Cooper towards the door. Haye hated the ex-cop with a passion, but he doubted even Cooper would have the balls to shoot dead a fellow member of staff then call a homicide captain from the crime scene.

Cooper decided to remain silent for the short journey back to police HQ, which suited Haye fine. Captain Sorrell was already waiting for them in the interview room. He began the proceedings before Cooper had even taken his chair.

'Lawyer?' Sorrell asked.

'Depends on what you have to say,' Cooper shrugged.

'What were you doing in Cliff Walker's apartment?' Sorrell said, getting straight to the point.

'Well, I know you fellas think I'm head of some prostitution cartel, but that doesn't pay so well, so my day job is head of security for the Baltimore City Hotel, in case you fucking forgot. Old Cliff lives alone. When he misses a shift for the first time in a hundred years or whatever, it's my job to check it out,' Cooper explained.

'Sounds feasible. Okay, let's move on. Give me the hooker's name. Now,' Sorrell demanded.

'I'm a fucking ex-detective. Don't you think I've asked her everything already? She was paid in cash by the guy wearing the hat. He kept it on inside the room. He had the lights out. She saw nothing. Believe me, I've gone over it a hundred times with her. There's nothing more to ask,' Cooper insisted.

'There's always more to ask. Her name or else,' Sorrell warned.

Cooper smirked. 'Or else what, captain? I thought the days of beating on suspects was long gone. That's why I left.'

'Talking of which,' Haye said, chucking several sheets of paper stapled together onto the desk in front of them, 'this is a sworn affidavit from TP. Says you beat on him while he was cuffed. You really are a lying scumbag, Coops.'

Cooper flicked through the pages quickly, before coming to Tre Paul Beckett's signature and scoffed, 'Who's gonna take the word of some yo, with convictions as long as his arm, over a former cop with an unblemished record? You guys are pathetic. You've shot your load. Time for my lawyer now,' Cooper said, leaning back and crossing his arms.

Outside the room, Sorrell kicked a wall in frustration. 'That is the most stubborn bastard that ever walked God's earth. He'd rather face certain death in jail than give us her goddamn name.'

Sorrell buried his head in his hands before sighing loudly, 'Okay, just let him go, Haye. This is getting insane. Tonight, I'm gonna need a beer. A lot of beer.'

50

#TrollHunting

Finance director Jack Portland sat in his favourite coffee house in downtown Minneapolis, enjoying his usual lunchtime double espresso. He had the air of respectability that came with his position as an executive of a major city bank, which provided a very comfortable lifestyle for his wife and two children.

Every day, Portland would peruse his copy of the *Wall Street Journal* before tapping away at his iPhone. To the casual observer, it looked like he was accessing the latest prices on the Dow Jones Index. In actual fact, he was switching his phone into airplane mode before using the coffee house's Wi-Fi with the new daily code printed at the bottom of his double espresso receipt. It was a procedure that he was convinced gave him complete anonymity and the confidence to ignore the tweet he had received from Baltimore Police ordering him to get in touch. He would then log on to his Twitter account as @TruthTeller and spout the vilest filth to any famous person who irked him.

His comments to pop star Miley Cyrus were creepy enough, but he had really enjoyed his spats with the late Bryce Horrigan, mainly because the television host took his bait and responded. Portland would spend most of his lunch hour trading insults, which would get more and more hate-filled with every response. Intellectually he was a match for Bryce, which is probably what intrigued the chat show host to keep the thread going.

But Portland crossed the line when he promised Bryce a most painful and agonising death. He went on to tweet Horrigan's New York home address, illegally obtained from the presenter's bank

146

account details from when Horrigan had been a customer with Portland's firm. Although he would never admit it online, when he saw Horrigan's eye-watering salary, over ten times that of his own quite considerable $120,000-a-year earnings, his hatred had amplified.

The address tweet had been their last exchange. Horrigan had alerted his company's security team, who had in turn informed the authorities. They had promised to investigate, but in truth did very little. However, with Bryce's death, all old leads would now be properly looked at.

Portland finished sending his filth to the female pop star not much older than his daughter, left a two-dollar tip, stood up and tucked the *Wall Street Journal* under his arm. What he hadn't noticed were the two men, in much cheaper suits, who were sitting behind him. One had been on his own cell phone, watching the live Twitter feed of @TruthTeller, while his colleague covertly filmed Portland sending the tweets, which would later be used in evidence against him.

'Jack Portland, I'm arresting you in connection with the death of Bryce Horrigan. You have the right to remain silent…'

Having his Miranda rights read to him and cuffs snapped on inside his favourite café was just the beginning of his humiliation. Jack Portland would eventually be absolved of any involvement in Horrigan's murder, but that would not prevent him from losing his job, with his career in finance in tatters. For as Portland would discover, no one, not even his favourite coffee shop, wanted to employ a troll.

The soon to be ex-finance director was one of seventeen Horrigan suspects arrested across America on the same day.

51

#HowTheOtherHalfLive

April arrived outside the address in Edinburgh's plush Barnton district with her nose twitching in anticipation. She couldn't wait to see inside. For April loved property – especially the houses of the rich and famous. Her biggest regret was that she once turned down the offer to be a staff writer for a property supplement at a rival newspaper. In the end the wage rise she'd been offered to stay where she was had been the deciding factor. But she'd been sorely tempted as she would not only have been setting foot in the high end properties, but also running the rule on the fine dividing line between money and taste.

April was convinced you could tell everything about a person by the way they lived. She remembered when she had once gone to interview one of Scotland's richest businessmen at home. He was a real boardroom bruiser known for his ruthless streak. But she'd been amazed at how ramshackle and downright filthy his sprawling converted farmhouse had been. This was a man who had launched numerous hostile takeovers with military precision, yet he lived in virtual chaos.

Many of April's door knocks were in Scotland's less salubrious districts, with their high-rise flats or condemned tenement buildings. April and Connor had a cruel nickname for such dilapidated council houses or junkies' drug dens, calling them a 'PP' – a Piss Palace – as they usually smelled of urine and sometimes much, much worse.

But there were no Piss Palaces in leafy Barnton; the Horrigan property was situated beside a private tennis court. The photographers who had been camped outside the Horrigan family home for the last couple of days were now gone. A notice hung on the gate by a friendly neighbour had informed the press pack that Mr and Mrs Horrigan were away and would like their privacy.

April approached the door, dolled up to the nines as usual, with her hair recently dyed, and layers of make-up desperately trying to cover the wrinkles. She always kept her demeanour friendly and bubbly, as that was her natural disposition, but she was professional and direct, telling whoever opened the door exactly what she was there for. The heavy wooden door was answered by an elderly woman, who was unmistakably Bryce Horrigan's mother – the presenter had taken her looks, for what they were worth. If she eyed April up and down in a slightly disapproving manner, she looked horrified when her eyes came to rest on the photographer Jack Barr, with his goatee beard and mane of long hair tied into the midlife crisis silver ponytail.

It was April who spoke first. 'I'm here about Bryce, Mrs Horrigan. We used to work with him. May we come in?'

Bryce's mother paused for a moment before she opened her door fully and stepped aside for the reporting team to enter. She didn't say a word until she had shown them into the dining room, and directed them to take a seat. April surveyed the decor, with its wooden panelled walls and old servant call box, where a light would indicate which room their paymasters were summoning them to. The table had white lace place mats. April guessed the Horrigans hadn't entertained anyone for a while.

'We apparently had camera crews outside day and night. Thankfully we've been away but goodness knows what the neighbours thought,' Mrs Horrigan sniffed.

April found it curious how people held onto things they perceived as being important even when faced with bereavement.

'I'm April Lavender, Mrs Horrigan. I worked with your son at the *Daily Chronicle* for a short while. I had a few staff nights out with him and Patricia.'

'Ah, Pasty, such a nice girl,' Mrs Horrigan said, with a flicker of happiness in her eyes, which quickly dimmed when she added, 'Such a shame what happened between her and Bryce. She loved him so much. Too much, in fact. I used to tell her she needed to keep a portion of her heart for herself, in case it should be broken.'

Flora Horrigan spoke in well-educated, clipped tones, like a Miss Jean Brodie character. April couldn't help but feel a little intimidated by her. She feared being in the company of smart people in case they should ask her a question she didn't understand. Despite being fifty-seven years old, April still felt in danger of being 'found out' due to her lack of education, having left school at sixteen to become a Royal Navy Wren, and having no formal journalism training. She had often confided her fears to Connor, who would actually dispense with his normal caustic quips to reassure her: 'Well, they've tried to bring in younger reporters with their degrees to replace you, and you've seen them all off the premises. There is only one April Lavender.' Of course, he'd usually ruin the pep talk by adding, 'Thank fuck,' under his breath.

'What happened between Pasty and Bryce, Mrs Horrigan?' April enquired, half for journalistic reasons, half because she was desperate to know.

'Please, call me Flora,' she said, visibly softening her demeanour. April took the opportunity of the change of tone to place her Dictaphone clearly on the table between them, pressing the red button to record. It didn't put off Mrs Horrigan. 'Fame is what came between them. My son became obsessed by fame.'

April had heard this before from Connor, who rated Bryce as one of the best newspaper writers he'd ever come across, and couldn't for the life of him understand why Horrigan was seduced by television. One day, Connor asked him outright and was surprised by Bryce's blunt reply: 'You can spend your whole life writing for the country's biggest newspaper, with your face printed in it every day and not one person will recognise you walking down the street. But a solitary appearance on a prime-time Saturday night TV show and even the taxi drivers are honking me in the street.' A little bit of Connor's respect for Bryce had died that day.

Now, here April was hearing the exact same thing from Bryce's own mother.

Mrs Horrigan continued, 'His father and I were astounded when he turned his back on being a lawyer. But we reluctantly had to admit he was very well suited to newspapers. He obviously had a flair for it. But then he moved to London and television came calling. He'd occasionally ring to ask what we had thought about his performance on this, that and the other television programme, but of course his father and I didn't even know what he was talking about. The television is rarely on in our house. If it's not *The Archers*, then we're not interested. We don't know if he took it as some sort of disapproval. Perhaps it was on our part, but his phone calls became less and less. Then he moved to New York. Very risqué as you don't know how those awful Americans will take to a Brit. But then he started all this pro-abortion stuff. I knew he was heading for trouble. I finally called him up and told him in no uncertain terms.'

'What did you say, Mrs... Flora? What did you tell him?' April prompted.

'The truth, my dear. That he would be murdered. That the Christian fundamentalists would find a focus for their anger in him. But I knew it was in one ear and out the other. He was revelling in the attention. That's why I feared the worse. I knew he would end up dead.'

April already had enough for a splash and a two-page spread inside. But she hadn't been expecting what came next.

'Then there was the sex,' Mrs Horrigan said, spitting out the word 'sex' as if it shouldn't be spoken, never mind done. 'He was getting lots of it. That's what he told me – his own mother. When I was warning him he should put his head back below the parapet, Bryce just laughed at me, saying, "But Mother, then I wouldn't get all these amazing girls. They're practically throwing themselves at me. If you're famous in America, it's like royalty. Some of them even think I AM royalty. Who am I to say otherwise if they want to bed a prince?" It was as if he was taunting me for some reason. *Look at me, Mum, I'm so rich and powerful and surrounded by women.* I couldn't believe my ears. That was the last conversation I had with my only son. In truth, he didn't even sound like Bryce anymore. He had changed; his accent, his personality, his morals, they were all gone. I didn't know the person I was speaking to. Like an echo of the man he used to be. Tragic, isn't it?' Mrs Horrigan said stoically, before tears filled her eyes and she began to sob.

April had sensed it was coming and produced a pack of hankies while the snapper cynically captured the mother's emotional low point on camera.

'Where is Mr Horrigan, Flora?' April asked.

'Donald? He goes sailing a lot now. He doesn't talk about it. He was never one to air his feelings, not even in private. But since Bryce's death he has become even more withdrawn. All he said was, "He should have studied at the bloody bar." Such a pity Bryce never wanted to be a lawyer like his father.'

April thanked Mrs Horrigan for her time and left with a very different impression of the Bryce Horrigan she had briefly known. She was starting to see why someone would want to kill him.

52

#BeerOClock

Haye and Sorrell walked the two blocks from police HQ on East Fayette Street to their local watering hole, an Irish pub on East Fairmount. They didn't talk much on the sidewalk, through a mixture of tiredness and suspicion they'd be overheard, but once inside the noisy bar, the first Guinness soon made them relax.

Haye ordered the crab dip with a side of sweet potato fries. 'I was so fucking busy I forgot to eat today, cap'n. Want something?'

'Nah. Food gets in the way of my drinking. Truth is, Denise has cooked me something. She'd kill me if I came home smelling of drink then refused to eat. Rather just get done on one count,' Sorrell explained, ordering another round of Guinness.

'I'm glad I don't have all that shit anymore. Don't get me wrong, cap'n, it suits straight shooters like yourself, but I'm not cut out for family life,' Haye replied, in between mouthfuls of food.

Sorrell smiled for the first time in days. 'And what makes you think I'm a straight shooter?'

Haye nearly choked on his crab dip. 'C'mon, cap'n, you're the straightest guy I know. I mean that in a good way. You wouldn't go beating the shit out of suspects like that scumbag, Coops.'

'The difference is, I did it where no one saw me,' Sorrell confessed.

'Fuck off. No way you be beating up on someone?' Haye said in amazement.

'Did too. I was new. Chased this yo for ten blocks. He ran out of steam before I did. I was a lot thinner and fitter back then too. I ran round this corner and BAM, he hit me with a right hook which dislocated my jaw. Sorest thing I ever felt. My legs turned to jelly and I was about to pass out. Know why I didn't?' Sorrell asked.

'Nope.'

'My shirt. I had just started dating Denise and she bought me this beautiful pink shirt. It was the first gift from a girlfriend,' Sorrell recalled.

'Pink? I'd have punched your lights out too,' Haye joked.

Sorrell ignored him. 'Anyway, I look down and it's ruined. Covered in my own blood. I thought, *What will I tell Denise?* So instead of passing out I flew into a rage and kicked the bastard unconscious. That was the first and last time I hit a suspect.'

'Jeez, cap'n, I never knew you had it in you. I'm not saying you're a soft touch. No way. But I just can't see you fucking up someone, like Coops. I guess every dog has its day,' Haye said, shaking his head.

'Know what?' Sorrell said. 'Coops was a good detective. I don't believe he framed anybody. But his methods were Stone Age. He didn't have the patience for interrogations. That's why he always beat on people. He was always in a hurry with somewhere to go.'

'Yeah, to check on his hookers down at his whorehouse,' Haye scoffed.

'You're probably right. I always reckoned if they could have removed Coops' evil gene, he could have risen to the top,' Sorrell concluded.

'That's what I like about you, cap'n, even after all these years doing this fucking job, you still try to see the good in people. Me? I think Coops is a lousy fucking dirtbag, who's going out of his way to dick us around and fuck up our investigation,' Haye replied, thumping his empty tumbler down on the bar, which brought an unwelcome glance from the bartender.

'I take it you two gentlemen would like another?' he asked.

Haye apologised. 'Sorry, long day, Andy. Yeah, two Guinness and two Scotch. Jura. Eighteen-year-old. Neat. One for yourself, too.'

The cops said nothing as Andy took his time to pour. Haye held his small glass of golden whisky admiringly up to Sorrell, and declared, 'Slanj-uh va.'

'What?' Sorrell asked quizzically.

'It's Scotch for "Your good health". I'm quarter Scotch myself,' Haye said proudly.

'Yeah, but only since you saw *Braveheart*. Before then everyone was Irish. They just swapped the Os for the Mcs.'

'I fucking loved that film, cap'n. "They may take our lives, but they'll never take our FREEDOM,"' Haye said in a terrible Scottish accent. 'Mel Gibson was fucking awesome. Before all the other stuff that came later,' he added almost sadly.

'I'll drink to that,' Sorrell replied.

Silence fell between the two men again as they drained their whisky glasses, before Haye spoke. 'Cap'n, don't you think we're taking our eye off the ball with chasing down Coops and shit? I could join the team looking through Horrigan's tweets full-time. Push them hard. Run down the death threats myself. I just think we're getting side-lined, while the bastard is still out there taunting us on Bryce Horrigan's own Twitter feed, for fuck's sake. Then there's your Baby Angel. We still haven't found out who they are. Gotta be linked, surely?'

Sorrell responded in a measured manner. 'Your freedom fighter, William Wallace – he wasn't just some barbarian, right? If I remember the film, he was educated. Spoke Latin?'

'Yeah. Sure. Where you goin' with this, cap'n?' Haye asked through bleary eyes.

'Coops is the same,' Sorrell declared.

'Fuck off. He speaks Latin? Fuck off,' Haye repeated, finishing the last of his Guinness.

'Believe it or not, he does. Catholic upbringing or something. He's real smart, too. Coops wouldn't want to have been arrested. To do the walk of shame in front of the TV cameras? Have his bosses ask all sorts of awkward questions? No way. He always wanted the easy life.'

'So?' Haye asked.

'So he's protecting someone,' Sorrell said, ordering another round of Jura and Guinness.

'The hooker?' Haye asked incredulously.

'That wouldn't make any sense if she was just a hooker. So she has to be something more than that.'

'His lover?' Haye said, the penny finally dropping.

'Slow. But you got there in the end, Haye, and that's all that counts. Listen, what's the first rule of homicide? Follow the facts. Every case throws up leads and we chase them down, right? That's what we're doing here. This Twitter stuff feels like a carrot on a stick. Someone is trying to tempt us away from where we're going. Well, last time I checked, I was in charge of this case. Not some crazy person on Twitter. Tomorrow, lean on Coops' ex-wife, Stephanie. A hard-faced bitch if ever there was one. Rumour has it she used to beat Coops up,' Sorrell smiled.

'No shit?' Haye said in amazement. 'No wonder he used to take it out on the suspects.'

Both men burst out laughing.

'Five minutes speaking to Stephanie and you'll wish you were in Coops' company again.' Sorrell smiled once more, feeling he'd been able to think straight for the first time since the death of Bryce Horrigan.

53

#TheLordsWork

Baby Angel @BabyAngel
Still reckon I'm a fake, captain?

Bernard Sorrell @BernardSorrell
I know you're a fake. Your name is not Baby Angel. The real you has yet to come forward.

Baby Angel @BabyAngel
Ah, dear captain, this is but a moniker I need to hide behind to do the Lord's work.

Bernard Sorrell @BernardSorrell
Funny, you've never mentioned the Lord until now. I don't believe you're the religious type. You're a phoney.

Baby Angel @BabyAngel
You have got me there. I never was one for Bible class. But that doesn't mean the rest isn't true.

Bernard Sorrell @BernardSorrell
I tend to believe if you lie about one thing, you can't trust the rest.

Baby Angel @BabyAngel
Tell me there wasn't a man matching Schroeder's description at that motel and I'll let you be.

Sorrell had discovered that not only was there someone matching Schroeder's description at the motel, CCTV footage had confirmed his identity. It was advantage, Baby Angel.

Baby Angel @BabyAngel
Well?

Bernard Sorrell @BernardSorrell
Yes, Schroeder was there. Now tell me how you know.

Baby Angel @BabyAngel
All in good time, captain. But first we have to catch our killer.

Bernard Sorrell @BernardSorrell
Suspect. Schroeder is a suspect.

Baby Angel @BabyAngel
Person of interest, suspect, whatever. I'll just call him The Killer. So what's our next step?

Bernard Sorrell @BernardSorrell
There is no we. This is a police matter.

Baby Angel @BabyAngel
Don't get so protective, captain. Remember, Baltimore Police wouldn't have heard Schroeder's name if it hadn't been for me!

The captain looked at his screen and muttered, 'Funny, I was just thinking the same thing.'

54

#TaxiDriver

Connor walked the full length of the taxi queue at Baltimore/ Washington International Thurgood Marshall Airport – a real mouthful of a title, understandably shortened to 'Marshall' by the locals. The taxi stand was located on the lower level of the main terminal, where only BWI Marshall-registered cabs could pick up customers – that gave Connor a realistic chance of speaking to the driver who had driven Horrigan to the hotel. He had a picture of the dead television personality on his BlackBerry, which he pushed through the drivers' windows, asking if Horrigan had been a customer.

He was utterly amazed by the huge range of nationalities and races behind the wheels. Back home in Glasgow it seemed all taxi drivers were white and Scottish. Here there were turban-wearing Sikhs, Asians, African Americans, you name it. But they did share one common trait with their Scottish counterparts: they were a bad-tempered bunch. Some would just shake their heads before Connor even asked a question. Another told him straight, 'If you're not hiring then fuck off, buddy.' Connor quite liked the friendly malice feel of adding 'buddy' to a threat. But, like any half-decent reporter, he persevered. When he had exhausted the queue of cabs, he simply waited at the end of the line for the next one to come in and try again.

He knew it was a long shot. It could be the driver's day off. Or he could be on vacation. Random thoughts started drifting through his head from a mix of jet lag and boredom, as he asked himself, 'How come, if they call it a vacation in America,

Madonna sang *Holiday*?' Connor had once held ambitions to work in the States, until someone told him most Americans only got two weeks' annual 'vacation' – three, if they'd worked for the same company for about thirty years. Connor couldn't do without his seven weeks' paid leave a year; eight, if you included getting back all the bank holidays he had to work, too.

The next white cab joined the end of the line, and Connor went through the motions again. 'Sorry to bother you, but did you pick up this guy?'

'What if I did?' came the shock reply. A shock because for once he wasn't being told to get lost.

'I'm a reporter. I'm trying to find out if he said anything?'

'Cops told me not to speak to the press.'

'I was Bryce's friend. I'm just trying to find out what happened to him.'

'What's in it for me?'

'$100?'

'I get $70 for every ride into town.'

'Okay, $70 for the ride, $100 for you?'

'Get in.'

The cab pulled out from the back of the line, earning the ire from his fellow drivers, who angrily tooted their horns and flashed their lights. Connor's driver flicked them the finger in return. 'Fucking assholes.' His badge said his name was Eddie Sandberg.

'So whatcha wanna know?' Eddie asked.

'Just anything you can tell me. Was he harassed? Worried-looking? Say much?'

'Worried-looking? No, he wasn't worried-looking,' Eddie said, before chuckling to himself.

'What's so funny?'

'Cops asked me the same stuff and I'll tell you what I told them. The guy was real relaxed. He was also here for some fun.'

'How'd you know that?'

Eddie chuckled to himself again. He had quickly started to

irritate Connor. Like someone laughing at an in-joke they refuse to share.

'Because when I asked him if he was here for business or pleasure, he told me, "Oh, I'm here for pleasure all right."'

'That does sound like Bryce,' Connor conceded.

'There's no way that guy was here on business. He was here on a promise.' Eddie's chuckle became a laugh. 'But someone had other ideas, right? Am I right?'

'Yes, I guess you're right.' Connor had had his fill of Eddie the twisted driver. He asked him to pull in a few blocks from where he was headed as he needed to get out. Connor took his age and a contact number along with a quick photo of Eddie leaning out of his cab window. It would do for a head and shoulders shot to go with his story of Horrigan's last taxi ride.

There wasn't much to go on, but at least now Connor had a good idea of his old boss's motives for being in Baltimore. And he just knew they were far from honourable.

55

#HungForASheep

Haye took the I-83 highway north out of the city heading to Lutherville, one of the most upmarket districts in the county. Stephanie Cooper's house was situated by Loch Raven reservoir, with views across the water to Towson Golf & Country Club. Haye pulled up his sedan outside the colonial-style home and whistled softly to himself. 'You wouldn't get much change out of a million dollars for that.'

But while the building and area reeked of money, its inhabitant was distinctly lower class. Before Haye even rang the doorbell, Stephanie Cooper flung open her door. 'If you've come to ask about Coops, I have nuthin' to say except he's a no-good piece of shit.'

'I know that,' Haye replied.

Stephanie cracked something that could pass as a smile. But it was only fleeting. 'What the fuck are you here for, then?'

Curiously, the soon-to-be divorced Stephanie Cooper was the same squat shape and height as her estranged husband. They even had similar aggressive personalities, more like siblings than spouses. *Maybe they are*, Haye thought to himself.

'I need some help. May I come in?' he asked politely.

Stephanie's dark beady eyes looked Haye up and down. He was good-looking for his age, even if he showed signs of wear and tear. 'You've got ten minutes before my hair appointment,' she said, showing him her back as she stomped into the depths of her home.

Haye looked at her boyish short haircut disappearing down the hall and thought Stephanie Cooper's hairdresser got money for nothing.

She stopped in the kitchen and gruffly asked, 'Coffee?'

'Sure, white, two sugars,' Haye said, scanning around. He could understand why she was so twitchy. There was no way Coops earned a plush pad like this on a cop's salary, even with a golden handshake from the homicide department. And Stephanie certainly didn't look like she came from money.

'So what's the cheating fuck done now?' Stephanie asked, peering at him with suspicious eyes over the top of her coffee mug.

'I can't be sure, but he won't give us the name of a hooker we think he's running from the Baltimore City Hotel. She might be able to help us with a case,' Haye said, keeping as much detail to himself as possible.

Stephanie started to laugh. Like everything about her, it wasn't nice. More mocking than jocular. 'This to do with that British prick?' she asked, already knowing the answer.

'Yeah, Bryce Horrigan. But please keep that to yourself,' Haye pleaded.

'Know why Coops left? I caught him cheating with one of the girls. Now, this goes no further, all right pretty boy? Because I'll deny everything, then claim you sexually assaulted me in my own home, gettit?' Stephanie warned and Haye knew she wasn't kidding. 'We had a no screwing rule when we worked the girls. Or blowies. No handjobs, either, okay? He was just to provide the security, make sure we weren't fucked around by vice squad and I looked after the rest.'

Suddenly it all made perfect sense to Haye. The expensive house. The lifestyle and Stephanie Cooper – a stereotypical don't-fuck-with-me brothel madam if ever there was one.

'But he broke the rule, didn't he? What's her name?' Haye said, going for the kill.

'A stuck-up little bitch who called herself Lindy Delwar. College student. At least she was until she discovered she could earn more as Coops' bitch than through her studies,' Stephanie said, pouring them both a refill.

Haye took out his iPhone to find the freeze-frame of the hooker counting her money in the hotel elevator. He showed it to Stephanie, who laughed again. 'I told her not to count out her bucks like that. It's crass.'

Haye thought that was rich coming from Stephanie Cooper. 'Where can I find this Lindy Delwar?'

'You can start by using her real name, Linda Delaney. They're shacked up together. They deserve each other, if you ask me. Coops has no other girls working for him. They all stayed with me. Loyalty means a lot to me. Here, you can have the little bitch's number if you don't want to speak to her handler. Rumour has it she likes to moonlight without Coops knowing. Drives him crazy. So she'll meet you if you pretend to be some rich punter,' Stephanie said, trawling through her iPhone contacts.

Haye took a note of Lindy Delwar's number, finished his coffee then politely rinsed it in the sink.

'So, you wanna go upstairs and fuck?' Stephanie asked bluntly.

'What?' Haye spluttered, before regaining his composure. 'I thought my ten minutes was up?'

'You can have another ten,' she said, making her way to the staircase.

'What about your hair appointment?'

'Let's be honest, this crop job pretty much looks after its fucking self.'

'And accusing me of sexual assault?' Haye asked, following her like a puppy.

'Only if you don't do me right,' she said, leading him into her bedroom by the hand.

56

#RecordTraffic

The tweet had a link to the *Daily Chronicle*'s website, which gave a teaser of April's 'World Exclusive', a tabloid tag reserved for what were the biggest stories. April thought it was a hugely overused newspaper term and something of an oxymoron. A footballer getting his wife and mistress both pregnant at the same time was a proper scoop, but only meant something on these shores.

However, her interview with Flora Horrigan was probably April's first true world exclusive as the murder of Bryce was still making headlines around the globe. Very quickly other news outlets would be running the quotes from April's interview, which was technically illegal and breached copyright. But such was the clamour for instant rolling news, the other media websites would simply credit the *Daily Chronicle* in their stories and include a hyperlink to the Scottish paper's homepage. If there was any fallout, they'd let the lawyers work it out later. April's exclusive proved to be something of a coup for her organisation, which saw its subscriptions suddenly go up at a rate of about 100 an hour – the fastest growth rate since they had gone behind a paywall a year earlier.

The splash in the print edition also had the world exclusive strapline and read: TV STAR'S MUM PREDICTED DEATH. Due to the constraints of page size and design it needed to be worded differently from the online version, simply to make it fit on a front page, which is measured in the centuries-old newspaper measurements of seven columns width – with 3.4 centimetres in each column. But online, the banner headline read, *The mother of TV star Bryce Horrigan talks exclusively about how she predicted her son's murder*. This was so Internet search engines would pick up on the words 'Bryce Horrigan' and 'murder'.

The editor from the online department excitedly burst into April's broom cupboard office and babbled, 'We've just seen a 300 per cent increase in subscriptions and passed the 51,000 hits mark for your story, too. Traffic is going through the roof.'

'Well done,' April replied as the online editor practically skipped out of her office. Not only had she failed to understand a single word that he'd said, she couldn't even remember his name. April only knew him as the lanky, curly-haired boy that 'did something with the computers'. When faced with the unknown, April just smiled. Usually she'd get away with it, unless Connor was around. He'd recognise that familiar vacant look and mutter, 'You haven't a fucking clue, have you?'

It was the same when they'd both bump into the paper's political editor in the breakout area. Connor would immediately engage him in debate about the latest events at the Scottish Parliament and playfully try to bring the oblivious April into the conversation, with fear etched all over her face. Afterwards she would ask Connor how he was always so up to date with everything that was going on. He'd shrug and reply, 'Because I actually read our newspaper.'

He had a point. Politics was carried daily on page two. April would just glance at it and glaze over. She had absolutely no interest in politics whatsoever, even though it still dominated television news. She couldn't even remember the last time she'd voted, but reckoned it was probably when she was still married to husband number two, who had been quite active with the Labour party… or the Liberals, she could never remember which. He was obsessed with politics, and insisted on talking about it morning, noon and night, until she could take it no more and ordered him to leave their home. When husband number two asked what he'd done wrong, April had snapped, 'You're actually boring me to death with your politics.'

He'd sniffed, 'But I thought you liked politics? I thought it was "our thing"?'

April had replied, 'Well "our thing" has got old, and life's too short.'

And that had been the end of that marriage.

There had been a time when April had her choice of suitors. Now all she had was the lecherous old Italian restaurant owner Luigi, who would propose to her, without fail, on every occasion she ate in his restaurant. She could usually laugh it off, but he was persistent. Unfortunately she didn't do much to put off her admirer as she kept insisting on eating there.

Now April felt hungry. She would definitely be stopping by Luigi's for dinner tonight. He may have been an old sex pest but he still owned the finest Italian in Glasgow.

57

#StreetWise

Haye called the number Stephanie Cooper had given him from her driveway, two hours after he first arrived. *That was a long ten minutes*, he thought to himself, before a female's voice answered the phone.

'Is that Lindy Del-war?' Haye asked, not sure how to say her surname.

'It's pronounced, "Del Wha". And it depends who's looking for her,' came the response. Lindy sounded streetwise.

'Someone with a thousand dollars to spare,' Haye replied coolly.

Lindy's demeanour instantly changed. 'Well, that's my kinda language. How can I help you?'

'I have two hours to kill before my next meeting and need a lie-down. I was hoping you could lie with me?' Haye asked.

'Well, you can lie down if you want, and I'll do the rest,' Lindy giggled.

Haye gave his own apartment's address, assuring Lindy, 'Don't worry, I'm divorced. I live alone. Can you be there in half an hour?'

'Oh I'm there, honey. But money up front, okay? No money, no touchy,' said a woman who had clearly been stung before. Her demands also suggested that she would be alone. Moonlighting, without telling her lover, as Stephanie Cooper had said.

'I can't wait, Lindy. See you then,' Haye said, before phoning the captain. He hoped tracking down the hooker would divert attention from the fact he had slipped off the radar for the entire morning.

He drove back to town, mulling over Stephanie Cooper's business offer. She wanted Haye as her new 'eyes and ears' to keep vice off her back. She had even come up with a plausible explanation: 'Tell them I'm your snitch. We'll throw them a name or two every now and then. A bail jumper who turns up looking for a girl. That's what Coops used to do.' Haye was beginning to wonder if the brothel madam had another agenda when she slept with him – after all, in her line of business, there's no such thing as a freebie.

Twenty minutes later, Haye was waiting for Lindy in his first-floor apartment. He watched at the window as a cab pulled up and a pair of high heels and long legs exited first, followed by the woman he recognised from the hotel CCTV – Stephanie Cooper had come up trumps. Lindy Delwar rang the buzzer and Haye let her in. She looked stunning and although in her mid-twenties, she could pass for being in her teens. Haye thought it was no wonder she could charge top dollar.

Lindy was all business. 'The money first, please.'

'What about these,' Haye said, producing a pair of handcuffs.

'We can do the kinky stuff later. Money first or I walk, mister,' Lindy replied, with the penny clearly failing to drop.

'How about I give you a lift downtown,' Haye grinned.

Lindy's smile vanished as she realised she'd been well and truly busted. 'Oh no, Coops is gonna kill me.'

58

#Commission

Captain Sorrell joined Haye in the interview room to quiz the girl they had been looking for. Any woman who lived with Colin Cooper would be used to the rough stuff, so the captain spoke in the softest tones he could muster. 'It's Linda, right?'

'I prefer Lindy,' she replied, sitting cross-legged like a petulant teenager.

'Okay. Lindy. You are not in any trouble – yet. But I can make trouble if you don't help us. I need to know about room 1410 and the night the television presenter Bryce Horrigan was killed,' Sorrell explained, like a father speaking to a wayward child.

'I told Coops, I saw nothing. He said he would tell you that. That you would leave me alone. I don't want to get involved in this shit. My family will go crazy,' she screeched.

'Okay. Let's take it one step at a time. How did the man with the hat contact you?' Sorrell asked calmly.

'Through Coops. That's how I do everything. Through Coops,' she insisted.

'But you don't do everything through Coops, do you?' asked Haye, lobbing in his loaded question.

'No. But room 1410 is always through Coops. He made me swear I wouldn't moonlight on my own. He said it was too dangerous. That I might get killed or busted. But he said he could always look after me at the hotel.' Lindy's words poured from her as tears tumbled down her cheeks.

'Lindy, tell us exactly what happened at the hotel that night,' Sorrell urged.

'I arrived expecting to perform for some white businessman. That's all the information Coops had. I got inside the room and most of the lights were out. I wasn't worried because I knew if any shit went down, Coops would be there for me,' she explained.

'Where was Coops?' Haye asked.

'In his control room. He's always there when we have a client for room 1410. Anyways, I go inside and this guy says he's not feeling up to it tonight. I'm thinking he's gonna go back on the money, but then he says he'll happily pay me for my trouble and hands over the envelope. I couldn't count it because it was so dark, but again I wasn't worried – if it was short, he'd have Coops at the door. I asked him if he was sure, as it was no skin off my nose, but he told me to go as he just wanted to sleep in the hotel room for a little while as he wasn't feeling well. And that was it. I got the elevator back down, counted the money – it was all there – then Coops and me headed home. We didn't see no TV star. We saw nobody else.'

'Do you remember seeing Cliff Walker that night?' Sorrell asked.

'Old Cliff? Yeah, he said hi. I used to always flirt with him for fun because he's gay,' she smiled.

'Did he know about room 1410?' Sorrell continued.

'Yeah. All the porters did. That's how we got our business. A guest asks a porter for a girl and then they speak to Coops. We'd always use 1410. Everything was cash, even for the champagne or whatever, so nothing shows up on their bill. Saves them getting grief from their wives or their expenses department,' Lindy explained.

'The porters take a kick-back?' Haye wanted to know.

'Yeah. It's like commission. I don't know how much, though. Coops handles all the money,' she replied, as if renting her body was like renting a car.

'That why you do a bit of moonlighting?' Haye continued. 'No cuts. No commission.'

Lindy's head and tone dropped. 'I guess. There's nothing wrong with liking money. I am going to get a proper job one day. Coops will go mad when he finds out. Please don't tell him you busted me. Please,' she pleaded as the tears tumbled yet again.

'I won't,' Haye promised, 'but we need anything else you can think of. Can you remember the guy's height? Build? Anything at all?'

'Maybe 5'10". He could have been taller. Or shorter. I just don't know. But I couldn't see his face at all. It was in shadow. He was still wearing his hat.'

'What did he sound like?' Sorrell asked.

'Weird,' she said thoughtfully.

'Weird how?'

'It was just strange, you know. Like nothing I'd heard before. South African, maybe? He just had a weird, fucked up accent.'

'Thanks, Lindy. You've been most helpful. Lieutenant Haye here will drive you home if you wish,' Sorrell offered.

'No, thanks,' Lindy said, 'I'll get a cab. But please don't tell Coops. I'm begging you,' she pleaded once more before leaving, the sound of her stilettos echoing long after she was gone.

'She wasn't helpful at all, cap'n. We've got fuck all,' Haye moaned.

'Maybe you're right. Or maybe you're not,' Sorrell said cryptically as he headed back to his office.

59

#Prohibition

April sat in the Peccadillo Café, eating her breakfast and reading the *Daily Chronicle*. It didn't take her long before she was in a rage – the source of her anger was a news report that her beloved menthol cigarettes were to be banned by the government.

'This is prohibition, that's what it is,' she spewed as she read on, incredulously shouting out remarks from time to time.

'Every year 700,000 people in Europe die from smoking-related diseases? So what? Every year thousands are killed on the roads. What are we going do, ban cars too? Oh, listen to this part,' April said to no one in particular, '"Menthol cigarettes have been targeted because studies show they appeal to younger smokers." Younger smokers? What about bloody ancient smokers like myself?'

She continued to mutter under her breath for the next few minutes, while taking huge chunks out of her bacon roll. All the regulars and staff were used to April's ramblings by now and didn't give her a second glance. The waitress, Martel, approached April's table with the bill and smiled. 'I'd hate to see what you'd be like if they banned fry-ups.' April looked genuinely aghast, before replying, 'I think you'd find me floating face down in the Clyde.'

Her phone rang. It was Connor. 'Oh it's yourself,' April said. 'I'm just chatting to Martel right now. What's the weather like? What time is it right now? Have you had a bagel and pepperami yet?'

'So many questions before I've even opened my mouth. But what the hell. Say hello to Martel for me. The weather is dry and sunny but with a cold front moving in from the west. The time, sponsored by Accurist, is 5.30am. It's a bagel and *pastrami*, not pepperami. And no I haven't had one yet, basically because the time difference screws up my body clock and my appetite.'

'Well, you should eat something. Force yourself or you'll run out of steam.'

'Yes, Mum. What news from the front?'

'Well, Big Fergie has been all over the shop. He's getting suggestions left, right and centre from the back bench. How did we end up with all these managers?'

'I don't know, but we're certainly not any better off for it. The problem with so many voices is they all want their say. They feel they must justify their existence. Instead of staying silent, or just saying the story is fine the way it is.'

'Exactly,' April said, stuffing more food into her mouth.

'I've told you before it's the height of bad manners to eat while talking on the phone,' Connor complained.

'I know, I know, but I'm starving.'

Strangely, the sounds of April trying to speak and eat at the same time made Connor slightly homesick. 'I miss the Peccadillo.'

'Well, find yourself a diner and get something to eat. You'll feel a lot better for it.'

'Yeah, yeah, whatever.'

'Whatever, yourself. You'll thank me for it. There's no problem that can't be solved with food.'

'Except morbid obesity,' Connor replied before hanging up on a throaty cackle from the other side of the Atlantic. April had her flaws but at least she always laughed at Connor's jokes.

60

#Alibis

'The arrests are piling up, cap'n. All have alibis that check out, though.'

'All of them?' Sorrell asked Haye dubiously.

'Yup, eyewitness alibis backed up by electronic alibis – state police were able to double check their cell phone locations.'

'So where does that leave us so far?' Sorrell asked his deputy.

Haye tapped away at his computer, before giving his boss the stats. 'Okay, there were 104,233 threats made upon Horrigan's life. Bizarrely, 3,095 of those were made AFTER he was murdered. We have also ignored the 34,560 that were made from outside of America, for obvious reasons. So that leaves us with a total of 66,578. Incredibly, almost 60,000 have already responded to our tweet, giving us their real names and addresses. They've also been asked to give their whereabouts on the night Horrigan was murdered. They'll be interviewed and checked out over time, but they're not the priority,' Haye said.

'Correct. If they've responded so quickly, they are not our targets. And the other six and a half thousand?'

'There have been arrests made in almost every state, cap'n. From a finance director who got his kicks trolling celebs, to high school drop-outs waging war from their bedrooms. The beauty is, local press have been all over the stories, which has prompted others on the list to hand themselves in. The number is going down and down, cap'n. We're getting there.'

'Good work, Haye. Send that info to me on an email. I'll forward it to the colonel. He surely loves all this Internet stuff.'

Haye was chuffed to bits. Sorrell rarely handed out compliments, which was the way Haye liked it. It meant when he got one it was fully merited.

'Once you've done that,' Sorrell added, 'we can get back to the real investigation.'

61

#QuestionTime

April was slumped in her favourite armchair, with a cold glass of G&T in one hand, and petting her cat Cheeka with the other. Like her owner, the moggy was getting on a bit. They shared other traits, too: their eyesight and hearing weren't the best; and, given the option, they'd both just eat and sleep the day away.

April felt every one of her fifty-seven years. Each night she arrived home from work feeling so exhausted she could go straight to bed. Instead, she would force herself to make something for dinner – although tonight she had eaten at Luigi's – then plonk herself in the armchair, where she would fall into a deep state of unconsciousness in a matter of seconds. All three of April's husbands had complained bitterly about her loud snoring, but Cheeka didn't seem to mind. The cat was now nineteen years old and had outlasted all of April's relationships.

This evening, after three hours' solid sleep, April had her second wind. She turned on the telly to find *Question Time* had just come on the BBC, hosted by David Dimbleby. 'Bloody hell, that bugger is older than me – yet he's still going strong,' she told the cat. Dimbleby was in fact a good nineteen years older than April.

She didn't care much for the current affairs and the smartass questions from the audience that were debated by a panel of guests. But she suddenly remembered how she used to watch Bryce Horrigan on the show. He had left the *Daily Chronicle* by then for London, but she had admired the way he oozed confidence and self-belief, and traded blows with government ministers and the token novelty member of the panel, which was usually a comedian like Alexei Sayle or Boris Johnson. It was amazing to think that Bryce was dead now after being such a high-flier.

April marvelled at the heartfelt passion from the younger members of the audience. She hadn't felt passionate about anything for years. She'd long ago decided getting worked up over things you can't change was a waste of energy. But she also recalled how it doesn't feel that way when you are eighteen and ready to take on the world.

Suddenly, April's brain clicked into action. She remembered a particularly tetchy exchange between Bryce and a young student activist on the show. It had been fiery and ill tempered, before Dimbleby had finally called a halt to it – not too quickly, mind you, as the old silver fox knew good TV when he saw it. Afterwards, there had been a story how the student had begun to harass Bryce, sending threatening emails then making late-night silent phone calls. He had been from Glasgow University and it had been Connor who had door-stepped him. The police had got involved after Connor's exclusive story and cautioned the student. After that, it'd all gone quiet.

April searched the chair for her reading glasses before finding them in their usual place, perched on top of her head. She put them on, then sent Connor a direct message, although she was still stuck in World War I mode, slowly tapping out her message like a telegram from the frontline. *What name student harass Bryce? Maybe killer?*

A few minutes later she received a reply: *Des Gilmour. Pompous rich boy masking as a socialist.* It was followed by Gilmour's last known address and one last tweet: *Clever girl. I forgot all about that little twat – now go get him.*

62

#LostInTranslation

Bryce Horrigan @BryceTripleB
Make sure you wear those knickers I bought you.
#Randyasfuck

Captain Sorrell was browsing through the tweets sent and received by the murdered television presenter.

'Haye, what the hell are "knickers"?' Sorrell asked, lamely attempting an English accent.

'Panties, cap'n,' Haye said, looking over his boss's shoulder. 'Bryce is suggesting to a follower she should wear the sexy panties he bought her.'

'Yeah, yeah, I didn't need the whole thing translated. I'm not a total dumb-ass,' Sorrell snapped.

'It seems to be his method,' Haye said. 'He flirts with them at first on his main Twitter timelines, then if he gets enough encouragement he moves to direct messaging them. We're still waiting for Twitter to give us access to his DMs.'

'How many women do you think he had on the go?' Sorrell asked.

'Twelve. But those are only the ones we know about from his public timeline. God knows what he had going on with his DMs.'

'Twelve Twitter lovers – the dirty dozen,' Sorrell said, chuckling at his own joke. 'We speak to them all?'

'Yeah, they all responded to our tweets, cap'n. All their whereabouts have been accounted for.'

'Then we really need those DMs. Any news on the warrant?' Sorrell asked.

'We're working it, cap'n.'

'And the warrant for his PC?'

'Still in the hands of the damn courts.'

'The story of my life,' Sorrell sighed.

63

#BossyBoots

Bryce Horrigan @BryceTripleB
This is a thriller – the cops can't catch my killer.
#KeystoneCops #CluelessCops

Yet another message was tweeted in the early hours from the murdered presenter's own account, appearing straight into the Twitter feeds of his ten-million-and-rising followers. It had prompted another panicky call from Colonel Cowan to Sorrell, before the captain had even stepped out of his morning shower. Sorrell listened to his boss's voicemail on loudspeaker as he got ready.

'Captain, it's Colonel Cowan here.' Whenever titles were used, Sorrell knew it was serious. 'There has been another tweet from Horrigan's account. I cannot believe that in America – the nation that gave the world Microsoft, Apple, Silicon Valley and Facebook – that we cannot, for the life of us, track one solitary hacker. The whole case hinges on this, yet our killer is tweeting and mocking us with impunity and we seem powerless, absolutely incapable, of doing a damn thing about it. I need – no – I *demand* answers.'

'And all this is before you've even got your shirt on, Bernard?' Sorrell's wife, Denise, frowned from the comfort of the marital bed. 'The sooner you retire the better.'

Sorrell appreciated his wife's concern. But he was not ready to jack it all in yet. Not while there was a killer to catch.

64

#TheList

'Eighty-four more arrests, cap'n. But get this: 1,477 more trolls have come forward, either by contacting local cops or by tweeting us back. We are now below the 5,000 mark – 4,939 to be precise – of those who remain unaccounted for,' Haye said with delight. 'The Twitterati have now got involved. They're bombarding the suspects that haven't responded to our tweets yet. They're on their case night and day.'

'Look at our notifications,' said Fidel, holding up his phone. 'They're totting up all the time. That's another 108 trolls responded in the last hour. It's working. Who says the net can't police itself?'

'Send me an email with the most up-to-date figures right away. I'll take them to the colonel,' Sorrell said, heading for his door.

Colonel Cowan normally looked like he had stepped out of a tailor shop's window. This morning he looked like he had been sleeping rough. Sorrell hadn't talked to the colonel since he had left his ranting voicemail on the captain's cell. It seemed Cowan had already forgotten his early morning outburst.

'Good news?' the colonel asked, barely looking up from the paperwork on his desk.

'I think so, sir. Out of the 100,000-plus Twitter threats, we have fewer than 5,000 unaccounted for.'

'What? Five thousand? Fuck me, that's enough to fill a sports arena.' Sorrell had never heard the colonel swear before. 'Have you cross-reffed them with the professor's profile? That should narrow them down.'

Sorrell truly hated the colonel's faith in the Professor Benedict Watson's spurious profiles.

'We're trying, sir, but we have to identify the trolls first. Police forces right across the states are picking them up daily. The more they arrest, the more press cover it, the more volunteers come forward – it's faster than waiting for a guy at his door, or arresting him at his work.'

'One of them is our killer, captain. We need to eliminate all but one from that list. Throw everything we've got at it.' The colonel returned to his paperwork, a none-too-subtle sign that their conversation was over.

Not for the first time, Sorrell would ignore his superior's order. He had other ideas and it didn't involve having all his available manpower sitting on Twitter all day.

65

#BalTaMoore

Tom O'Neill @DerryDude1887
Coffee time?

Connor was about to give April a quick call when he received a DM from Tom O'Neill asking if he fancied a coffee since they were both in town. Connor immediately replied how he'd rather it was a beer, but since they still had work to do they arranged to meet at a city centre Starbucks.

Tom was no longer the fresh-faced lad Connor remembered from their brief time working together in London. In the intervening decade he had aged badly. He looked old beyond his years, with a grey complexion to match his greying hair.

'Good to see you, Tom,' Connor said truthfully.

Tom gave him an equally warm welcome. 'Bloody hell, Elvis, I didn't think the next time we met would be in Baltimore,' Tom replied, with the word 'Baltimore' sounding more like 'Bal-ta-moore' in his thick Northern Irish accent, which had lost none of its strength over the years.

'Yeah, of all the places Bryce could have ended up dead.' Connor's remark rendered them both silent for a moment.

'I know. What a way to go. Someone certainly wanted him gone, that's for sure.'

'Do you know why he was here?'

'No, not yet. No one does. We've got the IT guys at the network going through all his old emails. But Bryce did most of his really private communications by DMs,' Tom said in hushed conspiratorial tones. 'Have you met the detective in charge yet? A real hard ass, but a little bit of a plod. Slow on the uptake, I reckon,' Tom added a little arrogantly – a trait that had probably rubbed off from his former boss.

Tom was right about Sorrell being a hard ass, but Connor would never have described the police captain as slow, even if he spoke in a lazy drawl. He decided to keep his own counsel about Sorrell.

'You okay if I do this up as a story? "TV bosses baffled by Bryce's trip to Baltimore", "Urgent email trawl", that kind of thing? It's not great, but it justifies me being here.' Connor was asking out of politeness as he would have written and filed his copy even without O'Neill's approval.

'Sure, just keep my name out of it for now though, will you?' Tom pleaded. 'I am technically still employed by ABT News and I can't be seen to be briefing the press.'

'No problem,' Connor said, meaning it this time. 'How long are you hanging around?'

'A few days, max. Probably until they release his body. Or what's left of it. Definitely won't be an open casket,' O'Neill said glumly. Again the mention of Bryce's death left them momentarily silent.

'Have they been able to track who posted the crime scene pictures yet?' Connor asked.

'Nope. They haven't even traced all the death threats, either,' O'Neill revealed, before leaning closer to speak quietly again. There was hardly any need as normal talking voices struggled to be heard above the din of coffee machines and constant chatter from customers. 'That's where they'll find the killer. You got to have seen the shit – literally – that used to get posted through the mail to the office. He had the fire-and-brimstone religious nuts on his case. But it was the pro-life lot who were making subtle enquiries about Bryce's whereabouts, where he lived, where he liked to eat and drink. They were the really scary ones. Put it this way, it spooked Bryce enough that he actually started changing his habits in the last month. He would take a different route home.

Never go to the same restaurant twice. And as you know, Bryce didn't spook easily.' Connor made a mental note to include that nugget of information in his copy, too.

'Any names I should check out?' Connor asked.

'Bloody hell, where do I begin? I'd say there were about half a dozen that we were keeping a close eye on.' O'Neill checked his iPhone, then jotted down some names on a piece of paper. The last on his list was @GeoffreySchroeder.

'That should keep you busy,' O'Neill beamed.

'Did you give these to Captain Sorrell?' Connor asked.

'Nah, we reporters have to keep some info to ourselves, don't we?'

Connor thought O'Neill's response was strange. Every reporter may be hungry for an exclusive, but most wouldn't withhold crucial information from a murder enquiry.

'Look, Elvis, I shouldn't be telling you this and you have to promise me you won't print this. Promise?'

'Promise,' Connor said reassuringly.

'Bryce's Twitter account was hacked a few weeks before his death. He only found out when one of his DMs had been read when he knew he definitely hadn't clicked on it.'

'Did he report it?' Connor asked.

'Only to me. He said somebody was spying on him, I told him to change his password. He was hopeless at Internet security. He'd always use the same password if he could get away with it. His office system made him change it every month and he'd write the new one down on a piece of paper in his top drawer, for Christ's sake. Figured it was safe because he was the only one with keys to his office, which was true. But Twitter and Facebook don't keep asking you to change passwords. So he never did until his account had been compromised.'

'Did you set up his new password?' Connor asked.

'No, he wasn't that stupid. He loved his Twitter account – he had a string of women on the go, sending him DMs all the time. He wouldn't trust anyone with that information. I reckon if someone wanted to find out where Bryce was going to be – in order to bump him off – all the clues would be in those DMs.' O'Neill leaned up straight again to finish the last sip of his skinny caffè mocha.

'Or in order to set him up? But that would have had to come from someone he knew.' Connor mulled it over, finishing his latte.

'His murderer is in those tweets, Elvis. Just ignore the obvious "I'm going to kill you" ones and concentrate on those who were looking for Bryce's whereabouts. That'll lead to your man,' O'Neill said before settling the bill with a smile. 'I'll pay while I still have an expense account.' They agreed they'd meet later on for a beer.

But before he went Connor suddenly had a thought. 'Is his body being repatriated to Scotland?' he asked, knowing a picture of the coffin leaving for home would make the front page.

O'Neill gave a wry smile. 'Yeah, it will be, eventually. I'll tip you off. For fuck's sake Elvis, you never switch off, do you?'

Connor smiled back. 'Bryce would have done the exact same thing.'

Now the talking was over, Connor had some serious Twitter trawling to do.

66

#IHateSatNavs

April hated with a passion the satellite navigation system her daughter Jayne had bought for her one Christmas. Despite being repeatedly shown how to operate it, every time she stared at its blank screen it perfectly mirrored her mind. Then she'd remember to press its one and only button to switch it on, before she was met with a series of icons that befuddled her all the more. When she finally found the 'Navigate to?' option, her stubby little fingers took an age to enter the postcode, as she would be pressing several letters at the same time.

But worse of all was the American accent that would 'order' her around. On more than one occasion she had remarked to Connor, 'And just how would an American know his way around Glasgow?' April had said it so often, Connor was no longer convinced she was joking.

Despite its US twang, the sat-nav did successfully direct April and her battered old purple Daewoo car to the address in Glasgow's Otago Street she was looking for.

She had called her newsdesk first thing asking if they wanted her to hit the doorstep of Bryce Horrigan's one-time student tormentor.

'Great idea,' her grateful news editor Big Fergie had practically shouted, as he was staring at a yet another nearly empty schedule. 'I should have thought of that. I'm surprised no one else has tracked him down already.'

'Connor said Gilmour wasn't on the voters' roll and he hasn't been on social media since the court ordered him off it,' April explained.

'Brilliant,' Big Fergie exclaimed, getting even more excited at the prospect of potential splash material. 'Although, how did Connor get his address?' he asked, suddenly getting suspicious. Ever since the Leveson Inquiry, newspapers now had to play everything by the book. There were to be no 'dark arts' in obtaining ex-directory phone numbers or blagging for information, such as when a reporter or associate called a number under false pretences.

'Bryce gave it to him. He got it from the Met, when the police interviewed him in London. Apparently, a helpful cop had left Gilmour's address clearly visible on his notepad. Bryce thought it would be too self-indulgent to send his own reporters to doorstep him. So he gave Connor a call instead.'

'Excellent,' the relieved news editor said, 'let's hit it.'

67

#AskONeill

Baby Angel @BabyAngel
I see you haven't arrested The Killer yet?

The captain sighed when he saw the direct message from Baby Angel. He now found their correspondence tedious.

Bernard Sorrell @BernardSorrell
Well done, you've read the news.

Baby Angel @BabyAngel
I don't need to read the news to know what's going on, captain. You of all people should know that.

Bernard Sorrell @BernardSorrell
Do you have some information or are you shooting the breeze? Cos I'm kinda busy, what with this homicide investigation.

Baby Angel @BabyAngel
You've met Bryce's deputy, Tom O'Neill. What did you make of him?

The captain was taken aback again. He hated anyone, including Colonel Cowan, knowing his business. He imparted case information begrudgingly even to members of his own team.

Bernard Sorrell @BernardSorrell
He was all right.

Baby Angel @BabyAngel
Feel he was telling you the truth?

Bernard Sorrell @BernardSorrell
Not the whole truth, but the version his bosses wanted to share.

Baby Angel @BabyAngel
Gave you a list of names, no doubt?

Bernard Sorrell @BernardSorrell
Yes.

Baby Angel @BabyAngel
Ask him about other list of names. The one with Geoffrey Schroeder on it that he gave to that reporter, Presley. See what he says.

Sorrell truly hated being played in this way. But for now he had little choice but to take part in a game where all the rules were being set by the mysterious Baby Angel.

68

#Everest

There was an intercom entry system to the crumbling old yellow sandstone building, but no need to use it, as the main door was permanently unlocked. April arduously climbed the three flights of steps to the top flat. She wondered if Edmund Hillary also broke out in a succession of hot hormonal flushes trying to make it to the summit. On each landing of the dingy stairwell, she was greeted by a different variety of odours that attested to the cosmopolitan tastes of the occupants, from the curry spices of India or Pakistan to Chinese culinary treats. It made April hungry.

She loved the way she had seen so many different nationalities settle in Glasgow over the generations. Unlike some of England's cities, by and large Glasgow had never been blighted by racial tensions. It was something that made her immensely proud of her little country, that it had such a big outlook on the world.

As she plodded her way up the final flight of steps with her thick thighs and lungs on fire, she was suddenly glad she had never lived in student digs. April had always been house-proud – from her days when she was a young mum living in a cramped council flat, to now, when three divorces had left her with a considerable property portfolio. Along with the lovingly restored old Victorian house on Glasgow's Southside, she had half a dozen flats dotted around the city, which she rented out to students and young families. She had bought them cheaply and in areas normally untouched by developers, and struck it lucky when the districts were targeted by city rejuvenation schemes, or in one case, the creation of a so-called media village, when the BBC and rival STV television stations moved in next door to each other.

But April wouldn't have bought this flat. She hated old tenement buildings as they were too reminiscent of her childhood.

She knocked on the door, which she guessed had been painted white at some point, but had turned almost yellow with the passage of time. The frame had been bust and repaired several times by the looks of things, from either break-ins or flatmates who had lost their keys and used the age-old master key of a boot to the door. She pressed the doorbell and wondered why she had bothered, as it emitted no sound. April decided to give another sturdy knock instead. Music could be heard from deep within the recesses of the apartment so she knew someone was home.

Moments later the door was opened by a girl in a short skimpy dress, which showed off her array of body tattoos. April's eyes couldn't help dropping to those on the girl's thighs. In the dim light of the landing, the body art looked like varicose veins.

'Hi,' April said as cheerily as she could muster, 'is Des around, love?'

April could not get her head around the modern phenomenon of tattoos. Her least favourite were the multi-coloured 'sleeves', with the 'ink art' covering the length and breadth of people's arms. In her day, tattoos were exclusively for sailors and convicts. And it baffled her why everyone wanted to look the same.

It was the turn of the girl to look April up and down, before she shouted over her shoulder, 'Dessy – someone to see you.'

'What?' came the distant reply.

'At the door. Someone wants to see you.' The girl gave a half smile as she told April, 'He's just coming. We're not normally up this early.'

The statement caused April to glance involuntarily at her watch. It had just gone 10.30am. Tattoo girl made way for Des Gilmour, who had a fine mop of unruly bed hair, and was wearing black skinny jeans and a student standard-issue faded T-shirt, with the name of some band April had never heard of, or wanted to.

'Can I help you?' he said in a passive-aggressive way, his chin jutted forward and his hands on his narrow hips.

'I'm April Lavender from the *Daily Chronicle*,' she replied, her hand outstretched. 'I wanted to talk…'

Des Gilmour cut her off. 'About that cunt Bryce Horrigan? What do you want to know? Did I celebrate his death? Damn right. I'm still hung over. Or do you just want to stitch me up again like that other reporter? "Oh, look at the weirdo student, who's calling the great, mighty Bryce Horrigan nasty names,"' Gilmour said mockingly. 'You wouldn't believe the shit that story caused me. My folks didn't talk to me for months. Said I'd embarrassed them.'

Cut off your allowance, more like, April thought to herself.

'So I certainly don't plan to go through all that again,' he added emphatically.

'I completely understand,' April said truthfully, 'but now Bryce is dead, maybe it would be good to give your side of the story? How it has affected you. Why you did it in the first place,' April said hopefully, desperately trying to convince the scruffy young man with a serious attitude problem to talk to her.

Des went to respond then thought better of it. Eventually he said, 'Okay, I'll tell you the truth on the absolute cast-iron assurance you won't print it.'

April maintained her smiley face but inside she was crestfallen. Post-Leveson, people who are interviewed can withdraw their consent at any time before it's published. So if you had someone confessing all to an affair with a public figure, they could pull their story at the eleventh hour, even though it was all recorded. In the old days, when journalists played hard and fast with the rules, if it was on tape then it was going in the paper. Consent or no consent.

April replied, 'Sure, I won't print a word. Legally, I can't now.' Deep inside she wanted to cut the meeting short. For what was the point in someone speaking if you can't use it? She also dreaded calling her news editor to tell him his much-hoped-for splash was now more of a plop.

It was Gilmour's turn to smile. 'Okay, come in – I'm about to blow your mind.'

69

#HelpingWithEnquiries

Tom O'Neill had been having an early morning coffee in the Starbucks across from the Baltimore City Hotel when he took the abrupt call from Lieutenant Haye.

'Cap'n wants to see you. Be here in half an hour.' The lieutenant hung up before Tom had a chance to ask any questions.

He knew from the tone and urgency it must be serious. But what could it be? Tom suspected Bryce's vastly abbreviated personnel file was probably the source of the captain's ire.

'So that list you gave us…'

'The personnel file,' O'Neill said, interrupting Sorrell, earning himself a deadly stare.

'No, the other list, with disgruntled employees, interns, etc etc.'

'Yes, I gave you that one,' O'Neill protested.

'What about the one with Geoffrey Schroeder's name on it?' Sorrell asked, staring unblinkingly at O'Neill, whose eyes darted from the captain to Haye, once again leaning against the wall behind his boss.

'Didn't I give you his name? It must have been an oversight,' O'Neill said, knowing how false and pathetic he sounded.

Sorrell stared at him for what seemed an age, before he finally replied, 'But it wasn't an oversight when you handed Schroeder's name to that reporter, Presley?'

'I must've got that information later,' O'Neill stuttered just as unconvincingly.

'I see. So you gave a list of potential people of interest to a journalist rather than the officers running the investigation?'

'It was just a list of nutters. Elvis… I mean, Connor had asked for some leads. I was only helping him out. Giving him some steers.'

'Let me give you a steer for nothing,' Sorrell said, pointing his finger at O'Neill's face. 'You get any more information then you come to me first. Get it? Now get out.'

O'Neill nodded his head in compliance.

'I don't like him much, cap'n.'

'There's not a lot to like, Haye.'

'Oh, and cap'n, I tracked down that bachelorette party. You know the one that got in the hotel elevator with 'hat man'? They were so wasted they couldn't even remember being in the hotel elevator, never mind some guy wearing a hat.'

'Sounds like some party. It was worth a try,' Sorrell said, his mind already elsewhere.

70

#LoveRival

Chrissie Hardie @HardieGirl89
Where shall I lunch today – any suggestions?

Patricia Tolan could recall the times she used to fly to America with Bryce, who boasted how he never turned right stepping aboard an aircraft. He always took left towards business or first class. But she'd had to get used to sitting in economy once his generous monthly allowance to her had gone.

She could remember the day it happened. Patricia had taken a call from her bank saying she had exceeded her overdraft limit. She always lived deep into her overdraft and needed Bryce's $4,000 a month to get her back in the black. On the very same morning she took the call from the bank, Patricia had lost the one and only major client for her PR business. It could have been paranoia, but she was convinced she had been dropped because she was no longer the girlfriend of America's fastest rising talk show host.

After being dumped by Bryce, it was proof of the old adage that bad things come in threes. Patricia had wandered from her soon to be ex-apartment in a daze. She was unsure where she had walked to or for how long, when she suddenly found herself standing outside her love rival's towering office block, not quite sure what she was going to do.

Chrissie Hardie was tall, blonde, excruciatingly pretty. Patricia had only discovered the name of Bryce's new flame the week before. That'd been when he had decided she should move out of their Manhattan penthouse. Patricia had exploded in a fit of rage, calling Bryce every name she could think of and some she made up on the spur of the moment. He had stood there like a typical man, just wanting the scene to be over and done with. She could see fron his demeanour that he had already moved on in his head, eventually saying, 'Come on, Pasty, we've had a good run. And it's not as if we still won't be friends.'

And that was it. The relationship, which began when they were eighteen at university, had ended twenty-seven years later with a casual shrug of his shoulders and the use of her nickname, which she despised. Suddenly, for the first time, she'd been able to see the loathsome creature standing before her. The man who she had defended at all costs. The man to whom she had been loyal, turning a blind eye to all his previous indiscretions. The man who had had his own way for too long and could move on from over a quarter of a century together as if switching to the next item on his chat show with a shuffle of his papers. Inside, she was experiencing every emotion, from pain, through devastation to anger, while Bryce glanced at his watch, eager to get off to the studio or perhaps to meet his new lover. God, how she hated him.

'Right, pull yourself together and take your time. There's no need to rush away. Just DM me when you've cleared out your stuff,' Bryce had said, as if concluding a car deal. 'Oh, and Pasty, don't even think of cutting up my suits – I've had them moved to a safe place.'

The door had closed behind Bryce. Patricia checked the huge walk-in wardrobes. He hadn't been kidding. All his precious designer suits, custom-made to try to cover his ever-expanding gut, had been removed. Which made matters so much worse as it meant it was all premeditated. 'Poor old Pasty was going to slice up my suits once I'd dumped her,' she said to herself, trying to mock Bryce's voice, 'so I had them locked away from the mad bitch.'

Patricia Tolan crumpled to the bedroom floor, where she sobbed uncontrollably for hours. Days later, she had found a far smaller apartment to move into across town. She'd only signed a three-month lease as she wasn't quite sure what to do next with her life.

Then she'd discovered the name of Bryce's new lover. Patricia had been standing outside ABT News, where her love rival worked as one of Bryce's PRs, when she saw Chrissie Hardie's post asking her followers where she should lunch. Patricia impulsively glanced across 42nd street to see a diner called Murphy's Bagels. She opportunistically tweeted back:

Patricia Tolan @PastyGirl70
@HardieGirl89 You can't go wrong with Murphy's down your neck of the woods.

Seconds later her post had been retweeted by Chrissie, with the added comment: *Murphy's it is.*

Patricia Tolan was just one of over 7,000 of Chrissie Hardie's followers. Which is one of the inherent dangers of social media – you can never be sure of who you are talking to.

71

#Clinique

April Lavender @AprilReporter1955
@ElvisTheWriter I need to talk to you.

'Hello, my perpetually hungry little friend. Tucking into your usual low-carb, high-fibre diet I trust?'

It was 4.30 in the morning Eastern Standard Time when Connor responded to the tweet from April to call her. By the background noise of chatter and clinking crockery, he had judged correctly that she would be eating the Peccadillo's full fried breakfast before starting work.

'Oh, it's yourself,' April said through a mouthful of food. 'What time is it there?'

'Half-four in the morning,' Connor replied.

'What are you doing up at that time?' April asked in her usual role of concerned mother.

'Still jet-lagged. Can't sleep. I'm knackered,' he said gloomily.

April gulped down a mouthful of milky, sugary tea, then spoke in hushed tones. 'I interviewed Des Gilmour, like you said. He told me some very interesting things about Bryce. Real eye-opener stuff.'

'Go on,' Connor urged, his curiosity suddenly perking him up.

'Did you know that after *Question Time*, Bryce met up with Des and his then-girlfriend outside the venue? He talked about perhaps hiring him as a columnist, dressed it up as Des becoming the newspaper's voice of the UK's students. Anyway, they met a few times socially after that. Apparently Bryce always made a point of saying to Des, "And feel free to bring your girl-friend along – I'll pay."'

Connor sat on his phone 3,000 miles away wondering where April was going with this.

'Anyway, it turned out that Bryce had no intention of hiring Des as a columnist, but had designs on his girlfriend, who had sat beside Des on *Question Time*. She was a goth, but beneath all that ridiculous black lipstick was one very attractive girl. She was also a very unfaithful girl. Bryce must have slipped her his phone number in the pub when Des was at the loo. All he knows is that at some point his girlfriend and Bryce began an affair. He kept flying her from Glasgow to London, putting her up in nice hotels and all the rest. Wait to you hear this bit though: Des only became suspicious when she began wearing "normal clothes and make-up".'

Connor laughed from the other side of the Atlantic. 'So her flimsy excuses to cover her weekends away didn't arouse his suspicions, but her new penchant for Clinique and Laura Ashley did? Brilliant.'

'I know,' April said excitedly, hurriedly gulping down another mouthful of sugary tea. 'That's when Des started his harassment campaign. He was desperate to spread the word that our Bryce was a bad bastard.'

The penny dropped with Connor: 'Bryce never got Des's address from the cops. He got it from Des's girlfriend. And the reason he got me on the case is that it was too close to home for him to be sending his own attack dogs. He played me like a Stradivarius.'

'You wouldn't be the first. I'm starting to think that Bryce Horrigan's whole reason for being was sex. That's what his mum said, too,' April said.

'Thank God you ditched lust for gluttony, huh?' Connor replied.

'Yeah, most people eventually get bored with sex but I never tire of eating. Anyway, better go. I don't want my fried eggs getting cold.'

Connor smiled again. April and her appalling eating habits always cheered him up. 'Can you try to track down Des's reformed goth?'

'Already have,' April replied, her mouth now half full of drippy egg yolk. 'Des helped me out. Get this: she moved to New York about the same time poor old Pasty was being shown the door. '

'He should have had revolving doors fitted to his apartment,' Connor quipped. 'What's her name?'

'Chrissie Hardie. She's in PR,' April said almost incomprehensibly, as she gave a square sausage a square go.

'Public Relations. The one-size-fits-all job description. Be great to speak to her,' Connor said.

'You betcha,' Connor heard April mumble as her desire to eat outweighed her need to communicate.

It was becoming clear to them both that Bryce had liked the thrill of the chase: there were plenty of willing partners to choose from, yet he targeted the goth girlfriend of a student who had berated him on *Question Time*. Bryce would have enjoyed his revenge, for he took any public humiliation as a personal slight. Connor now had some concrete leads to trade with Captain Sorrell.

72

#Tetchy

Baby Angel @BabyAngel
So what did O'Neill have to say about the other list?

Sorrell was beginning to loathe how Baby Angel knew his every move. Haye had suggested that perhaps the captain's emails were being hacked, but Sorrell always preferred a simpler, more logical explanation.

Bernard Sorrell @BernardSorrell
No more games. Reveal yourself.

Baby Angel @BabyAngel
Oooh, we are in a tetchy mood. Get outta bed the wrong side this morning?

Bernard Sorrell @BernardSorrell
I'm getting bored with this.

Baby Angel @BabyAngel
I'm not. Now tell me what O'Neill said or you'll get no more guidance from your guardian.

Bernard Sorrell @BernardSorrell
He said he was just throwing Presley a bone as Schroeder was one of the many on a watchlist.

Baby Angel @BabyAngel
But something doesn't add up, right?

Bernard Sorrell @BernardSorrell
You could say that.

Baby Angel @BabyAngel
I do say that. What didn't add up, captain?

Bernard Sorrell @BernardSorrell
Schroeder.

Baby Angel @BabyAngel
Why doesn't that add up?

Bernard Sorrell @BernardSorrell
Because I don't believe he killed Horrigan.

Baby Angel @BabyAngel
So what was Schroeder doing in Baltimore? Hmmm?

Bernard Sorrell @BernardSorrell
I think you're playing me for a fool. You're wasting my time.

Baby Angel @BabyAngel
You stupid black bastard. The truth is staring you in the face.

Bernard Sorrell @BernardSorrell
What's my color got to do with it?

Baby Angel @BabyAngel
Nothing. Sorry. The only colour that matters is your grey matter. Use your brain.

Sorrell stared at the screen with a quizzical expression. And it wasn't the insult that was puzzling him.

73

#OddManOut

Connor was doing some Internet research, sitting in his hotel room systematically working his way through the Twitter feeds from the six names passed to him by Tom O'Neill. The first five fell into the Bible-bashers category. They were all a bit too obvious: either damning Bryce Horrigan to eternal hell and warning he'd pay for his sins, or starting in a biblical vein before moving on to torrents of abuse and threats.

But Connor thought the sixth must have been some sort of mistake – compared to the others, it was relatively tame. Although Geoffrey Schroeder was one of Bryce Horrigan's ten million followers, his timeline revealed he had had just one major online spat with the TV presenter, which had ended with a very abusive slanging match over Bryce's pro-abortion stance. It was just heat-of-the-moment stuff, nothing particularly startling compared to the chilling nature of the others on the list. Connor could even track the moment Schroeder calmed down, explaining why he had flown off the handle at Bryce because he lost his wife and unborn to an abortionist. Although his tweets were dripping with emotion, you could tell he was being genuine in his sorrow and beliefs. Schroeder had recently retweeted the pictures of Bryce's death scene, but that was about it.

Connor checked who followed Geoffrey Schroeder. It was a quick search as he only had a dozen followers. But the last one – Baby Angel – caught his attention. He clicked on the profile, which read, *God's assassin. My mission is to destroy all baby killers.* The Twitter profile certainly had a fire-and-brimstone feel to it, but it was the timeline that intrigued the reporter: Baby Angel had first made contact with Schroeder three weeks before Bryce's death.

Connor thought long and hard before deciding he had no other option but to take a chance. He wrote:

Connor Presley @ElvisTheWriter
@GeoffreySchroeder we may be able to help each other?

Connor posted the innocuous tweet not really knowing what to expect. A minute later, he was notified he had a new follower. Geoffrey Schroeder was online.

74

#CallMe

'April, it's Lacey Lanning. I need to speak to you. It's important. It's about Bryce. Something I never told you. I'm in trouble. I have no one else to turn to. Hope you get this message.'

April had missed Lacey Lanning's call as her phone had been at the bottom of her bag, as usual. It wouldn't be the first, or last, important call April would miss. It always amazed the journalist when she went to check her mobile, after a few hours of forgetting about it, to find reams of texts and voicemails of increasing urgency.

April called Lacey back, but this time it was the turn of the DJ's mobile to go to voicemail. A minute later, April received a text from Lacey: *Thanks for calling back. I'm on air until midnight so can speak to you after then. xx*

April knew there had been more to the story. Now she couldn't wait to hear Lacey's unedited version of events.

But someone else was also keen to hear what Lacey had to say for herself, when they accessed April's voicemail. Even after the 'hacking scandal' that forced the closure of the red-top tabloid *News Of The World*, listening into someone's voicemails was still surprisingly easy as long as you had their mobile phone number and four-digit PIN code. Despite several warnings from Connor to change her voicemail PIN code, April had never got round of it, meaning it was still set to the factory default of '0000'.

Not knowing whether April had listened to Lacey's message, the hacker deleted it and hung up. They needed an urgent plan of action before the DJ said too much.

75

#TheWholeTooth

Baby Angel @BabyAngel
Ask Tom O'Neill about Operation Molar.

Captain Sorrell stared at the DM from Baby Angel, but didn't quite know what he was looking at. He DM'd back, *Molar?* and waited for a reply. None was forthcoming. As usual Sorrell hollered Haye into his office.

'You know, there is a perfectly good intercom system, cap'n?' Haye pointed out.

'And why do I need an intercom when I can use my voice?' Sorrell said by way of a rebuke, before adding, 'Look at this.' Sorrell swung his PC screen so Haye could see it.

'Molar?' Haye said thoughtfully. 'I guess it must be a code for something.'

'Well, I figured that out,' Sorrell said impatiently.

'I'll call Tom O'Neill again and tell him to come in right away, cap'n.'

'Yeah, but don't say what it's about. I want to see his reaction when I mention it. And this time he better not hold out on me.'

Lieutenant Haye showed Bryce's deputy into Captain Sorrell's office in silence, before the loyal detective took up his usual spot leaning on the wall by his master's desk. Sorrell ignored his visitor as he continued to type at his PC, before hitting 'Send', leaning back in his chair and placing his reading glasses on top of his head. He studied Tom O'Neill down the end of his nose for what seemed an age, before saying the words, 'Operation Molar.'

The colour drained from O'Neill's face.

He had been sure he had thrown the captain enough dirt to keep them satisfied. But he'd been wrong. There were very few people who knew about the incident referred to as Operation Molar – a comical-sounding title that did nothing to reflect its serious nature. O'Neill tried to weigh up how much he could reveal without implicating himself. The captain seemed to see right through him.

'This is the third time I've had to interview you, so before you think about spinning me some bullshit again, just think what a charge of withholding information from a homicide investigation will do for your chances of a green card.'

Tom O'Neill's shoulders visibly sagged. He knew the game was up. He would still try to paint himself in the best possible light – after all, the only person who could dispute his version of events was dead. 'There had been complaints about Bryce's behaviour. Lots of complaints. One PR girl in particular alleged Bryce had bitten her. Fuck it, there was no "alleged" about it, he had bitten her bad. She looked like she'd been attacked by one of those devil dogs. Her ears, neck, breasts. Hell, he left one of her nipples practically hanging off.' Tom shuddered at the thought.

'Sick fuck,' Haye said, speaking for the entire room.

'The HR department had had to deal with many issues over the years at ABT News, but it's fair to say this was the first time they'd handled a staff biting issue. Bryce's defence was he had simply got carried away during sex. But her photographic evidence said otherwise. He had attacked her, plain and simple. He confided in me later he'd been off his head on crystal meth. He claimed he couldn't remember a thing.'

'Ain't that always the case,' Haye snorted in disbelief.

'The girl threatened to go public unless Bryce was reprimanded, and he was… of sorts,' Tom said, hoping his explanation would draw a line under the matter. He was wrong.

'Of sorts?' Sorrell asked.

'Well, he was told in no uncertain terms that it must never happen again... but that was it, really. Business as usual. They got rid of the PR instead. Made her sign some waiver. Gave her some money, I don't know. But she understandably felt short-changed. She was more than just another lover, she was living with him. When she was in hospital being stitched back together, Bryce had her things moved out of his flat. After that, she wanted revenge. Big time. She threatened to leak her photos online.'

'So Bryce Horrigan made plans, didn't he, O'Neill? What did he do?' Sorrell demanded.

This was the area of the story O'Neill hadn't planned to visit. But he was left with little choice.

'He wanted her photographic evidence destroyed,' Tom replied quietly.

'Which you did for him?' Sorrell asked, already knowing the answer.

O'Neill felt like the captain had slit his body down the middle and read his soul.

'Yes,' he replied shame-faced. 'She had taken them on her iPhone. She showed them to me. I then deleted them when the opportunity arose. Without the photographs she still had her scarring, but much more difficult to prove was *when* they happened. But the iPhone pictures were stamped with time and place, showing she had taken them in Bryce's apartment. In his bathroom, as it happens, when she cleaned herself up while Bryce slept off his meth high. No photos, no case,' Tom concluded.

'But that meant you needed to betray her trust?' Sorrell said, hitting the mark yet again.

'Yes,' O'Neill replied softly, now staring at the floor. 'And I've regretted it every day since. I was scared. Scared if this got out, Bryce would be sacked and I'd be out of a job.'

'So you destroyed evidence of assault and battery, to cover your own ass?' Sorrell said with disgust written all over his face.

'I didn't say I was proud of myself. But I was desperate,' O'Neill protested.

'And how did you manage to do it? How'd you get that close?' Sorrell enquired.

'It was sort of a date,' O'Neill replied, again unable to make eye contact with the captain.

'A date? Or "sort of" a date?' Sorrell asked, his eyebrows arched in anticipation.

'Bryce sent me to console her. He said it would be the perfect opportunity to destroy the photos. He even made me buy a new iPhone, to switch with hers. Just to make sure. She had this glittery phone case. So all I needed to do was put it on the new phone and take her old one. It was easy enough, as she kept crying all the time. She was a wreck, and no wonder after what he did to her. She even showed me the nipple that had been stitched back on. She said it made her look like the Bride of Frankenstein. That's when she broke down again and went off to the bathroom to compose herself. I then switched phones and told her I had to leave on urgent business. You probably think I'm a total shit, don't you?'

Both Captain Sorrell and lieutenant Haye stared at Tom O'Neill with empty expressions.

'What's her name?' Sorrell asked.

'Who?' O'Neill said absent-mindedly.

'The complainant. What's her name?'

'Hardie,' O'Neill replied, 'Chrissie Hardie.'

Captain Sorrell continued to stare in total silence. Eventually he lifted his pen and told O'Neill to spell her name, which he did.

'Chrissie H-a-r-d-i-e,' Sorrell repeated back before looking at the name he'd written in his notepad. 'You sure?' the captain asked, staring intently at O'Neill again.

'Of course. I'm unlikely to ever forget her, am I?' O'Neill snorted.

Lieutenant Haye showed O'Neill the door, slamming it behind

the Northern Irishman. He then turned to face his captain. 'How come every time we speak to that lying fuck we get a different story? First he withholds the name of Geoffrey Schroeder, now this,' Haye snarled.

'That usually means we're getting closer to the truth,' the captain said, placing his reading glasses back on his nose. 'And I like the truth, Haye.'

76

#Contact

Connor wasted no time following Schroeder, then sending him a direct message:

Connor Presley @ElvisTheWriter
I'm a reporter from Scotland in Baltimore. I'm told you may be able to help me with info on Bryce Horrigan murder?

Geoffrey Schroeder @GeoffreySchroeder
Who said I could help? The police?

Connor knew Schroeder would be twitchy as hell. He tried to reassure him as best he could.

Connor Presley @ElvisTheWriter
Not police. A friend. I haven't spoken to police – or anyone – about you.

Geoffrey Schroeder @GeoffreySchroeder
You tell me who your friend is and we'll talk. I'll give you a story. Might not be what you want to hear though.

Connor Presley @ElvisTheWriter
You know a reporter NEVER reveals their sources.

Geoffrey Schroeder @GeoffreySchroeder
No name. No deal. No more contact until I know who
your friend is. Don't make it up, I'll know.

Connor was perplexed. He hadn't expected a response at
all, never mind this one. Schroeder was behaving like a hunted
animal, which he no doubt was. He even read Connor's thoughts
about making up the name of an imaginary friend.

'You're up to your tits in this,' Connor thought out loud. But
what difference would it make even if he did give him the name
Tom O'Neill? They were from different worlds.

Connor was in a dilemma. He wanted to interview Schroeder
so badly. He just knew he held the key to everything. Besides,
until now, he had got next-to-nothing on this trip. But he couldn't
hand the name of a fellow journalist over to a suspected killer just
for a story, could he?

Connor typed out another DM before looking at the screen for
several minutes.

'Fuck it,' he said, and pressed 'Send'.

Moments later he got the response:

Geoffrey Schroeder @GeoffreySchroeder
Okay. Let's talk.

Schroeder's next tweet was a set of directions:

Geoffrey Schroeder @GeoffreySchroeder
Head up state. I-83 to Maryland border. Turn off on Old
York Road. 2nd left into industrial park. Alone.

He finished by sending an ominous warning:

Geoffrey Schroeder @GeoffreySchroeder
I'll be watching.

Geoffrey Schroeder searched for Tom O'Neill's name on Twitter. It didn't take him long to find the one he was looking for, with a profile that read, *Derry dude, living in New York. Journalist, lover, not a fighter, and deputy to @BryceTripleB – my views are definitely not HIS.*

Geoffrey scrolled through O'Neill's timeline. He wasn't as prolific at tweeting as Horrigan had been, but he was still a heavy user. Schroeder decided to abandon any plans to cross the Canadian border once and for all. There was a good chance he would never make it anyway.

Instead, he stared at O'Neill's avatar picture and decided he needed to make his last stand in Maryland. And he would start with Connor Presley.

77

#TheDMs

Lieutenant Haye burst into Captain Sorrell's office without knocking, which always meant he had urgent news.

'Twitter just got back to me and it's hot stuff. I mean really hot stuff – we've got all his direct messages AND the ones he deleted.'

Like many detectives, Haye wanted to boast about how clever he had been first, before getting to the point. 'I remembered how this real slimeball football player was sending DMs to a girl I was dating. He'd met her at some function and looked her up afterwards on Twitter then began messaging her, asking for her cell number and a date,' Haye explained.

'I hope there's a point to this story about your social life, Haye?' Sorrell sighed.

'Yeah, cap'n. Basically, every time he sent her a DM he would delete it in case his wife found out. Apparently, she was the suspicious kind.'

'With good cause,' Sorrell replied.

'Anyway, I suspected Bryce Horrigan would have done the same with his more salacious DMs. And he did.'

'Or his hacker did,' Sorrell reminded Haye.

'Correct. Some were deleted from his account after his death, but we've got them all back. Every single DM and it's dirty stuff.' Haye smiled – a little too admiringly for the captain's liking. 'Turns out he was a scratcher and biter.'

'What?' Sorrell said as if he was hearing things.

'He liked to bite and scratch women during sex, just like Tom O'Neill said. Horrigan sent loads of apologies explaining he just got carried away and hoped their "markings" weren't "too painful", Haye said, before quickly tapping at his iPhone. 'Get this, according to the *Kama Sutra*, there are eight different levels of biting. They range from "the hidden bite" to "the biting of the boar". I'm guessing Horrigan was more the boar type.'

The captain shook his head in disbelief.

'It gets better, cap'n, a lot better,' Haye said with excitement rising in his voice. 'Apparently, Horrigan came to Baltimore on a promise,' the lieutenant said, now smirking like a school kid.

'A promise of what?' Sorrell asked.

'A foursome!' Haye beamed.

Sorrell instantly recalled the four filled but untouched champagne flutes at the crime scene.

Haye turned his iPhone screen to Sorrell. 'Three women had been sending Bryce DM's with nude photos, too – look!'

Haye opened up one of the pictures, forcing Sorrell to turn away in disgust. 'Jeez, I'm not a gynaecologist, Haye.'

The lieutenant laughed at his boss's discomfort. 'That's Chrissie Hardie. The other is Patricia Tolan and the third is a new name to us, one Lacey Lanning. Looks like she's based in Scotland. Anyway, they all arranged a rendezvous with Horrigan for a dirty weekend in Baltimore.'

'Was he really so shallow he would fly from Manhattan to Baltimore just for sex?' Sorrell asked.

'Cap'n, I have friends who would *walk* from New York for a handjob, never mind a foursome. But what I can't figure out is, why Baltimore? Why not stay in New York?'

'Because the killer has no connection with Baltimore. They do with New York,' Sorrell said matter of factly. He studied the direct message exchanges before saying thoughtfully, 'Looks like Bryce Horrigan invited his killer to his own party.'

78

#GoingCommando

'Lieutenant Haye? It's your friendly, blue-faced, kilt-wearing, Sassenach-hating, Scottish policeman – and yes I have gone cunting commando,' Crosbie said from his office on the other side of the Atlantic.

'Sounds like you've gone over the edge, if you ask me,' Haye replied glibly.

'Ha, knew you Yanks had a sense of humour. Everyone says Americans don't do irony. But I always thought that was total horse cock. America has produced the best TV comedies of all time. *The Simpsons, Seinfeld, Curb Your Enthusiasm, 30 Rock…*'

Haye cut Crosbie off. 'And Police Scotland clearly had a sense of humour hiring you. Did you have any luck with that cell phone number?'

'Sorry, I'm such a digressing dickhead. I guess I'm just so excited speaking to a real-life Bawlmore detective. Tell me, is your job anything like *The Wire*?' Crosbie asked hopefully.

'Nope. The cell phone, detective?' Haye said, his voice rising.

'There I go again. They don't call me the "Off on a Tangent Twat" for nothing. I traced the number to a woman called Lacey Lanning. She's a DJ based in Inverness. According to reports in the press, she was Bryce Horrigan's former lover,' Crosbie reported.

'Small world. I've just been looking at an interesting picture of her.'

'Was she in the nip?' Crosbie asked enthusiastically.

'Excuse me?'

'The nip. The scud. Her birthday suit. Could you see her dirty pillows? What about her growler? Sorry, minge. What's the American word again? Puss…'

'What the fuck is wrong with you, Crosbie? Yes. She was naked, as it happens,' Haye finally said, exasperated. 'Her name has come up before; could you bring her in? There're some questions we'd like you to ask…'

'Now hold your plums,' Crosbie interrupted with a terrible John Wayne impression, 'Miss Lanning has gone missing. Disappeared last night shortly after finishing her show. Her car is still in the staff car park, so something's not right.'

'Shit,' Haye cursed loudly.

'Shit, indeed. Apparently she's been having personal problems, but her disappearance is totally out of character. We could put out a nationwide appeal through the media if you're that desperate?'

'Yes, we are. Good idea, detective, thanks,' Haye replied genuinely.

'So is this what you'd call a "red ball" situation? Has the chief been breathing down your neck? Busting your ba…'

Haye's moment of gratitude passed as he once again slammed the phone down on his Scottish counterpart. The lieutenant had serious doubts about DCI Crosbie's sanity.

79

#CoopsConfession

'I told you she had nothing,' Colin Cooper said after being transferred through to Captain Sorrell's office, 'but the big-I-am Captain Sorrell wouldn't listen.'

'What is it, Colin? I'm busy.' Sorrell wasn't in the mood. He had got all he needed from the ex-detective.

'Why did you do it, captain? Why bring her in? I had interrogated her. Tall guy, short guy: she didn't have a fucking clue who she met in that hotel room,' Cooper said angrily.

'You never did have the patience for interviews, Colin. Lindy proved to be most helpful. She could even be our chief witness,' Sorrell said, trying to wrap up the call.

'Not anymore. I told her not to talk. Not to moonlight. It's not my fault. It's not my fault. You forced me to do it,' Cooper said chillingly.

Sorrell immediately picked up on the worrying change of tone. 'What do you mean, Colin?'

Cooper didn't reply, but Sorrell heard him sniff, as if he was crying.

'What have you done, Colin? Colin, speak to me, what have you done? Colin? Colin? COLIN!' Sorrell boomed down the phone. But all he heard was the sound of the ex-detective sobbing down the line.

It was the cry of a guilty man.

80

#DealMaker

Lacey Lanning @RaceyLaceyDJ
Bryce, I have tried to move on but I can't. Maybe sex with my ex will help??

Bryce Horrigan @BryceTripleB
You have my full attention. Go on.

Lacey Lanning @RaceyLaceyDJ
I don't want it to end the way it has. There was more to us than that.

Bryce Horrigan @BryceTripleB
Yes, it was unfortunate. I won't be trying Meth again. I was off my tits.

Lacey Lanning @RaceyLaceyDJ
Yes. And my tits nearly came off!!! What is it about you and biting everyone's breasts?

Bryce Horrigan @BryceTripleB
I am truly sorry. But yes. We should meet up again. Maybe I should invite all my exs?

Lacey Lanning @RaceyLaceyDJ
It'd have to be a large restaurant. More like a banqueting hall.

Bryce Horrigan @BryceTripleB
I'm thinking more of a very large bedroom!

Lacey Lanning @RaceyLaceyDJ
I bet Pasty and Chrissie wouldn't say no?

Bryce Horrigan @BryceTripleB
You think? Thought they hated me.

Lacey Lanning @RaceyLaceyDJ
We've all hated you at some point. I reckon one last fling won't do us any harm...

Bryce Horrigan @BryceTripleB
All of you together?

Lacey Lanning @RaceyLaceyDJ
I'm sure we could be persuaded – if there's a free trip to New York in it?

Bryce Horrigan @BryceTripleB
Nah, not NY. I'm too well known here. Somewhere nearby. An hour flight. Tops.

Lacey Lanning @RaceyLaceyDJ
DC? Baltimore?

Bryce Horrigan @BryceTripleB
Wire country? Sounds wild.

Lacey Lanning @RaceyLaceyDJ
Wild and dangerous – like me. I could fantasise you're Jimmy McNulty.

Bryce Horrigan @BryceTripleB
And I'll pretend you're Kima – she's gay too, right?

Lacey Lanning @RaceyLaceyDJ
I'm not gay. I just like to swing both ways.

Bryce Horrigan @BryceTripleB
Now you're talking. Okay, Baltimore it is. You sort it out
and I'll get Tom to book the flights.

Lacey Lanning @RaceyLaceyDJ
Tell the thieving bastard that Chrissie wants her old
iPhone back.

Bryce Horrigan @BryceTripleB
Shit, forgot about that, sorry. But needs must. I'll make
it up to her. In more ways than one.

Lacey Lanning @RaceyLaceyDJ
Spending money for us, too? Say a grand each.

Bryce Horrigan @BryceTripleB
Jeez, a couple of hookers would be cheaper.

Lacey Lanning @RaceyLaceyDJ
Yes, but riskier – in every way.

Bryce Horrigan @BryceTripleB
True. It's a deal then.

Lacey Lanning @RaceyLaceyDJ
Good. But NO BITING!

Bryce Horrigan @BryceTripleB
Promise.

Lieutenant Haye and Captain Sorrell stared once again at the exchange of direct messages in near disbelief. Twitter had informed them they had been deleted from Bryce's account AFTER his murder, and no wonder – they had lured Horrigan to his death.

'Someone didn't want us to see these, cap'n. And now Lacey Lanning has disappeared off the face of the fucking earth,' Haye said.

'Maybe our Scottish reporter can help. Bring him in,' Sorrell instructed Haye, before returning to his thoughts.

81

#NorthAgain

Edwina Tolan @QueenBee
Would you be interested in information that shatters
the Bryce myth?

April Lavender @AprilReporter1955
Was always told you shouldn't speak ill of the dead. But
then again, the dead don't sue! What myth?

Edwina Tolan @QueenBee
His pro-choice myth.

April Lavender @AprilReporter1955
Go on...

Edwina Tolan @QueenBee
I have got proof from two Bryce exs that he ordered
them to have abortions.

April Lavender @AprilReporter1955
Proof?

Edwina Tolan @QueenBee
Baby scan proof. Sent them to a private clinic to avoid
bad publicity. All during his pro-choice rantings about
that dead cheerleader.

April Lavender @AprilReporter1955
Wow, can you email me the scans?

Edwina Tolan @QueenBee
No. Shall only meet face-to-face. I'm at my holiday
lodge in Aviemore.

'Great, another trip north. That woman's a control freak. And I'll need to take the bloody car this time as she's in the back of beyond.' April was moaning to herself when she was interrupted by her ringing mobile.

'Miss Lavender, it's your number one police confidant,' DCI Crosbie said loftily.

'Hello, detective,' April replied in her usual cheery manner. 'Do you have a nice little story for me?'

'No. I have an April Lavender-sized story – i.e. fucking huge,' Crosbie replied, straight-faced.

'Oh, you are a cheeky one,' replied April, who was not only used to insults, but also familiar with DCI Crosbie's Tourette's syndrome manner.

'Do you remember that washed-up DJ you interviewed in Inverness recently? The one who had been shagging Bryce Horrigan and probably anything else that moved,' Crosbie said.

'Lacey Lanning? Of course. Why?' April asked.

'I'll tell you why. The stupid cow has only gone missing,' Crosbie said.

'Oh no!' April said, the colour draining from her face. 'She left a voicemail last night saying she desperately needed to speak to me. She had something important to tell. She promised to call me after her show. I fell asleep in my chair waiting for the phone to ring. She never called back. I was going to call her again this morning.'

'You're not going to get her. Her phone is in her car, and there's no sign of Lacey,' Crosbie explained. 'I'm assured she wouldn't have walked out on her job at the radio station, as I understand it was something of a last chance saloon as far as her career goes. Have you still got the voicemail message from her?' he asked hopefully.

'Here's the thing, I went to listen back to it this morning and it's been deleted. I could have done it accidentally but I specifically remember pressing the "number two" to save it as I knew it was important.'

'And I thought it was only journalists who hacked people's phones. Anyway, we're going public with it later today, but thought I'd give you a heads-up first. Just keep me in the loop if she gets in contact, would you?' Crosbie asked.

'Thanks. I'll tell the newsdesk. You caught me just in time. I'm actually heading back up north shortly. Aviemore this time, to interview Edwina Tolan. Pasty's mum. Yet another of Bryce Horrigan's ex-lovers. There seems to be plenty of them about.'

'Mind me asking what the story is?'

'You know I'm not supposed to, but if you promise not to breathe a word to anyone else?'

'Cross my arsehole and hope to die,' Crosbie replied.

'Think you got your idiom a wee bit muddled there, but anyway, Edwina says Bryce ordered his lovers to have abortions. Can you imagine that? The courageous campaigner for women's rights,' April said excitedly.

'You do love a bit of scandal, don't you? Well, stay in touch. Especially if you hear anything about Lacey. And be careful on the A9. It's deadly. As the Doors once sang, "Keep your eyes on the road, your hands upon my cock".'

'Er, I don't think they did actually. But thanks all the same for your concern,' April smiled. She reminded herself to DM Connor with the developments before heading for her car.

82

#TheFinalCountdown

'Cap'n, we're down to our final trolls,' Haye said, as he entered Sorrell's office with Fidel.

'How many?' Sorrell asked.

'We have 422 unaccounted for,' Haye said almost apologetically.

'Our trolls handing themselves in has dried up, too,' Fidel added. 'We're getting two or three a day, but that's all.'

'And we've done all our usual checks? The Wi-Fi and the CCTV and all the rest?' the captain asked.

'The 400-odd left are more professional. They've masked their IP addresses. Just like Baby Angel and Bryce Horrigan's own account too,' Fidel explained.

'Professional trolls, who'd have thought?' Sorrell said, shaking his head. 'The colonel isn't going to like this. He's convinced our killer will be one of them. Goddamn Twitter. What is its purpose? I mean, really? I might be an old stick in the mud, but for the life of me I'll never understand it. Never.'

Haye and Fidel thought better of trying to give an answer. The captain had left them well and truly stumped.

As Sorrell predicted, Colonel Cowan was incandescent with rage. '422? We have 422 suspects we simply can't find? What other homicide investigation would have 422 suspects unknown?'

'This isn't like any other homicide investigation, sir.'

'I know that, Sorrell. Don't point out the blatantly obvious.' His voice was almost at fever pitch.

'Then don't tell me how to run MY homicide investigation,' Sorrell snapped back. He had never spoken to his superior that way. He had never needed to. It stunned the colonel into silence. And Sorrell wasn't finished. 'Now will you please let me get on with solving the case my way? I am following some definite lines of inquiry. And I can do without all this Twitter crap.'

The colonel leaned back in his chair and wiped his brow. He was a chastised and defeated man. All he could muster by way of a reply was, 'Keep me up to speed with any developments,' but there was no conviction in his voice.

Sorrell left his office without saying another word. But the colonel was left in absolutely no doubt that Bernard Sorrell was nobody's bitch. It would be the last time he ever shouted at his captain.

83

#SpillingTheBeans

Connor had just received April's DM about heading north when he took a call from Lieutenant Haye, who was as forthright as he'd been with Tom O'Neill.

'Connor Presley? This is Lieutenant Haye, from Baltimore Homicide. We need to talk. Be at Captain Sorrell's office for 2pm.' Connor checked his watch. It was already twenty-five to two. '2pm. Sharp,' Haye added, as if reading Connor's mind, and with no apology for the short notice. Connor had met many policemen over the years, but none as straight-talking as this pair.

He hoped they were still unaware of his contact with Geoffrey Schroeder. Connor dare not mention the prime suspect as any police involvement would see any chance of his world exclusive scoop disappear.

The journalist arrived right on time and was shown into the captain's office by Haye, who took up his usual position by his boss's side, like a loyal guard dog. Connor strode towards Sorrell's desk, but before he could offer a handshake, he was asked by the police captain to take a seat. He obviously wasn't the handshaking type.

'What can you tell me about Bryce Horrigan? And, please, spare me the sugar-coated version. I want to know what he was really like, what he got up to with his women,' Sorrell said.

Connor had to make a quick calculation. They didn't seem to know about his Schroeder contact. They were still concentrating on the women. So, after recounting a quick version of their professional relationship, Connor moved onto Bryce's love of the high-life and women.

Sorrell and Haye each looked more bored than the other, until the captain interrupted. 'I've heard all this power's-an-aphrodisiac stuff. I need more than he was a big-headed, womanising pain in the ass? What you got?'

Connor had to marvel at this detective's ability to get straight to the point. He also had the physical presence that made you want to tell the truth. 'I don't know if you've been told this, but two of Bryce's ex-lovers have ended up back in Scotland with similar injuries,' Connor said, then let the sentence hang in the air to see the reaction.

Lieutenant Haye suddenly stopped using the back wall as a support. But Sorrell's demeanour didn't change. Connor would hate to play him at poker.

'What sort of injuries?' Sorrell asked.

'Kind of like scratches. Or bites. Around their breasts, neck areas,' Connor explained.

'Any of these women been to the United States lately?' Sorrell asked.

'Well, Patricia Tolan was living with him in New York before it all turned sour.'

'Yeah, we know about her,' Sorrell replied.

'And Lacey Lanning told my colleague she also went to see him in New York, but she didn't say when. Only in the last six months,' Connor heard himself say. 'And then there's Chrissie Hardie. Bryce wooed her from some student he clashed with on television. She moved to New York, too. PR, I'm told. I've got a number for her but haven't been able to get hold of her yet.'

Captain Sorrell abruptly concluded the chat. 'Thank you for your help, Mr Presley. If you have any other information, please call me.' Sorrell then added reluctantly, 'I guess I also owe you one. If this leads to anything, you'll be the first to know.'

Connor couldn't help beaming from ear to ear. 'Thank you, captain.'

Sorrell waited until the reporter had left before he turned to

Haye and cracked a rare smile. 'We already had the three women. Now we have three motives. Let's close this thing down, Haye.'

84

#Retribution

North Branch Correctional Institution was in lock-down after the guards had struggled to control the inmates. Even the longest serving staffers couldn't remember when the prisoners had been this crazy before. The place had been buzzing since they heard about their new arrival, with the sense of anticipation crackling through the air like electricity. The prison warden feared the worst. He'd had enough of his men attacked lately and ordered that all inmates were to be confined to their cells indefinitely. It did nothing to dampen their spirits.

Finally, the focus of their attention arrived. Ex-detective Colin Cooper was wearing his prison issue orange jumpsuit, as he was led through the facility. His cocky stride had been replaced by the slump-shouldered trudge of a broken man. Just the merest sight of the hated former cop, who loved to beat suspects, sent prisoners into a frenzy. They goaded him with cries of 'Welcome to hell, Coops,' and shouted obscenities, throwing items ranging from tea cups to their own excrement in his direction.

It was more like a Roman coliseum with a condemned Christian marching to his death. Cooper was to be held in solitary confinement for his own safety. But the warden knew he couldn't protect him forever. Sooner or later he would require the solitary cell for another prisoner, leaving the ex-cop to his fate. Colin Cooper didn't care. He had beaten to death the woman he loved because he couldn't control her.

Control was the reason he had left Stephanie. He had wanted a woman who would do exactly as he said. To fuck when she was told. To earn money. To love, honour and obey, as the old marriage vows go. Instead, he had had to beat a confession out of Lindy that she had been caught in a police sting, going behind his back once more even though she had promised, on her mother's life, that she wouldn't moonlight again. Worse still, she had told the cops everything about their lucrative business with room 1410. That was tantamount to treason as far as Cooper was concerned. He had hit her, then hit her again, before he lost all memory of what happened next. The Chief Medical Examiner's autopsy report said the victim had sustained injuries 'consistent with an automobile accident'. Her once beautiful features were only able to be identified through her dental records.

Cooper could have put a bullet in his brain but that would have been an easy way out. He wanted to die for what he had done. But he wanted to suffer too, the way his poor Lindy had.

One week later, the ex-detective would get his wish when he was transferred from solitary to the main facility. The inmates had cleared a cell as a 'reception room' especially for him. He was led there by a throng of black prisoners, almost all of whom he had put away, after dishing out his customary beating in custody. Waiting for him inside the cell was Tre Paul Beckett, his boxer's hands already swathed in the bandages he used to wear before donning his gloves for the ring. But the gloves would remain off this time. Colin Cooper stepped into the cell surrounded by the baying mob, fully resigned to his fate.

TP would never get the early release he'd been promised by Lieutenant Haye, to resume his fighting career. Not after he had a life-term added to his sentence for beating to death the former Baltimore Homicide detective, Colin Cooper.

85

#ReverseBug

'Cap'n, we've found the computer Horrigan's tweets are being sent from,' Haye said excitedly.

'About time,' Sorrell said.

'Yeah, but you may need to sit down for this one. They are being sent from Bryce Horrigan's own office computer in New York.'

Sorrell's face was a mass of confusion. 'Back up a minute. Not only are these tweets being sent from a dead man's Twitter account, but they're also coming from his own PC? How is that even possible?'

'Remotely. NYPD's computer crimes unit finally got the warrant to confiscate his PC, right? But as our guy was about to unplug all the equipment, he spotted some sort of device sticking in a USB port that he just knew shouldn't be there. Turns out it was a bug that allowed the hacker to switch on and access his computer to send the tweets,' Haye explained.

'How come we didn't trace it sooner?' Sorrell demanded.

'It was tricky. The user never stayed on too long. They also hopped around a lot. They would bounce around the world until they reached Horrigan's PC, then bounce around some more. The PC was just the middle link of the chain. The tweets were finally sent from some public Wi-Fi hotspot in Prague.'

'What now?' Sorrell asked, knowing he was way out of his depth when it came to technology.

'Okay, this is the really cool part,' Haye said, struggling to contain his excitement. 'NYPD have installed a reverse bug. All we now have to do is wait until the hacker accesses Bryce's computer again. Not only will we be able to instantly trace back to where they really are, it will also install our own surveillance program into the hacker's machine. It will set off like a homing beacon every time they go online. We've got them by the balls, cap'n,' Haye beamed.

'An electronic trap,' Sorrell said in amazement, although his mind was already elsewhere.

'Uh-huh. So, that's the good news. But there's bad news as well: Chrissie Hardie has turned up dead. Shot in her apartment. No sign of forced entry.'

'What about her old injuries? The bite marks. Did they check for those?' Sorrell demanded.

'It's all there, cap'n. Along with the gunshot wounds to her head, she had extensive scarring to her breasts, including one of her nipples. The Bride of Frankenstein description fits, just like O'Neill said. His story about switching her cell phone stands up, too. She did have a new iPhone. And guess what? The number matches one of the calls to Horrigan's phone you took on the morning of his death. She may have hated Bryce, but she called his cell to find out if he was really dead. Along with one from Lacey Lanning and one from that reporter, Presley.

'Her name hadn't shown up on Bryce's phone because it was a new number. I think knowing Bryce Horrigan was very danger-ous for your health,' Sorrell concluded.

86

#TheSkiSet

April felt tired and hungry as she pulled into the Highland tourist resort of Aviemore. It was just a two-and-a-half hour drive from Glasgow up the notorious A9 – Scotland's longest road. Someone, in their infinite wisdom, had made the carriageway just two lanes wide for the majority of its 150 miles, meaning that the entire A9 had become an accident black spot as drivers risked extreme overtaking manoeuvres just to avoid getting stuck behind a caravan or slow-moving truck.

April had actually enjoyed the journey north again, barely driving over 50mph – well below the A9's speed limits of either 60mph or 70mph. As she barely used her mirrors and had next-to no peripheral vision, she was blissfully unaware of the huge tailbacks of frustrated drivers behind her – a perfect example of what causes so many accidents on the road in the first place.

Although the ski season hadn't kicked off properly yet, April could see the Cairngorm mountain range was already completely white in the distance as she took the turn-off towards Aviemore's town centre. She thought to herself how she would have loved to ski. Not necessarily for the skiing itself, but because she had always romanticised about being part of the whole winter sports scene. Those young sophisticated go-getters with their 4x4s, impossibly white teeth and looking like they'd just stepped out of a catalogue, even after a day's exertion on the slopes.

She had once secretly taken a batch of ski lessons at a dry slope in Glasgow's Bellahouston Park. Despite being not much more than a mound, April had been terrified when she finally reached the top after many comical attempts to master the Poma lift. Her instructor had told her to keep her skis in the V-position – or snowplough. She had managed to carry out those instructions to the letter for about the first two seconds, until she felt her skis straighten themselves into the parallel position, which soon had her gathering speed and hurtling straight down into the crash wall below. April hadn't hurt herself badly, apart from a burst lip when she had raised her hands just before impact, smashing the ski pole handle into her mouth. Connor had been his usual sympathetic self the next day, when he remarked that her fat lip was the worst trout pout he'd ever seen. That had been the end of skiing as far as she was concerned, but now, seeing the sun setting over the snow-capped peaks, she wished she hadn't been so hasty.

It was April's second trip north in a week, after her Inverness journey to interview the now-missing Lacey Lanning. She hoped the DJ was all right, but somehow knew she wasn't.

April planned to check in to the Cairnmore Hotel, get something nice and bountiful to eat, then sleep, before she hit Edwina Tolan's doorstep at nine the next morning.

She pulled into the hotel's car park, situated near the old-fashioned railway she'd passed through on the train recently, with its wrought iron bridge crossing the track. April stepped outside her car and breathed deeply. 'Ah, such fresh air,' she announced to the world, before promptly lighting up. The hotel was like an old country manor. It looked inviting, with its busy pub and restaurant, and the tartan-wallpapered reception festooned with stag heads and various other animals shot in the name of sport.

She liked this place, especially the smiley welcome from the innocent-looking Highland lass, whose nametag said she was called Morag. After checking in, April took herself for dinner, ordering the venison from the hotel restaurant. It was so delicious she could have eaten it all over again. Instead, she decided to take herself for a walk along the main street, where she spotted a lively bar.

As April took her seat she couldn't help noticing the size of the hamburgers being served. She hesitated for a moment, before ordering a burger and a large glass of red wine. April was feeling rather pleased with her deceit, as if anyone really cared that she was on her second main course of the evening.

The smell of the grill from the kitchen practically had her salivating. But as she took the first bite out of the oversized burger, a familiar face walked through the door. April couldn't place her at first, as she was out of context, but then the penny dropped. It was Morag, the receptionist from the hotel.

Morag gave April a little wave, and called out, 'Good evening, Miss Lavender. Was the venison not filling enough?'

April turned scarlet; she had been well and truly busted.

'The chef who's on duty tonight is pretty stingy with his portions,' Morag confided. 'No wonder you needed something else to eat.'

April swallowed her mouthful and smiled. 'I am an awful glutton, aren't I? I put it down to the fresh air up here. And it's so cold – too cold to snow, as they say.'

'I wouldn't be too sure of that. Aviemore has its own weather system. It's very hard to predict. Don't be too surprised if it's all white by morning,' Morag warned, before a large, rough farmer type came through the door and gave Morag a cursory peck on the cheek.

Morag's kindness convinced April more than ever that Aviemore was a charming place. It was buzzing and filled with various nationalities. April could see herself retiring here. She figured the day wouldn't be far off when she got a tap on the shoulder from management. Connor, for all his jibes and slagging, had once told her the problem was she was too good. That had been a nice and very unexpected compliment. But since one of the senior news subs had retired, she was now the oldest member of staff at the *Daily Chronicle* and felt very exposed.

April finished up, tipped the waitress generously then sent a round of drinks over to Morag and her beau. As she stepped outside the bar, she felt the cold air sting her whole face and shuddered. 'I think Morag could be right about the snow.'

87

#HiredCar

'Hi, Tom, where are you?'

'In a coffee shop waiting for someone, Elvis. And you?' Tom O'Neill replied.

'Listen, I did a shitty thing so I'm phoning to warn you and apologise,' Connor said sheepishly.

'Ha, this sounds interesting. Right, sock it to me, buddy, as they say over here.'

'I gave your name to Geoffrey Schroeder. I'm sorry. But he would only agree to speak if I told him who had put him in the frame. I reckoned there would be no harm in lifting your name as he wouldn't know you from Adam. Again, I'm sorry,' Connor said, full of remorse.

There was silence down the line and Connor fully expected a verbal bashing that would be both justified and deserved. He was surprised by Tom's response. 'Have you met him yet, Elvis?'

'No, I'm going tonight. Need to hire a car first,' Connor said, more to himself.

'Fuck it, you can have mine. Where are you staying?'

'The Baltimore City Hotel, right on the harbour.'

'I'm in the Yellow Tree Hotel on University Parkway. Get yourself a cab and she's all yours. And, Elvis, remember, this guy is dangerous. Very unstable. Do you want me to come with you?' O'Neill asked.

'No, Tom. He's twitchy as hell. He'll run a mile. I need to speak to him. If what he says is of interest, I'll tell him to turn himself into Sorrell.'

'Good plan. But call me if you get into any shit. I'll tell the captain and let him know where you are. And don't worry about using my name. Had the blue suede shoe been on the other foot, I'd have dropped you right in it too, Elvis,' O'Neill said reassuringly.

88

#Timing

Bryce Horrigan's office computer screen once again flickered into life, shortly after 3pm EST. The first safety check the remote user tested was the PC's webcam, to satisfy themselves the room was empty, before the username 'BHorrigan' was typed in followed by the password in the space below. The user accessed the Twitter home page, but instead of typing Bryce's username and password to log into his account, they entered another identity: @BabyAngel. They then typed out a DM to one @BernardSorrell.

One hundred and ninety miles away in Sorrell's Baltimore office, the captain, Fidel and Haye watched the live feed from an NYPD camera set up to monitor Horrigan's PC. They watched in real-time as the remote user DM'd the captain.

'That explains why the Horrigan and Baby Angel tweets were usually sent at the same times,' Fidel said. 'The Horrigan tweets were roughly around 3am, give or take an hour or so, when they knew for sure the office was empty. But Baby Angel needed to engage with the captain during the day, so chose 3pm.'

Haye added, 'Get this, 3pm is when the ABT News team always have their afternoon conferences. So our hacker would be fairly confident that Bryce's office would be empty at both 3am and 3pm. They'd use the webcam to make sure, too.'

'They'd also need to know that there was a 3pm conference in the first place,' pondered Sorrell.

Fidel took a call from his IT counterpart at NYPD. 'The reverse bug worked. They've traced them. We've got the hacker's current location,' he said, scribbling down on a notepad the information from New York.

'Well, I'll be damned,' Sorrell said as he raised his massive bulk onto his feet, opened his drawer and placed his police standard issue Glock 22 .40-calibre pistol snugly into his shoulder holster. 'I think it's time to catch our killer.'

It was the first time a direct message from Baby Angel to the captain would go unanswered.

89

#Solitaire

Connor took a cab to the Yellow Tree Hotel as instructed. But on the way there he received a DM from Tom: *Slight change of plan, Elvis. I have to shoot off for a meeting. I've left the keys with the valet. They'll get the car for you. Good luck.*

Tom quickly sent another: *There's a full tank of gas. Just remember to tip the valet, ya mean Scots bastard!!*

Connor retorted, *Rather be a mean Scots bastard than a bog-trotter.*

I'm from Northern Ireland, remember? The bog-trotters are over the border, Tom wrote back.

The valet arrived with Tom's Ford Focus. Connor tipped him as instructed then familiarised himself with the controls before driving on the right side of the road. He found it easy. He didn't understand what all the fuss was about.

Connor recalled April telling him a story of her dream holiday to Saint-Tropez on the French Riviera. She had hired a villa and planned to live like a film star for a week. The only problem was negotiating the hire car and driving on the 'wrong' side of the road. After nearly causing two pile-ups just leaving the airport complex, she returned the car back to the hire desk and took the bus instead. 'Six hours it took me to get from the airport to my villa. And what did I do all week? Played solitaire because I had no car to go anywhere.' Connor had remarked how he was sure the film stars also played solitaire on the French Riviera too… after all the sex, booze and drugs.

He chuckled to himself. 'I miss the crazy old bat – shit, I'm even talking to myself like her now.'

90

#AvyMore

'Detective Crosbie? It's Lieutenant Haye here,' the detective said
as he made his way to his car with Captain Sorrell. 'NYPD's computer crimes unit have got a trace on Bryce Horrigan's hacker.
It's a UK IP address. Located in Scotland. Somewhere called Avy
More?'

Crosbie sat bolt upright in his chair. 'Aviemore? Are you sure?'

DCI Crosbie then spelt out the place name with his own
unique version of the phonetic alphabet. 'Asshole. Vagina. Idiot.
Ejaculate. Minge. Orgasm. Rimming. Ejaculate?'

'Jeezus, yeah, that's the place. Are you all right in the head,
buddy?'

'Never been better, thanks. I feel tip, titty, twatty top. But
now I've gotta go, sport,' Crosbie said, which was his idea of an
Americanism.

For the first time it was the Scottish detective who slammed the
phone down on his US counterpart.

91

#WhiteOut

April woke early with a strange light in her room that even the hotel's black-out blinds failed to keep out. She opened them to find a white blanket of thick snow over everything. Down below one of the porters was trying to dig out the hotel mini-bus with a snow shovel. It looked at least a foot deep. April stared at her high heels beside the bed and mumbled, 'Well, those bad boys aren't going to cut it.' She needed to go shopping for more climate-appropriate clobber before hitting Edwina Tolan's doorstep this morning.

April dressed, ate and spoke to the porter, who she saw come through the door with the snow shovel. He had successfully freed the minibus and April asked if he would give her a lift to the nearest outdoors shop. She also asked if he would kindly dig out her own car.

Then she took a call from Kenny Black, the photographer from Inverness she was due to meet. There was no way he could make it through – the snow ploughs were battling to clear the A9 and he estimated it'd be late afternoon at the earliest before he could make it. But with more heavy snow forecast, even that wasn't guaranteed. 'Oh well, on your own again, April,' she sighed. The porter smiled. April wasn't the only single ageing female guest he'd seen talking to herself over the years.

Even though the porter was used to the conditions, his mini-bus slipped from side to side, clipping a kerb, as he dropped April off at the nearest outdoors shop. Tottering in her high heels, she gingerly made her way to the front door, only to slip over as her inappropriate footwear sent her flying. Two members of staff rushed to her aid, taking considerable effort to help her to her feet, as April had winded herself and was incapable of moving.

Finally she was able to gasp, 'Thanks… I always like to make an entrance.'

After a seat and a glass of water, she was able to ascertain that nothing was seriously damaged. 'Plenty of padding,' she said, patting the many folds of her stomach. 'Now I need you to find the right clobber to cover it. You might want to start with a tent and work backwards.' Forty minutes later, a new April emerged into a fresh blizzard, looking like the Michelin man. She was dressed from top to toe in Berghaus clothes, from the ski jacket to the salopettes, hat and boots. Her thighs made a 'swoosh, swoosh, swoosh' sound as she walked back to the hotel, fearing she would spontaneously combust.

Her car had now been cleared. She tipped the porter a tenner, then, studying her mobile, asked, 'Is there a problem with the signal? I've no bars on my phone.'

The porter laughed. 'There's always a problem up here. It's temperamental, to say the least. And when the snow comes down like this, forget it.'

April may have been wearing the right gear now, but she found conditions underfoot still as treacherous and her car was not fitted with winter tyres. In fact, the tread on the front wheels was barely legal. She strapped herself into the driver's seat and hoped for the best. This was going to be even more of a white-knuckle hair-raising drive than usual.

DCI Crosbie's powerful police BMW was having an equally tough time of it, with its rear-wheel drive practically useless in the near white-out conditions on the hazardous A9.

'This minge mobile is no more than a motorised sledge in the snow,' he cursed to himself. He repeatedly got April's 'out of service' message as he tried her mobile from his hands-free. Suddenly he received a call from a local sergeant in Aviemore he'd asked to go and intercept April at the hotel.

'Sorry, DCI Crosbie, we've missed her. The porter didn't know which direction she was going in. We have her car registration from the hotel records, so we'll keep a look-out. But as you can imagine, we're pretty busy up here today. This is the worst weather I've seen in years.'

DCI Crosbie hung up, gripped the steering wheel tightly and put his foot down as he ploughed northwards in a hail of snow and expletives.

April's Daewoo was also crawling through the snowy conditions, towards Coylumbridge and the mountains. The snow ploughs had been working hard, but it was still a losing battle, with fresh white powder quickly replacing the stuff they'd just pushed off to the side of the road.

The radio was issuing regular police warnings only to under-take essential travel. Well, this was essential as far as April was concerned. She managed to fall in behind a snow plough on the road leading to the ski centre. Following the plough was both a curse and a blessing as it cleared the snow but also showered April's already chipped windscreen with red salt. She needed her wipers on the fastest setting to have any hope of seeing anything, but with the snow falling even more heavily, she was basically driving blind.

April was about to give up when her sat-nav announced that she was approaching her destination. She neither liked nor trusted the device, even though she had no sense of direc-tion whatsoever. She still felt guilty over the fact she once sent a blind man with his guide dog traipsing towards the wrong side of town. April only discovered this when she had proudly announced to Connor back at the office how she'd done her good deed for the day.

'A blind chap couldn't find Princess Square so I sent him to the top of Buchanan Street, telling him it was just past the Underground,' she'd beamed.

'That was nice of you,' Connor said, still typing without taking his eyes off his computer screen, 'but Princess Square is at the bottom of Buchanan Street, opposite Fraser's.'

April froze in horror. 'Where did I send him, then?'

'Buchanan Street Galleries. You're going straight to hell, I hope you know.'

The sat-nav sprang into life again, announcing April was to take a left turn in a hundred yards. She slowed down, letting the plough disappear into the distance when she spotted the name *The Cairns* written on a slice of tree trunk. She had barely turned onto the untreated forest road when her car came to a shuddering halt. The vehicle was lying at a crazy angle. April figured she must have veered off the narrow road into a snow-filled ditch. She got out and looked at her old Daewoo, knowing any attempt to move it would be futile.

'Oh well, old girl, you got me here at least. Now this old girl will need to walk.'

92

#TheFinalPost

Patricia Tolan tried to start every morning in a positive state of mind. But her drink-and-drug-addled brain was unable to put aside the hurt and anger caused by her ex, Bryce Horrigan. She had believed and hoped that his death would bring her some relief, but it hadn't. Now she kept reliving the moment of his assassination over and over again.

Patricia replayed the media file on her laptop once more. The GoPro camera attached to the end of a gun barrel lit up Bryce Horrigan's frightened face before there was a flash then a bang. When the screen cleared, Patricia's former lover, the man who had once vowed never to leave her, was left clutching at the awful wound in his neck. There were seven other flashes as Horrigan's body was pumped full of bullets, but the look of terror soon left, leaving only vacant, unfocused eyes.

It was the final file she would post from Bryce's own Twitter account to his millions of followers in a few hours' time, but until then it was for Patricia's eyes only. She would then check if Geoffrey Schroeder had responded to her other persona, @BabyAngel. She had been trying to contact the pro-lifer for days now, but he had gone to ground.

But Patricia's mind soon refocused on the cause of all her anger. She played the media file, frame by frame this time. Bryce had died all too quickly for her liking. She had needed more pain. More realisation of the hurt he had caused so many people. His suffering had been brief. Merciful, almost. But Patricia's anguish lived on in her own world of despair.

She tried to force out a laugh, which just sounded false and unnatural. It soon made way to loud wailing as she put her face down on her desk and cried, collapsing to the floor in a foetal position, where she lay caressing her tummy and empty womb, thinking of the baby that would never be.

Patricia 'Pasty' Tolan was not a well woman.

93

#NanookOfTheNorth

April had never done so much exercise in her life. Even going through fourteen hours of labour to deliver Jayne hadn't felt as exhausting as this. She didn't know why she was pushing herself so hard. A reporter half her age and weight would have turned back by now. Maybe she was trying to prove a point that she wasn't past her prime.

'I may be over the hill, but I can't let the bastards know that,' April shouted slightly manically into the wilds, where the trees were being blown sideways by the fierce winds and painted white by the snow. She couldn't even hear herself in these violent conditions, especially with her hood up and pulled tight by two toggles to perfectly circle her moon face.

The blizzard was relentless. April wasn't even sure she was going in the right direction after leaving the sat-nav and the safety of the car behind. But almost as soon as the snow had come, it stopped, swirling away towards the top of the mountains. Bright sunshine and a patch of blue sky broke through, bathing April and the surrounding land in a blinding light. Her eyes took time to adjust, and she wished now she had bought the Oakley sunglasses the sales assistant had attempted to flog her in the outdoors shop.

'£120 for a pair of shades – you must be joking,' she had told him. *But who's laughing now?* she thought to herself as she tried to see where she was going through the slits in her eyes.

April continued her slow trudge along the forest road, before eventually rounding a corner to see her goal – The Cairns lodge. It was like a picture postcard, a Hansel and Gretel-style cottage with a layer of icing cake snow on the roof. Surrounding the lodge was a wooden deck, which April could imagine would be glorious in the summer – if you could brave the dreaded Scottish midge, the little cousin of the mosquito, whose swarms have been known to drive mad both man and beast.

April clumped her way onto the decking to the front door where the snow abruptly ended under the roof overspill. She stamped her feet to clear them of the slush that had stuck to the soles.

'Ah, you made it. Plucky little you,' said Pasty's mother, Edwina Tolan, as she opened the front door.

'I know, look at the state of me. I'm like Nanook of the North,' April said in her bright and breezy way.

'Well, our little Nanook, why don't you come in to our wee cranny?' Edwina said.

However pleasant Edwina tried to sound, April could never warm to this woman. 'Don't mind if I do,' she smiled as she stepped over the threshold, with Edwina locking the door behind her.

April was shown into the farmhouse kitchen, which she would have loved to nosey around, poking into drawers and cupboards at will. For she truly loved interior design. But the atmosphere was not conducive to a chat about wall colours and decor.

'Tea, coffee, sticky bun? I'm sure a woman of your carriage can never turn her nose up at any sort of cake,' Edwina Tolan sneered, looking down at April.

Ouch, April thought to herself, *I'm barely through the door and she's already ridiculed my weight.* The cruelty with which Edwina had delivered her putdown made April almost crave Connor's caustic comments.

'Coffee, please. And as I always say, it takes a lot of effort to stay this size,' she replied, trying desperately to keep the mood light.

'Quite,' Edwina replied sharply. 'Patricia, dear,' she shouted in the direction of another part of the cottage, 'would you come and prepare coffee for our guest?'

Edwina had caught April unawares. She had no idea her daughter would be here too. A moment later, Bryce Horrigan's former lover entered the room and made her way straight to the oversized, brass-bottomed kettle, filled it with what must have been about a gallon of water, and returned it to the top of the Aga stove to heat. Patricia left a smear of blood on the kettle's handle and returned in the direction she'd come from, not once making eye contact with April.

'Hello, Patricia, have you cut yourself, dear?' April said, to no avail – there wasn't even a flicker of recognition from Patricia that the journalist had spoken.

'Manners, Patricia,' barked Edwina, making her daughter jump with fear.

'Sorry, Mama. I was in a daze. Nice to meet you again, Miss Lavender. I'm quite all right, thank you,' Patricia said robotically. 'What do you take in your coffee?'

'Plenty of milk and five sugars, but don't stir it as I don't like it sweet,' April replied with a lame joke, trying desperately to keep the conversation upbeat, lest it went to the dark place she feared it was heading. Neither of the Tolan women said anything in the long minutes before the giant brass kettle began to bubble and boil. The silence chilled April. She knew something was wrong. Very wrong.

Patricia eventually handed over a mug of coffee, and her mother suggested April take a seat in the next-door lounge. 'We have another guest,' Edwina smiled again, 'someone you've met before.'

April was shown into the adjoining room, where a young woman with her back to the door sat slumped in a chair, her head tilted to one side, watching a silent television. There was an overwhelming sickly stench that April couldn't put her finger on at first. It smelled like iron.

'Aren't you going to say hello, Lacey? After all, you two had plenty to say to each other before,' Edwina sneered once more.

'Eeelp meeee. Eeelp meeee,' the figure on the chair croaked as April took a step towards her. Lacey turned her head and looked up at April, who now knew what the source of the sickly iron smell was: blood had trickled from the DJ's mouth and run down the entire front of her body and pooled around her bare feet.

'Eeelp meeee,' she croaked louder, as a fresh gush of red spluttered from her lips.

April dropped her coffee mug, which smashed loudly on the floor.

'Your little friend here won't be doing much talking in future, not since we cut out her tongue.' Edwina smiled manically. 'I warned her what I'd do if she went blabbing. But she wouldn't listen. So after my darling Patricia intercepted Lacey's message on your voicemail, we decided we needed to speak to her first. It was dark by the time she left the studio. Didn't take much for us to bundle her into the car. Simple, really. You see, Lacey was part of our little plot. She had agreed to send Bryce those naked pictures of herself. To say she wanted to be part of a foursome in Baltimore. She bought our story that we just planned to humiliate Bryce, nothing more. Lacey even let Patricia use her Twitter account to set up the sordid little session. All the time Bryce thought he was flirting with Lacey, he was actually sending DMs to my daughter.'

Edwina paused for a moment and glanced at Patricia.

'They shared a common bond, you see. Bryce had sent them both to that butcher's clinic in Switzerland to have their bastard babies terminated. Patricia then worked her magic on Bryce's other bit on the side, Chrissie Hardie. She was an angry young woman, especially when Bryce was still on TV every night being his usual smug self after what he'd done to her. She also developed a deep bond with my daughter after Patricia showed her the injuries Bryce had given her, too. Chrissie could see for herself that Bryce had mauled others and got away with it. Patricia then logged on to Bryce's Twitter account and showed Chrissie all the sleazy DMs he had been sending other women while poor Chrissie was living with him. She hadn't needed much encouragement after that to take part. She also let Bryce know she was up for his sordid little foursome. Amazingly, he believed it. Of course, there's nothing more sobering than a murder, and Chrissie got cold feet after Bryce turned up dead. Started to panic. We needed to put her out of her misery too.'

'You are quite mad. Both of you,' April gasped.

'It's true, poor Patricia is quite mad. And I have my moments too, don't I, dear?' the mother said, turning to her equally psychotic daughter.

'Yes, Mama. Do you remember that cyclist when you were taking me to school?' Patricia recalled while staring into the middle distance.

'Of course, dear. You never forget your first. Lycra-clad freak. He kicked MY car just because I cut in front of him. Well, let me tell you, when it comes to car versus bike, car wins every time.'

'And then there was our neighbour, wasn't there, Mama?' Patricia continued.

'Ah, yes. Old Mr Goodier and his constantly barking dogs that'd just drive you insane,' Edwina said as she and her daughter walked towards April from either side of the room, like a pincer movement.

'I think you were barking before the dogs,' April said, edging her frame back out of the living room door into the kitchen.

'That's not fair, Miss Lavender. An insane person wouldn't have been able to cover up their crime. An insane person wouldn't have pushed Mr Goodier down his stairs to break his neck, then close the door. His dogs didn't bark much after that. Why would they when they had plenty to eat? There wasn't much left of poor Mr Goodier by the time I phoned the police as a concerned neighbour.'

April had backed into the thick wooden farmhouse table. She

edged her way around it, refusing to take her eyes off the Tolan women as they continued their slow advance.

'You see, I found I had a knack for killing,' Edwina continued, 'I was good at it.'

'A classic mistake, I'm afraid, pet,' April replied. 'You got lucky with the cyclist. You were cowardly with an elderly neighbour. And you've screwed up with Bryce Horrigan – or I wouldn't be here, would I? My colleague Connor and I figured it out. The game's up.'

'Elvis and fatso have brought down the killer queen, have they?' Edwina laughed. 'Poor Elvis, any moment now he'll be shot dead by a crazed pro-life nut job, who unfortunately will turn the gun on himself before he can be questioned about killing Bryce Horrigan. And it will all be played out for millions online,' Edwina said, her eyes darting to the ultra-thin, expensive-looking laptop on the table. 'Amazing thing, technology. What you can do with it. Expands the horizons, I feel.'

'Overrated, if you ask me. Some things never really change. A killer is still a killer, in my book. I guess I'm old-fashioned that way,' April said defiantly.

'You certainly are, dear. No one buys papers or books these days. They download them. Click. Same with a washing machine, a sofa, your groceries. Click, click, click. And I've discovered it's just the same with murder. Click, you're dead.'

Edwina and her daughter instantly froze at the sound of someone stamping the snow off their feet on the wooden porch outside, followed by a rap at the door.

'Excuse me, we appear to have an uninvited guest. Don't let her move, Patricia,' Edwina said sternly, as her daughter took a blade from the block of knives. April noticed there was already one missing. 'Won't be a tick,' Edwina said jauntily as she headed for the front door. April quickly weighed up her options. She was at least twice Patricia's size, so figured she had a decent weight advantage. Instead, she decided the best option would be to scream for help from the visitor. But she didn't get the chance. Edwina Tolan opened the door, to be met by a red-faced man, carrying a large, heavy photographer's bag.

'Hello, I'm K...'

Before Kenny Black even said his name, Edwina viciously thrust a kitchen knife into the snapper's throat, with such force it came out of the back of his neck. He stumbled backwards, toppling over the snow-covered bannister into the white garden below. Before he'd even hit the ground, Edwina had closed the door, safe in the knowledge he was quite dead.

'Now, where were we?' she said, returning to the kitchen. 'Ah yes. It's time to carve up a fat little piggy.'

April felt her backside press up against the warmth from the cast iron cooker. She had come to the end of the road and could go no further. Each of the Tolans was brandishing a knife, the mother having retrieved another after leaving her last one in the neck of the poor unfortunate photographer who had valiantly battled through the snowdrifts to meet up with April. They now stalked their prey, with Edwina coming round the left of the farm-house table and Patricia on the right flank. They stared at April intently, watching her eyes dart between them. April would have given anything to have called Connor. Not to save herself, but to warn him. If only she could buy more time.

Edwina was now within six feet of her, and took a fresh-air swipe at her with the blade, then laughed when April flinched. Like a cat toying with a mouse, Edwina was enjoying herself. April's hands fumbled behind her, hidden by her rotund frame. She braced herself for the imminent attack, knowing it would be swift. She just hoped it wouldn't be too swift. Her eyes darted towards Patricia, who had stopped in her tracks, clearly waiting for her mad mother to initiate the move when they would both finally attack, plunging their blades into her body.

Then it came.

Edwina lunged surprisingly quickly for a woman of her age,

with those regular gym work-outs clearly paying off. She sent a flash of ten inches of steel thrusting towards the trapped reporter. At the same time, April retaliated by swinging the heavy copper-bottomed kettle towards her attacker, having already removed the lid behind her back. More than a gallon of scalding hot water hit Edwina Tolan directly in the face and body, drenching her and forcing her to drop her blade as she fell to the floor screaming.

Her daughter looked on in horror and shouted, 'You've killed Mama,' before lunging at April, who swung the kettle upwards at full force, catching Patricia perfectly under the chin, delivering a knock-out upper cut blow like a heavyweight boxer.

With both of her attackers down, April immediately went for her handbag to retrieve her mobile phone. She was in luck, she had two bars of signal. She called Connor, hearing the international dialling tone connect. It rang three times before he answered.

April didn't wait for him to speak, shouting, 'Pasty and her mum are in on it. It's a trap, Connor. A TRAP.'

'I know,' her colleague coolly replied before the transatlantic call was cut off.

April dialled 999 asking for police and an ambulance, while she picked up the knives that were intended for her, putting them in the bin. Seconds later the door was kicked down, and DCI Crosbie rushed in, covered in a light dusting of snow, leaving a trail of slush from his hiking boots behind him.

'That was fucking quick,' April said, as she slumped against the cooker. 'How'd you find me?' Crosbie snapped cuffs on the two Tolan women and admitted, 'It was tricky. There are hundreds of these fucking chalets up here. So I asked the snow plough driver. He recalled seeing "some crazy bitch in a purple banger weaving all over the road" behind him. He helpfully told me where you pulled off.'

'And the snapper?' she asked.

'He's been iced, I'm afraid,' Crosbie replied. 'Anyway, how do you like these silver bracelets, ladies? You're goin' downtown.'

'Been watching too many cop shows, detective?' April observed correctly, as the heat from the Aga enveloped her like a warm blanket.

'Yeah,' he confessed. 'Got masel' a homeboy in Bawlmore, too,' he said, giving his terrible American impression.

'I have no idea what that means, my strange detective friend, but glad to see you all the same.'

April looked at the Tolan women lying prostrate on the floor. Patricia was still out cold, while Edwina sobbed and whimpered like a wounded animal. April rummaged around in her bag again until she found her pack of menthol lights and her lighter. She sparked up and inhaled deeply before closing her eyes, humming the song *Ding-Dong! The Witch Is Dead*.

'Or at least very badly scalded,' DCI Crosbie added wryly.

94

#TooLate

Connor Presley had taken April's call just a fraction too late – he was already staring down the barrel of a gun when he was forced to hang up. Geoffrey Schroeder stared at the reporter intently, assessing if he posed any danger.

'I'm unarmed,' Connor said, raising his hands slowly in the air.

Geoffrey placed his forefinger to his lips and replied, 'Shhhh.'

The warehouse had long been abandoned. Wind blew through the cracked and missing windows, with broken glass scattered everywhere. It was the perfect place to kill someone. No CCTV cameras. No witnesses. No one to help. Connor was beginning to think this had been a bad idea.

Schroeder indicated with the barrel of the gun that the journalist should move to the right. The crunch of their footsteps on the broken glass could be heard above the wind rattling through the old building as Schroeder herded Connor behind a bunch of old pallets that were haphazardly stacked about eight feet high. Connor wondered why they were trying to hide. If Schroeder wanted to shoot him, he could have done it there and then.

Behind their makeshift wooden cover, Schroeder stopped pointing his gun at Connor and whispered, 'I didn't shoot Horrigan. I wanted to, but I guess someone hated him more than I did. I got a tweet from someone called Baby Angel telling me he was going to be in Baltimore. They told me to go to his hotel. But it didn't feel right, so I backed off. Next thing, he's dead. Someone wanted me to shoot him or take the rap for it. That's why I wanted to know who gave you my name. I've been set up.'

They both heard a noise at the other end of the warehouse. 'We're not alone,' Schroeder said, raising his gun in readiness.

Connor feared that Schroeder may think he'd set him up. He protested his innocence. 'I swear I didn't tell anyone where I was coming. No one. Not even the cops.'

Schroeder looked distracted and didn't seem to take any notice of Connor's declaration of innocence. 'It's no cop. We need to get out of here,' Schroeder said, as he crouched down to peek around the edge of the pallet stack.

Suddenly Schroeder flew backwards. A loud bang cracked around the warehouse walls, leaving a ringing noise in Connor's ears. The pro-lifer writhed in agony, clutching his face, before another bullet struck, blowing blood and matter out of Schroeder's side across the floor. Connor attempted to pull him back to safety, but it was too late. Geoffrey Schroeder lay lifeless.

His gun was within grasp, but Connor had never fired a weapon before. He was also up against an expert sharpshooter, so knew that any thought of a movie-style shootout, with him blasting his way to safety, would be futile. Instead, he decided to use what he was good at, and all he had left. Words.

'I'm coming out. My hands will be in the air. I have no weapon. Repeat, I am unarmed. Okay. I'm coming out now,' Connor announced loudly. *Here goes nothing*, he thought to himself. Connor stepped from behind the pallets to show he wasn't about to make any sudden moves.

'I was always waiting for you to "come out", Elvis. I've had my suspicions about you.' Bryce Horrigan's former deputy, Tom O'Neill, smirked at Connor.

Connor ignored the gay jibe and asked with genuine interest, 'How the fuck did you find us?'

'I was in the boot of my car. Or the "trunk", as they say over here. I even tweeted you from it. Nice touch with the valet parking, don't you think?' Tom said, pleased with his ingenuity.

'And where did you learn to shoot like that?' Connor asked.

'Well, duh, I am from Northern Ireland,' Tom replied in his thick Derry accent. 'We've got more fucking guns than the Yanks. At least I don't have to hide them here. God bless America and the Second Amendment. The right to bear arms is the best thing about this country. I keep mine in the boot. You're not supposed to, but it came in very handy, don't you think?'

Connor decided to change tack. 'Murder, Tom. Really? Bryce may have been a pain in the arse, but bitch about the boss over a beer, for fuck's sake – you didn't have to kill him.'

'That's what I thought too, but when you're offered the perfect plan to literally get away with murder… well, frankly, it was just too damn tempting,' Tom replied, his powerful-looking gun pointing directly at Connor.

Connor scoffed. 'Get away with murder, Tom? You lured an unarmed man to his death, stared him in the eye and shot him in cold blood. You've crossed the line, buddy. You going to do the same when you fall out with your next boss? How about the boss after that, Tom? Where would we be if we all did that? You're fucked, mate.'

'You think so?' Tom snorted.

'I know so. Bryce wasn't the only one lured in, pal. Or that poor pro-life fucker lying over there in his own guts. Don't you think Pasty and her insane mother have a contingency plan for you too, you dumb twat?' Connor saw Tom flinch at the mention of his co-conspirators. 'They can expose you with a single tweet, fella. And don't think they won't. They might have hacked Bryce's Twitter account, but you pulled the trigger. You've been lured in, just the same as Schroeder.'

Tom's gun barrel dropped ever so slightly. He may have been the one holding the weapon, but suddenly he felt very exposed. It made perfect sense that the Tolans would dispose of him now. He was the only one who had fired the shots. He had killed Bryce, Chrissie Hardie and the hotel porter, Cliff Walker. It was only meant to be Bryce. It had been all so simple when they'd laid it all out. It was only now he realised he was just another pawn in the Tolans' lethal game.

Tom finally responded to Connor. 'Bryce was right about something: I could never fill your boots, Elvis. You are good. A real operator, as they say in the trade,' he said as he raised his rifle up to eye level and took aim at the rival reporter.

Detective Sorrell listened to the entire conversation on his iPhone, recording the confession on the free 'Call Recorder' app Haye had installed for him. Connor had phoned the captain's cell from his BlackBerry before stepping out from behind the pallets. Sorrell had been about to hang up on the reporter when he heard him say he was unarmed. Realising a situation was unfolding, he had hit the record button.

Haye had already been driving Sorrell towards the warehouse, at the head of a fleet of police vehicles, even before they'd taken the call from Connor. That's after they had triangulated Tom O'Neill's location from the strength of his signal between cell towers, in the same way they had been tracking down all the Internet trolls.

Sorrell had his phone clamped to his ear, listening to the events unfold in the warehouse he could now see in the distance. But he was too late: a single shot rang out, abruptly ending the transmission. 'Shit,' the captain swore as he thumped the dashboard in frustration.

Connor Presley's BlackBerry had shattered into several pieces when he dived to the floor as Tom O'Neill had taken aim and fired. But the shot that rang out hadn't struck. Instead, when Connor looked up, Tom was spreadeagled on the floor.

'Got the motherfucker right between the eyes.'

Connor looked behind him to the prostrate figure of Geoffrey Schroeder. The pro-lifer lay lopsided, one half of his body a bloody mess, his rifle propped up on a broken piece of brick, the butt under his good arm. He was still staring through the telescopic sight, the effort of manoeuvring into position sapping the last of his energy.

Captain Sorrell and his trusted lieutenant found them that way. Connor desperately needed to call April. He picked up the bits of his BlackBerry and stared at it despairingly.

'Here, use my phone,' Haye said, offering his cell.

'Thanks. But I can't remember her bloody number. I'll tweet her instead,' Connor said as he struggled to familiarise himself with the iPhone's touchscreen, having been so used to the BlackBerry keys. He logged on to his own account and sent a DM to April:

Connor Presley @ElvisTheWriter
Are you all right? Situation here resolved. O'Neill was the killer. He's dead.

Connor pressed 'Send', before writing another:

Connor Presley @ElvisTheWriter
Also need your mobile number. My BlackBerry is knackered.

He sent his second message believing it was a futile gesture as April would never have the wherewithal to check her tweets. He was about to dial his office when he received a DM:

April Lavender @AprilReporter1955
What took you so long? I've sorted psycho mum/ daughter. I'm bloody starving.

Connor shook his head slowly from side to side. 'Will wonders never cease,' he said to himself.

95

#HeadlineNews

Daily Chronicle @DailyChronicle
TV star's 'killer' shot dead in US. Two more suspects arrested in Scotland after one man killed and woman seriously injured.

It was certainly a headline that caught the attention of both the dwindling newspaper-buying world and the Twitterati. Tom O'Neill's death had already become worldwide news, but the information on the agencies and news sites was sketchy at best.

That wasn't the case for the *Daily Chronicle*. They reported that the radio DJ Lacey Lanning had been found gravely wounded while a freelance *Daily Chronicle* photographer was discovered dead at a remote Highland chalet. What's more, Bryce Horrigan's ex-fiancée and her mother had been arrested at the scene.

From the other side of the Atlantic, Connor Presley reported how he had found himself in the middle of such dramatic events, managing to capture a full confession on his phone from Tom O'Neill before Bryce Horrigan's deputy had been shot dead. There were even some glowing quotes from the publicity-reluctant Captain Bernard Sorrell, praising Connor Presley's bravery and assistance in the conclusion of Horrigan's homicide case. The report also contained a first-person piece by Connor, who painted the shoot-out scene like a movie finale. It led to dozens of requests for interviews pouring in to his newspaper's offices from media outlets across the UK and US. Even a Japanese TV crew wanted to speak to the Scots 'hero' for their news feed. Then there were the publishing houses, desperate to do book deals.

'I feel like I've gone over to the other side – being interviewed instead of asking the questions,' he told April as he was getting ready to head for Marshall Airport to catch the first of his flights back home.

'Well, maybe you have. You going to write the book about it, then? It'd be a bestseller,' April said through her customary mouthful of food.

'Only if you write it with me. It needs the Scottish half of the story too, and that's all down to you.'

'Oh gosh, yes. My dream come true – to finally be a published author. Should have done it years ago when I was your age, when I still had the energy.'

Connor caught sight of himself in his room's mirror before he left. He looked wiped out, with grey skin and bags under his eyes. 'Energy?' he laughed. 'If only you could see me now. Anyway, I'm off to the airport to see if my newfound celebrity status extends to getting an upgrade.'

96

#Farewell

Captain Sorrell was waiting for Connor in the lobby, catching the reporter's attention as he went to check out.

'Give you a ride to Marshall?' the detective offered.

'Thanks, captain. Would you mind if I asked you some questions on the way?' Connor asked hopefully. 'It would make a good follow-up piece.'

'You damn journalists never switch off, do you?' Sorrell smiled, which was as close to a 'yes' that Connor was going to get. 'You've met my driver, Lieutenant Haye.'

'Is that all I am to you, cap'n?' Haye laughed.

'Do you actually have a first name, lieutenant?' Connor asked.

'Harry. It's been so long since I've been called anything other than Haye, even I had to think for a minute there,' he joked.

'So Dirty Harry it is. Most people call me Elvis,' Connor said back.

'When's your flight, Elvis?' Haye asked.

'I'm on the 17.00 to Newark.'

'It's just gone noon. Fuck it, we've got plenty of time. Shall I take him some place, cap'n?' Haye said with a glint in his eye.

'Why the hell not?' Sorrell replied.

Minutes later they pulled up outside the detectives' favourite Irish bar on East Fairmount. 'You gotta try the crab dip, Elvis,' Haye recommended. 'It's fucking A.'

The three men took a booth, ordered their food and drinks, before Connor produced his Dictaphone from his man bag. Sorrell chuckled. 'This guy is all business, ain't he?' Their drinks arrived, with the trio sinking their first Guinness almost before the waitress was back at the bar.

'Something has been bothering me, captain. You and the lieutenant were already on the way to the warehouse when I called you. So you were either keeping tabs on me, Geoffrey Schroeder or Tom O'Neill – which one?' Connor asked.

'Well, we didn't have a cell phone for Schroeder. And it would have been too easy to track you down – all I'd have to tell you was I had a big story, and you'd have given up your location and sold me your grandma at the same time, right?' Sorrell said, smiling again.

'So it was O'Neill you were on to. But how?' Connor wondered.

'Lots of circumstantial things, really. The first was Lindy Delwar. She told me the 'hat man' in the hotel room had a really weird accent. South African, or something. Now, Lindy Delwar had not been outside the city of Baltimore in all her twenty-four years, so how would she know what a South African accent sounded like? It hadn't been an Afrikaner she'd spoken to. It had been a Northern Irishman. Hell, I could hardly understand O'Neill when he came in to see us.'

Sorrell took a gulp of his Guinness before continuing. 'The next was the bug plugged into Horrigan's office computer. It could only have been done by three people: his deputy O'Neill, his ex-girlfriend Patricia Tolan or lover Chrissie Hardie. So that narrowed it down again. It also turned out that Horrigan had DM'd O'Neill, sending him to Baltimore to set up his little orgy. So we knew O'Neill was in the vicinity.'

'Bryce must have smelled a rat,' Connor said. 'He would've feared he was being set up, so he sent his trusted right-hand man to make sure it was all right,' Connor figured.

'More pimp than deputy,' Haye smiled. 'What Horrigan didn't know was, he had just sent his own killer to lay the trap. O'Neill booked room 1410 through Coops, pretending he needed a hooker. But all he really wanted was an unregistered room. He even set the scene with the four champagne glasses so his boss wouldn't be suspicious. It was bothering us why Horrigan hadn't run a mile when a man had opened the room door to him. Unless he'd sent the man in the first place.'

'Bryce sensed danger but his dick overruled his head,' Connor concluded.

'Chrissie Hardie then turned up dead. O'Neill told us Chrissie had complained to Horrigan's bosses about his biting. They turned a blind eye. He pretended to be a shoulder to cry on, when really he was setting her up as bait. Part of the foursome to lure Bryce to Baltimore. Chrissie was more than willing at first as she wanted revenge. She'd been promised Bryce would be left humiliated. But when Bryce turned up dead she no doubt freaked out. She called Bryce's phone, but hung up when the captain here answered. Her phone records then show she called Tom O'Neill, most likely demanding answers. Of course he would have promised to come round to sort it all out. And he did, driving from Baltimore to New York to shoot her in the head.'

'And back home in Scotland, Lacey Lanning also called Bryce's phone,' Connor said. 'She too hung up when she heard the captain's voice. So she got onto Patricia Tolan demanding answers too. That's when Pasty and her psycho mum took over. Told her to shut up or they would make her shut up. But Lacey still had some fight in her. She did the interview with good ole April Lavender – as a warning shot, to show that she was prepared to talk to the press. So mental mum Edwina made sure she'd never talk again by cutting her tongue out.'

'But the crucial piece of evidence was when my "driver" checked out the CCTV footage from the hotel,' Sorrell said. 'O'Neill turned up to ask the duty manager if there were any of Bryce's personal effects the police hadn't taken away that could be returned to the family. It was a total bullshit excuse, of course. He'd have known forensics would have lifted everything from room 1410. It was a fishing exercise. He was doing a clean sweep, making sure he hadn't left any loose ends. But O'Neill then bumped into the old

273

porter, Cliff Walker, who said something like, "Nice to see you again, sir." Cliff was known for never forgetting a face. And he was right. He had seen Tom O'Neill before Bryce Horrigan died. It was O'Neill who had approached him about some female company and old Cliff did what he always did and called Coops. But then their little scheme with room 1410 all blew up in their faces when Horrigan ended up dead. Coops warned Lindy and Cliff not to say a thing as he would handle everything.'

Sorrell paused, downing the last of his Guinness. 'Unfortunately for old Cliff, he didn't put two and two together straight away: that the 'hat man', who asked him for a girl, was the same guy in a suit he saw coming out of his manager's office a few days later. It was probably the hat that threw him. O'Neill wasn't wearing one for his return visit, of course. O'Neill would have been worried that the old boy would wake up at five in the morning and suddenly remember that he was 'hat man'. So he sat in the Starbucks across the street and waited until he saw Cliff walk home after his shift. He shot him with the same gun he used to kill Bryce with, just as Colin Cooper had predicted,' Sorrell concluded, ordering another round.

'You know what, cap'n? Coops was a good detective, as you said. He was just a bad motherfucker,' Haye said philosophically.

'Ironic. Tom O'Neill was a good reporter,' Connor said. 'Who'd have thought he could have been a triple murderer. And for what? Because he hated his boss? Just move jobs. Tell me this though, captain: when did you know the case was connected to Scotland? When I told you about Lacey and Pasty's scarring?' Connor was now thinking more about his book than any newspaper articles.

'Well, that confirmed it. But I knew there was some sort of connection when Baby Angel was being racist to me in a tweet and she wrote "colour" in the British way – with a "u" – instead of the American spelling. It was a small point, but it made me think I was corresponding with a Brit. When you told me about the other women's injuries it all clicked into place,' Sorrell explained.

'Poor Pasty. They reckon her mother is too insane to stand trial so Pasty will be the only one in the dock for this whole sorry mess. The thing is, I could understand Pasty's bitterness towards Bryce, but the mum was a bigger psychopath than the lot of them. What makes people like that? What turns them into killers?' Connor pondered.

'That's the million dollar question,' Sorrell replied. 'And it'll drive you crazy trying to work it out. All I know is people do bad shit. End of.'

'One more for the road, cap'n?' Haye offered.

'Yeah, but you better lay off. You are my designated driver, after all.'

Lieutenant Haye didn't mind. It was the first time he'd seen his captain so relaxed and happy in years.

97

#TheBaltimoreBlues

A bleary-eyed, jet-lagged and slightly hungover Connor Presley sat in the Peccadillo Café opposite his perpetually cheery colleague.

'Look at you, you're never happier than when you're eating,' he remarked.

'You're very astute,' April replied, sending flecks of food in his direction. 'I do love my food.'

'You're amazing. Truly. No matter what happens to you, you just bounce back. Nearly stabbed to death by two insane bitches? Water off a duck's back to April Lavender,' Connor remarked.

April sensed he was feeling down. 'What's up? You look tired.'

'I'll tell you what's up. I've been shot at. I've had about eight hours sleep in the last few days. And what have I got to show for it? I'm sitting here again with you stuffing your face as usual.'

'Don't take your jet-lag foul mood out on me,' April protested.

'Don't you see?' Connor continued. 'Nothing changes. Not even working the biggest story of my career. It's still just back to the grindstone. I haven't moved on. All I do is work. Run. Drink. Get my leg over, every blue moon, and that's it,' he said, earning a sly glance from the waitress, Martel.

'Uch, yer arse. I think you've just got too big for your boots, now you're an international superstar,' April suggested.

'Well, this "international superstar" is about to turn forty next week,' he replied gloomily.

'Ah, finally, the crux of the matter. You know it's only a number. Age is just how old you feel,' April said reassuringly.

'That's fine when you're an ancient relic like yourself. But I'm forty feeling sixty. And that's not the point. Who really cares that I've reached this landmark?' Connor moaned.

'I care. I'm sure Martel cares. Anyway, the big Four-Oh is not all it's cracked up to be. Do you know what I got for my fortieth birthday?'

'A gramophone?' Connor retorted.

'No. Nothing. I told my third husband not to get me anything so that's exactly what he got me. Nothing at all.'

Connor loved the way April never referred to her husbands by their names, but only as One, Two and Three. 'Well, you told him you wanted nothing and got nothing. What's the problem?'

'I'll tell you what the problem was: it was my fortieth and I got nothing. I was absolutely furious. That was the end of us, let me tell you.'

'Did you file for divorce on account of him being unreasonable?' Connor smiled.

'Yes, I did actually. Nothing for my fortieth, just what was he thinking?'

'That'll be more than I get,' Connor said.

'Oh, snap out of it. The problem with getting older is you start to think of your own mortality. Well, I say to hell with growing old. To hell with birthdays. And to hell with technology. Do you know all that matters? Being able to put words together in roughly the right order. So let's write our book. And stop thinking so much – it works for me,' April said with a flash of her gold incisor.

Connor smiled back. 'I love the way you put everything into perspective. How could I ever get too big for my boots, sitting here being lightly speckled with particles of your breakfast and looking at your big moon face with food stuck between your teeth?'

'Anyway, with your big book advance, you can buy me a decent wedding present,' April said, a huge smile all over her face.

It was Connor's turn to spit out his food. 'Luigi? You haven't said yes, have you?'

April flamboyantly displayed her diamond-encrusted engagement ring.

'Why, Miss Lavender, I do believe you are blushing.'

'I haven't actually said yes yet, but he told me to wear the ring until I make up my mind,' April explained. 'I think I could get used to it. Will you give me away?'

'Gladly.'

They left the Peccadillo with Connor singing a jaunty little tune. 'Here comes the bride – hips six feet wide.'

Acknowledgements

Thanks to David Simon for his book *Homicide: A Year on the Killing Streets* (originally published by Houghton Mifflin in 1991), which gives incredible insight to Baltimore's detectives. It is a book that today, in this age of Leveson, would probably never be written – so much for a free press?

The time I spent with my own Maryland detective was invaluable. He is a true gent and a man on the front line, still living everything Simon wrote about in the early Nineties.

Finally, thanks to Colin for his geeky technical advice, my dear colleague Yvonne, Sara for taking a punt and Craig for his expert editing.

About the Author

Matt Bendoris is a senior journalist with the *Sun* newspaper who is already making waves with his electric style of crime fiction writing. His first novel, *Killing With Confidence*, attracted fantastic plaudits, and he is already working on his third book. He has also ghost-written two showbiz autobiographies, including The Krankies' *Fan Dabi Dozi* (John Blake Publishing, 2004), and Sydney Devine's *Simply Devine* (Black and White Publishing, 2005). He lives in Scotland with his wife, Amanda, and their two children, Andrew and Brooke. In his spare time he enjoys running and he's completed four marathons.

CONTRABAND

Contraband is the crime, mystery and thriller imprint from independent publisher Saraband, the inaugural Saltire Society Scottish Publisher of the Year. We offer readers an eclectic range of writing – from pacy detective stories to intriguing psychological thrillers – and give a platform to the most exciting and talented new authors. For more info, please visit www.saraband.net, and connect with us on Twitter: @SarabandBooks or Facebook.

Falling Fast 9781908643537
SHORTLISTED, Deanston Scottish Crime Book of the Year 2014
FINALIST, Dundee Int'l Prize

The Storm 9781908643872
'Cracking pace, great cast of characters and satisfyingly twisty plot. A great read.' JAMES OSWALD

The Guillotine Choice 9781908643407
Based on the moving true story of a survivor of Devil's Island: *Papillon* meets *The Shawshank Redemption*.

Beyond the Rage 9781908643704
Kenny O'Neill is raging... meet Glasgow's answer to Tony Soprano.

'Redefines the term unputdownable.'
CRIMESQUAD

LITERARY PSYCHOLOGICAL THRILLERS

The Disappearance of Adèle Bedeau
Graeme Macrae Burnet 9781908643605
'Intelligent and stylish' THE LIST

Oh Marina Girl, Graham Lironi
9781908643919
The death sentence of a spaceman.
'A book you could become obsessed with'
ALASTAIR BRAIDWOOD